A COLLECTION OF YOU
AND ME

A COLLECTION OF YOU AND ME

BRENNA JARDINE

Brenna-leigh Jardine

To anyone who has ever felt out of place or alone in their own house, to the ones who feel forgotten or disregarded.
To anyone who has ever felt the kind of love that people write stories about, and to the ones still trying to find out what love actually means; and to anyone who's had to hear the deafening silence which comes after death,
To anyone who finds themselves somewhere in the pages of this book,
I promise, you *are* going to make it.

August 7th.

You died on August 3rd.

When I was younger my parents used to say that as long as we followed the rules, our lives could be *anything* we wanted them to be; We could be stepped on and disregarded, or we could become speakers in front of masses who made a *real* difference in the world. But the more I grew up, the more I realized how *completely* full of shit they are. Our lives are *constantly* being subjected to unconsented change. Even if we play every card right, and make every single hard decision, in the end it just—*it doesn't matter* because we all inevitably end up in the exact same place. My therapist asked me to write this; for some reason she seems to think that being able to talk to you again, even like this, is going to somehow sooth the gapping void in my lungs that holds me unable to breathe. I don't believe her, how can *anything*—let alone this stupid book, make me feel like a person again when you are just—

But here we are I guess, this is it; nothing left but you and me, and the inescapable history that lies between the two of us. This is the story I can't believe I lived through, the one you never saw the end of, and the one my therapist will never be able to understand the details of.

I

Sunday, September 2nd

Nothing matters—especially not this stupid exercise, but if I have to write it—because apparently, I do, I might as well start from the very beginning. I was 16 years old.

I was in grade 11 and constantly stuck in my head. There was always another test or paper, always another way I could somehow destroy my carefully guarded GPA, I endlessly worried about things that hadn't even happened yet so that I would be prepared in the off chance they did. Essentially, I was your average high school student stuck in the endless repetition of small-town public school. But one day I was running late to my AP Bio class and of *course, that* had to be the day I forgot something. I stood in the hallway only half aware of where I was, due to the copious amounts of caffeine running through my bloodstream due to the test I wasn't nearly prepared for; it's a miracle that I made it that far at all. There I was; 16 years old and filled with nothing but pure existential dread over a future I could have never predicted. I remember throwing around the contents of my bag, then ripping through my exploding locker haplessly while at the same time trying to look as though I wasn't a single breath away from a complete meltdown. But no matter how hard I looked; I *couldn't* find a pencil. Not only that, but every tool I could possibly use as a substitute had miraculously disappeared with it leaving me standing there with nothing but loose paper and old garbage. Out of all the things I could have possibly lost that day, leave it to me to always lose the one thing I can't go on without. To my absolute horror, even my backup pencil seemed to be lost in the abyss of my locker

I helplessly looked around the empty halls as though I was searching for a piece of dry land while swimming in the middle of the ocean. I just needed one person; *anyone* I even remotely knew, but I was already running late and the hallways were empty. Well, they were empty other than you. There you stood with your perfect hair and blue shoes; with your easy smile and crinkled eyes. Even back then you were an intimidating force to look at; a mix of safe arrogance and unwavering self-confidence that I didn't dare to question. During the 11 years that we had been in school together, I had never, not once, seen you look anything less than in perfect control of any given situation. You basically owned everyone in high school; always walking around with your entourage as though you already knew that one day you would do something bigger than us all. I really wanted to hate you for it, but I couldn't, none of us ever could because we saw it too, no one doubted that you would live an incredible life once you were able to get away from our town, and you did—but no one ever thought the life we dreamt for you would be so short.

For some reason that day you felt me staring at you in the empty halls, though I'm not surprised, because I must have been looking for over a minute. Before I could turn back with embarrassment to my spiraling existential panic about my failing grades and missing pencil, you turned to look at me. Before that one moment, I didn't realize that you even knew I existed but there you were, smiling at me as though the whole time we had been playing a secret game no one else knew the rules to. I remember that I foolishly looked behind me, as though trying to find the person that smile was meant for because there was no way it could possibly be directed at me but there was no one else. Just you and me, and the papers trying to fall out of my locker. I turned back quickly, feeling the heat rush to my face as I contemplated trying to squeeze myself into the space between old lunch meat and used gym clothes just to avoid having your green eyes locked on mine. But my pencil was still missing, and I still had a test to fail. So in a moment of false confidence, I took a deep breath instead of running away and found your eyes. It was insane. I tried to think of some impossible story to share as to why you; a beautiful, popular, and smart senior, needed to help me; a boy, a year below you who was five seconds away from accepting the fact I was never going to escape high school. My mind spun with stories I could spill; something filled with drama and tragedy like the Greeks did that might make you take pity. But then your lip twitched the way It always did before you spoke, and the words all died in my throat.

"Can—can I borrow a pencil? I have this test and—"

"Course." You didn't let me finish, something that would have driven me crazy had I not been so focused on watching the slight shade of gold in your hair turn white as the sun streamed through the door. I felt like we were breaking some unspoken rule about the savage hierarchy of high school; like someone was about to burst through the door and tell me to stay in my own grade away from people like you, but instead, you reached into your pocket and gave me exactly what I had been missing as though you had done it a million times, then you walked away before I could say thank you.

I couldn't do anything but stupidly stand there, watching as you walked down the hallway while trying to understand exactly *what* had just conspired between the two of us. That is until I remembered why I was standing at my locker in the first place. I then continued to run to my class with an apology to my instructor already on the tip of my tongue.

. . .

After our strange first meeting in the hallway, I started to notice you in places I didn't think you existed. Like the same way you don't feel sick until someone points out how pale you look. I realized you and your friends sat in the back of my Bio class; that you and your lab partner had laughed at me after I threw up while having to dissect a pig heart. I watched as you drove past me on your way to school while I walked alone in the rain because I didn't have the money for a car. But most shockingly, I saw you walk through the wooden doors of my church on Sunday mornings. You always wore an ironed button-up shirt and your clean blue shoes, I don't know how I never noticed that was you, but somehow, I had completely missed your constant presence in my life. The problem came from the fact that once I realized it, I couldn't unsee it even though I desperately wanted to. Even in the days where I barely knew your name, it always seemed to be the two of us circling the same life; almost as though a mirror for what we would one day become, more importantly, who I would become. But even at sixteen, I wanted to know you, although I was far too scared to ever say anything about it.

It wasn't until almost two months later that we finally spoke again. Through some twisted idea from fate, we had been paired up as lab partners. I'll never forget how nervous I was sitting down in the small space beside you but I made a pact with myself that no matter how much I wanted to, I would *not* give you the satisfaction of knowing that the only thing I could think about was the way your eyebrows drew together when you listened to the teacher talk. Instead, I tried to write notes on the human body as my hands shook hard enough that after I could barely make out a word.

"Your name is Andrew, right?" You said once the class was getting ready to leave, your voice was deep and soft but certain. I doodled on the sheet of notes I had given up on writing.

"Yeah, but—but everyone calls me Collin."

"Alright, Collin then." I wanted to punch myself when I felt my face heat at having your sole attention on me, but the way you said my name was unlike anyone else had ever said it.

"I'm Sebastian," You gave me your most charming smile which I'm sure worked on everyone back then, it worked on me.

"I know." I honestly considered throwing myself off the stool as the words came without my mind's permission, it was not what I wanted to say.

Of course, I knew your name, *everyone* knew your name. Sebastian Morgan; the perfect child who teachers loved to hate and every student wanted to be with. I said the name over and over again in my mind, trying to get used to the way the words felt while trying to find something to say that would make you realize I wasn't a stalker. It seems unbelievable to think back to the day I said your name for the first time.

"It's—your lab book—" I pointed to the book on the table in Infront of us that luckily, did in fact have your name scribbled on the top of it. You nodded your head in understanding but the smile on your face made me doubt whether or not you believed it.

"Right." I was, quite literally, saved by the bell that rung loudly above us. The class moved quickly to get away from the dreaded classroom as soon as they possibly could, all exempt you. Instead, you sat there as though waiting for me to say something else, something that was profoundly going to change the course of our lives. In some ways you did, even if we didn't know it yet.

"See you around, Collin." You smiled and left me there wondering how on earth I was ever going to pass this class with you sitting beside me.

2

Monday, September 3rd

It must have been a full month after you learnt my name that we finally spoke again. I for one, seemed to be more then okay living in the tense silence that constantly seemed to surround us; we were two people who had thousands of things to say yet every word always got caught on our lips before we could speak them. But in the silence, I learned a lifetime of things about you. For example; The way you smiled when you were nervous or uncomfortable, or that you had a freckle on the inside of your left hand and that you mouthed each word as you wrote it down in your notebook. I also learned that out of every sport in the world, you chose to fight people. And I mean in a ring, against other people who were trained to hurt you. You were on an actual fight team, which I didn't know existed and apparently you were pretty good at it. It took some time but slowly I found that I wanted to ask you about all of it, I wanted to hear you tell me every little detail about your life because it made you, well *you*. I had always been one to hide behind my own fears, never the one to step up or speak out, but for those thirty days where we built towards something more, I, for the first time, didn't want the fear to drown me like it used to.

The day that started our path of either ruin or salvation was a normal Wednesday. We were cleaning up from a lab that I personally wanted *nothing* to do with even though you thought it was interesting, you thought *everything* was interesting back in those days.

"Alright class; there is a unit test on Monday so please, I beg you, start studying now and don't wait till Sunday." Our desperate teacher said, not that the class would listening as the bell was already ringing. Suddenly the room turned into a stampede that not only could but *would* instantly crush you if you got in their way. I could feel my heart beating hard in my chest at the thought of yet another test, the last one still kept me up at night because my mark was nowhere near what I wanted it to be. I had to get at least a B on that next one and for a second, it was the most important test of my entire life. I knew I was spiraling fast as I tried to think of how I was going to tell my parents that I had failed out of school and that my life was ruined and I was never going to leave—but then you put a hand on my shoulder; the simple action immediately removed me from the panic about school and instead threw me into a new sense of panic because; your hand was on my shoulder.

"This stuff is going right over my head; you think you could help me out?" I wanted to laugh because I was just as, if not more, lost than you but for some reason, you thought that I was in some way prepared for that test, even though I knew you saw me look at your notes in class but then you were looking at me with those stupid eyes and your hair was falling in front of your face the way it always did back then and I couldn't say no. Who cares that I would most likely lead us both to an impressive failure, I couldn't say no.

"Sure—yeah." Your eyes lit up as you pushed your books into a bag without noticing the panic rising because I had absolutely no idea how to help you; I couldn't figure out how to get myself to pass, let alone someone else. Instead of commenting on what I'm sure you could see growing on my face, you just smiled.

"Perfect, tomorrow after school then." It wasn't a question because you gave me no time to answer, instead, you just walked away as though you knew I couldn't say no, as though I had already somehow said yes though my mouth was still closed.

I remember going home that night and reading the textbook back to front into the early hours of the morning because I refused to get it wrong in front of you, not when I stupidly told you that I knew the answers. I would get this right because there was no way I would ever be able to speak to you again if I got it wrong.

To be honest, I don't remember most of that day, my mind was too busy trying to stay awake let alone deal with the mundane issues that were happening to my fellow high school subjects, but even so, the day felt never-ending. My anxiety was slowly eating me alive at the thought of hanging out with you, Sebastian Morgan, outside of the classroom, I couldn't believe it; a part of me thought it was all some prank that was going to end in a disaster like an 80s rom-com except that I had no secret powers to save me. But even if every part of my body was yelling at me to back out last minute, I knew it was a chance you were only going to offer once. Sometimes I think about what would have happened if I just went home that day. I met you after school at my locker in the same place we first met but this time you knew my name. I only stood there for a few minutes but I swear it seemed like hours; every second that went by made the voice in my head confident that I was being stood up and by the time I saw you I was already planning how I was going to move schools in order to avoid the embarrassment of seeing you again. But there you were; with your messy hair and constant energy, the people around you hung off your every word. You smiled as you approached me, pushing away the people trying to gain your attention without so much of a word. They left quickly, but I could feel their eyes on me as they walked away.

"Let's go." You didn't stop to wait for me, instead, you made me run to catch up with your long strides.

"Where are we going?" I asked, looking around at the tall trees that had always made me feel impossibly small. You didn't say anything, only kept walking with a knowing look in your eyes. You really loved to be all brooding and mysterious back then, something I grew to love as we got older and even more so when the familiar spark in your eyes faded. You didn't stop walking until we came to the old school ground we used to play on when we were kids. Although due to the current condition of the structure, I doubted that kids went there anymore.

"This is the place I go when I need to get away." You said before walking over to dump your stuff onto one of the many platforms and I was shocked, to say the least. The great untouchable Sebastian Morgan hung out on abandoned overgrown playgrounds when he needed to escape.

It was either really creepy, or something so insanely personal that even telling me about It seemed like a raw admission. Despite knowing better, I followed you up the shaking ladder to sit on a small platform covered in moss. It was on the verge of rotting, and I don't even want to think about the germs and horrible diseases I'm sure were woven into the fibers of it because it didn't matter. At that moment I didn't care about the stability of the structure or the fact that there were a thousand things we could catch from sitting on it, I didn't even notice the clouds slowly filling the sky because it was just us, you and me for the very first time and you were looking at me with those big eyes that begged to answer any question the universe could ask. I wanted to look away from you but I couldn't because the moment was intense in the way things had never been before; this was more than you catching my eye by accident in the hallways or one of the many times you caught me staring, this was you holding my eyes on purpose because you *wanted* to. The side of your mouth twitched, as though you were about to say something important.

"So, what's the chemical formula for photosynthesizes?" I let out a laugh while opening my textbook, thankful that there was something to read off of instead of having to somehow find the right words to say to you.

Soon I forgot about the knot forming in my stomach or the way my throat got tight when you sat back against the makeshift wall and your leg rested against mine; I forgot about all of It and got lost in trying to make it sound like I had even a clue what I was doing and not as though I was trying to recall the lines through a caffeinated haze. I told you about how and why water can do what it does, why humans breath or blink their eyes, I told you absolutely everything I could and tried to answer your questions even if I had no idea what I was saying. That is until the rain started to fall around us, only slight at first but it quickly became something biblical. Before I could panic about my ruined notes, or run home as I assumed we would, you laughed and ran over to the old swing set that looked as though it under no circumstance would it hold your weight, but somehow it did, and you started swinging back and forth like a child who was seeing the outside world for the first time.

The rain soaked your t-shirt, making the fabric cling to your chest defining every dent and imperfection and I wanted to take a picture, even then I knew I always wanted to remember the moment.

"Come on!" You yelled over the sound of the rain, and it was one of those moments that has the power to change your life.

It would have been easy to walk away; I owed you nothing and I was freezing cold, but for the first time in my life I wanted to do the reckless thing and stay. Against my better judgment, I knowingly dropped my books on the ground to be destroyed by rain and ran to join you. In that one moment, despite the rain, our joy was bright enough for the whole world to see it. The two of us were almost adults yet we got to pretend as though we were only children who didn't have to care about anything yet. You couldn't stop laughing as you threw yourself off the swing like the older boys used to do in grade school before motioning for me to follow. I didn't tell you I was terrified of heights, or that the worst possible outcome I could have imagined for myself was jumping off that godforsaken object, I didn't tell you because I knew it didn't matter; I would have done anything you asked me to do in those days due to the fact I wanted you to think I wasn't afraid of anything. So, I did what I never thought I would do, I felt the rain hit my face as I jumped, and before I could understand what was happening, I was on the ground with your hands on my waist as though to make sure I didn't fall over. I felt the heat of your skin through the thin shirt that was now soaked through but I wasn't cold anymore, the rain that would leave me chilled for weeks seemed to dissipate because there you were standing *so close*. Close enough that I could feel the heat radiating from you like my own personal heater and for a moment neither of us said anything, too caught up to care about pretenses or games. Before I could really understand the moment, you were gone, walking back to where our ruined books laid, but I knew you were smiling. I stood there for a second longer, trying to understand what had just happened between us because things like this, moments like those, didn't happen in the real world. But then you turn back to me and I realized I was standing in the rain like an idiot while you were waiting for me. I didn't waste another second before following you, our books were long forgotten as you lead me under the platform we once sat above.

This time when you opened your mouth, I knew it would have nothing to do with science.

"What do you think of the rain?" I looked at you as though I was searching for the right answer to an unanswerable question, how does one form an opinion on something like the rain?

"What do *you* think of the rain?" I asked your question back because I knew your answer was going to be better than whatever half-assed one I could come up with on the fly. You looked at the ground before meeting my eyes.

"Honestly, I think there are different kinds of rain, and I think if we watch closely, it can tell us the story of the world," I didn't say anything out of fear that I would accidentally miss the words you hadn't said yet. "You know the days when the sky is bright, and the rain is falling softly outside your window and the world gets that smell that makes you feel safe? I think that when it rains like that, it's the world giving us a new start; it's letting us try again." As though on cue, a cloud of thunder rattled the ground and I knew that you wanted to ask If I was okay, but instead you leaned your foot against mine. I'd be damned if I let you know this early that I was afraid of thunder—or that really, I was afraid of everything.

"What about this kind of rain?" I asked instead to take my mind off of it, you smiled shyly.

"When the rain is pounding like this, I think it means that some great tragedy has occurred, even if we can't understand it, the world does. It's morning something that we will never know" At first, I honestly thought you were crazy for how could someone really think there was that much meaning to something like the rain? But the more I thought about it, the more I thought about how much easier it was to be sad when the skies were grey and the rain was falling against the windows making everything harsh and violent, or how clean and new the earth smelt in the morning when the storm had passed. Slowly I looked at you with something like wonder; how could someone like you, possibly have grown up in the same world as me and still have the innocents to think something as pure as this? I think a part of you thought I was going to say something negative from the way you looked away when I didn't respond

"You're right, how could anyone think that the rain is just rain?" Your smile was bright enough to conquer the thunder outside. It took five seconds to decide whether or not you wanted to let me in.
You did.

started to tell me about philosophy and your thoughts on the impossible questions it presented, I had never thought about things the way you did, you spoke with such a passion that I couldn't help but live in the words you said even if I didn't understand any of it. I think it's why I fell in love with the impossible because that night you made it real. I never truly realized how smart you were until that day, but you were by far the smartest person I had ever talked to, far smarter than me but you still asked me questions as though you really did want to know what I thought about them. Never once did you look at me as though you were disappointed with my answer. I found out that you were reading the Iliad, and listened as you argued about the point of war and how it was truly a story of human tragedy instead of destruction. I found out that you fought and trained so hard in hopes of being able to get a scholarship and that it was your only way out of the hellscape we lived in, most of all, I learned that you had a little brother named Christian who wouldn't live to see his sixteenth birthday. I couldn't help but lay out my story after you so poetically told me yours, most of the things I said that night were things that I had never before said out loud, let alone to someone I barely knew but there were different rules that night under the cover of thunder. I told you about the violence in the walls of my house, of my father's loud voice and strict views, I told you that I wanted to learn about absolutely everything even though I was horrible at actually learning it. For some reason, I felt safe under the rotting wood while the world cried about another one of its mysteries.

By the time the sun had set I stopped waiting for you to counter my every word with a sharp remark, or to interrupt my thoughts with something you thought was better and stopped thinking that maybe I had said too much because you looked at me with the same look in your eyes that I had never seen in anyone else. That was my favorite thing about you; no matter what insane thing I said next you never made me feel as though I was saying something wrong, I never felt as though I needed to be someone else for you to listen. I wanted to tell you everything because I had never met anyone like you before, and my darling, I promise I will never meet anyone like you again.

We sat there in the rain all through the night, caught up in the words that created our own secret world. That is until I finally thought of my parents who would be sitting at the dinner table waiting for me to come home and that we had to be at school in a few short hours, but I couldn't find it in me to be upset about anything.

"I'll walk you home." You said in a gentle voice, I knew something was forever changed between us, the shy quiet tone of earlier had been replaced by an ability to speak as freely as we both wanted to.

"You really don't have to; I *can* find my own house." I didn't want to leave our hiding spot yet.

"You can't change my mind." The thing was, I didn't want to.

We started out on the journey to my dark home and the rain made it hard to see. It took five seconds for you to watch me pull in on myself, trying to create some kind of heat but just like that as though we really were some kids in a movie about love, you draped your relatively dry coat around me and I thought that there was no way this could possibly be happening to me; things like this never happened to people like me, not in the real world but there we were; as real as could be. I didn't want the night to end because a part of me was terrified that the morning light would break the spell, that like a ghost you would be gone the second the light hit and everything that had just happened would cease to exist.

I stopped in my front yard and leaned against the lamp post, I don't exactly remember what it is that I talked about, most likely something that had no meaning as it was just a nervous ramble because I didn't want you to leave yet. I do remember the moment when you took a step closer to me, taking your time as though you were giving me a chance to move away, I didn't.

I looked at you, but your eyes were already on me, running down my face to land on my lips as you moved a fraction of a breath closer. The air around us was on fire with what was about to happen, like a spark waiting to ignite. Looking back on it, that moment in front of my house was inevitable, it was always going to happen but, in that moment, I thought I was about to wake up. The air around us grew hot and tense making it harder to breathe by the second. I felt it run down my spine and fill my lungs, but I wanted to live in the moment, the feeling of knowing what was about to happen between us and knowing there was nothing that was going to stop it. You were so close, closer than anyone had ever been outside of my family and it felt like I was about to jump off a cliff, the feeling of doing something irreversible sat heavily on my chest yet I couldn't move. You were so warm, and the air around us was so cold. Before I could talk myself out of it, or truly think about the consequences of what was about to transpire, you closed the small gap between us with a breath. It was barely an idea of a kiss, lips barely touching but it was enough to set my soul on fire. As though you finally realized what you had done you moved away quickly, I'm sure there was panic growing in your eyes but for the life of me, I couldn't open mine to see it, not when the feeling of you so close was still so real.

"I'm sorry." You breathed in a voice that was more unsure than I had ever heard you speak. "I should have asked—"

I didn't respond. Instead, in a moment of pure stupidity, my hand found the way to the back of your neck and I was pulling you closer. This time when our lips met it was real, both of your hands found their way to the side of my face, my hand grabbed onto the hair near the base of your neck. I remember thinking that yes, *yes* this is what it is supposed to feel like. I had never kissed anyone before, not like that with the rain falling and the dark skies hiding us from the rest of the world. I felt your thumb rub small circles on the side of my face and even in that first moment, I never wanted to lose that feeling. Every nerve was on fire and I couldn't think of anything other than your body being so close to mine, lips together in the same way I had been thinking about for weeks. The need for air became too much to ignore so I pulled away but you didn't let me get very far before pulling me back, it was as though time had stood still for those few moments like we were both nowhere and everywhere all at once.

The moment, however, couldn't last forever as we both jumped when the lights inside my house turned on, and just like that, you were gone as though I had only imagined it. I watched you look at the house for a moment before moving closer, you took my hand gently.

"I've wanted to do that since the day you asked me for a pencil." I didn't have time to reply as before I could, you were walking away just like the first day. But I could feel your hands on me like a whisper as I watched you turn around for a final look.

All these years later and I still remember every detail about that day, every feeling and word that was spoken, it's something I don't think I want to share with anyone else because it was *ours*. I knew my parents would be waiting at the kitchen table with anger written on their every feature; I knew there would be hell to pay for what I had done, but when I thought of the feeling of your lips on mine, I knew without a doubt that I would happily pay it.

3

Wednesday, September 5th

I fell in love with you the same way the rain fell that night; slowly, but then all at once.

After that one night when the falling rain ruined my science notes and you kissed me under the secrecy of night, we started playing a game but only you and I knew the rules and we couldn't afford to ever lose. Every day I would walk down the busy hallways and see you standing at your locker surrounded by people who wanted you and all I could think about was the way your lips felt when they pressed against mine or the way your hands moved when they ran down my back. You would always look at me with a secret smile, your eyes reflecting the same thing as mine, yet to everyone around us, it was barely a friendly glance. We would sit at our shared desk in Biology and you would lean your leg against mine under the table to make me smile as though it would declare you the winner. It was always a dangerous game; we both knew the consequences would destroy us if anyone found out but we stupidly didn't care, we were young and felt invincible because we had each other. Now as an adult I can say with certainty that it was the most stereotypical thing I ever did because how on earth did we think we were ready to deal with the outcome of our actions? Did we really think we could hide it forever, or that for some reason we would be spared from the horrors of our world?

My childhood friend Malcolm used to bug me in gym class about the brown-haired girl who the entire school knew was crushing on me, I would go back to my war zone of a house and be pelted with questions about the blond girl from church. Her name was Sally and I remember she always wore red shoes and when we were fifteen, she put her number in my pocket like a dare. I would nod along and joke about the possibility of interest, giving fake answers and hollow hellos, they never realized that I snuck out of the house each night to walk down the block to where your car was parked. Thinking back on it, maybe they did know, but maybe their intense denial made them want to forget.
On Sundays, we would both be pushed into the church to sing about a god only one of us believed in. We would sit there with our families wearing our best clothes and listen to the man up front preach about the meaning of sin; but instead of thinking about God all I could do was think about the way you laughed when I kissed the right spot on your neck, or the way your hair, no matter how hard I tried, would never lay flat near yours ears, the people around me had no idea that the definition of religion had been tied up in the meaning of you.

One memory that sticks out from the rest of them was one night we were sitting at that same old playground that had started everything, you had a six-pack of beer sitting on the floor between us and you were quiet. You were never quiet.

"What's on your mind?" I asked, my mind automatically running over the worst possible outcomes I could come up with before you had a chance to surprise me with it, you took a deep breath and I was ready for the worst.

"It's about God," I was a little taken aback by the statement because it was something we didn't talk about, our family's views had no place in the haven that we had created ourselves.

"Okay?"

"You go to church every week and pray; your sing their songs and mutter their words back to them and I don't understand, how could you possibly believe in something that doesn't believe in you? How can you say their words back to them when they are laced in condemnation?"

Your face looked as though you were trying to understand the answer to a question you thought was impossible. There was something sharp laying in the soft edges of your voice. I took a moment to think about it, the question one that I had struggled with since grade school because my family would have looked at us as something unholy, as something that went against the very nature of the universe, but nothing in my entire life had ever felt as real as you; as when you wrapped your hands around my neck and kissed me as though there was never a question as to why.

"Because I need something bigger than me to believe in," I told you the truth, at the young age of sixteen religion was still something that I was confused about, not yet old enough to understand that I was allowed to make it whatever I wanted It to be. I couldn't imagine going through my life believing that I was completely alone in the world, maybe it was teenage angst, but I needed something to believe in outside of my vicious house, it gave me hope that things could change one day. You grabbed my hand gently as though telling me it was okay, your thumb rubbed a circle over the old cigar burns that still felt hot, and I wanted to tell you everything I had always been too afraid to say out loud, the things I was too afraid to tell myself. "What do you believe in?"

It was a bold question, something I only asked because I was caught up in a moment of bravery. It was the only thing I had been too afraid to say because I knew it would do nothing but bring up the pain that you were not so secretly trying to hide. You looked down at the ground in an action so fast that had I not been looking for it, I would have missed completely. Suddenly I had this overwhelming urge to take the question back, to tell you that you didn't have to answer because I hated the way you struggled for words, your eyes grew darker than they had been before and for a moment I thought that you weren't going to tell me.

"I don't think I believe in God, like how could I believe in something that condones people being killed for who they are, who lets violent wars be fought in their name," you played with the bracelet your brother gave you. "Who lets children die from disease before they are given the chance to live," your words broke my heart as I thought of Christian, he had just been put back in the hospital and I knew you were struggling to stay positive about it. I gripped your hand tighter and all I wanted was to protect you from all the things you never deserved to deal with because you didn't—you didn't deserve any of it my love; not then, and not now. Your eyes carefully meet mine. "But I do believe in life; I believe in the love a mother has for her child or the old man who always helps bag groceries down at the market, I believe in good people, and I believe in us."

There were no words that I could find to sum up the words filling my throat. So instead, I moved closer and leaned my head against yours letting myself live in the space between us, because at that moment despite my fear of the future, I believed in us too. I wanted to ask more, I wanted to hear about your brother but I knew you had already given too much of yourself away, we were still too new for me to push the crumbling boundaries between us.

"I believe in us too," I said back instead, the words feeling right as they left my lips, and soon your hand was on the back of my neck, lips crashing into mine like a boat against the harrowing sea. I wanted to tell you that I believed in *you*, but there were no words big enough to fit all the ways in which you made me feel human so instead, I put my hand against your face and kissed you as though I would never kiss anyone else again. At that moment we were teenagers drunk on the idea that love would save us, and I guess in a lot of ways it did.

Eventually, you pulled away and returned to your drink as though the moment had never happened. I took a sip of my own even though I hated the way it tasted. Neither of us should have been drinking, I was a minor and you had a fight coming up that took most of your attention.

"I'm gonna win." You said when I asked if you were ready. Your words were confident and real, something which made me laugh through the overwhelming fear I felt for you because you were going to get in a ring and punch someone—even worse, they were going to punch you back.

"Let's just get you through it," I wasn't able to think past the first punch let alone the ending. I never told you how nervous I was, that every time you stepped in the ring it made my head spin with fear and anxiety, every punch made me want to run into the ring to somehow save you. I'm sure you knew, but I refused to speak the words. Instead, I smiled.

"I can't wait to watch you do what you love," I knew how much the sport meant to you, I saw it in your eyes when you talked about the way the canvas felt under your feet or the way you knew even then, that you were better than the rest of them. It should have sounded arrogant but when it came from your soft lips it couldn't be anything but the truth.

"You're gonna be there, yeah?" You asked as though it was a question even though you had bought me the ticket yourself to make sure I would be there. It was the first time that I was going to see it in person.

"I wouldn't miss it for anything."

. . .

When the day of the fight actually came, I woke up early with a text telling me that you had made weight and it felt like a breath of air had been pushed from my lungs. I had watched you struggle in the gym for days, weeks even just sitting there watching you cut the weight while trying to get my math homework done. I knew it was going to be close and I was so glad you made it, but you making weight meant that it was all real; that there was nothing else standing in the way of you getting in the ring. I took some deep breaths. Of course, I had watched you fight before, i had watched you hit and get hit in return, but this was different, this was *real*. I knew that people died in that sport, and although unlikely the thought made me want to throw up. It's crazy now to think that there was ever a time I was uncomfortable at the idea of fighting, as I've now spent most of my adult years involved with gyms but that November morning, I was more than afraid of what the night would bring.

I wanted to slow the movement of time, as though if I just tried hard enough, I could somehow delay the inevitable but before I could blink twice, I was sitting amongst a group of people, at a fancy venue with music blaring so loud that I could feel it in my chest. I looked around for anyone I might know, not surprised to see the group sitting in front of me was your groupies from school. I put my head down in order to avoid being seen by them as I'm not sure what I would have said If they spotted me. I looked anywhere other than the giant ring that seemed to tower over everything else. *Breathe,* I told myself, looking over the hundreds of people who had no idea about the moment they were truly witnessing. I looked to the room I knew you were warming up in or whatever it is that you did, but you were already looking at me through the window with a smile on your face. The sight of you, still looking like you despite the space calmed me enough to smile back. It took everything to stay in my seat. I could barely hear the music over the sound of my heart pounding in my ears, you gave me a thumbs up before walking away and I turned my attention to the ring where the first fighters were taking their place. I tried, I swear I tried to pay attention to them, but then you and your coach walked into the main room to hit some light rounds and all I could focus on was the way your hair moved when you landed a punch, how serious your face looked as though you were thinking about both everything and nothing at the same time. I didn't think about how much I wished I could be like the rest of your friends and run over to greet you. I turn back to the current fight with pain, not wanting to think about the fact that all too soon it was going to be you standing in that ring, *you* getting punched, I looked down at the ground.

By the time you were being called, I wanted to throw up. I watched as your opponent walked to the ring, his face made of stone; calm and focused, he looked like a fighter; something I never thought of when I saw you. You and your messy hair and large sweaters had no place beside that man who looked the part. I honestly thought you were doomed, that is until I saw you finally walking to your spot. It was as though we had entered a completely different universe when your friends sitting in front of me jumped up from their seats with your name on their lips. The boy who loved to read ancient literature, who held me in his arms tightly when I came broken and bruised from my father's harsh lessons, looked like a stranger to me; your normally soft eyes were hard as steel, your hair was tightly pulled back as though to erase any ideas of mercy. At that moment I understood what I previously had not; the man in front of you was going to lose.

You walked with your back straight; your head held high as though you were Achilles himself about to march into battle with the knowledge that he was untouchable. I couldn't look away, for a moment I completely forget about the violence and focused on the pure beauty of it all. That is until you were standing in the ring. I watched your friends sitting right up front, the girl who was always at your side standing up with a cheer. When the bell rang it felt like a car crash was happening right in front of me and I knew there would be no survivors but I couldn't look away, no matter how much I wanted to.

The world started moving in slow motion while you both circled each other, both waiting to see what the best course of action would be. You threw the first punch, I felt my heart catch in my throat, it must have landed perfectly as around me the crowd cheered, your friends stood up on their seats. I couldn't take my eyes off of you. Every punch you threw made me breathe a little easier, watching the way you moved and blocked, every motion as fluid as water, you made it look so incredibly easy that it was almost hard to be afraid for you. That is until your opponent threw a head hook that pushed you back, I had to put a hand over my mouth in order to keep my composure my heart immediately went to the worst-case scenario, but you didn't fall down, instead, you grabbed him harshly and knead until the ref broke you apart and I almost forgot about the pain of seeing you hurt. When the round ended, I sat back in my seat, taking a deep breath in order to calm my racing heart. I couldn't help but overhear the same girl in the front row talking about how attractive you looked under the lights, and how she swore you looked at her before the fight. I wanted to laugh, to tell her how wrong she was but instead our secret stayed ours because no matter how badly I wanted to rub it in her face, it was something no one else needed to know.

The second bell rang and this time I found myself watching without covering my eyes or looking away, I watched a smile grow on your face after you threw a shot that made your opponent falter, it's always been intoxicating to watch; the round wasn't even halfway over yet the entire room knew you had won. You were a picture of controlled danger, something I had never seen but couldn't get enough of. It was almost no surprise when halfway through the second round you threw a head kicked and followed it up with a perfect right hand, we all stood up and cheered as your opponent fell to the ground. The place was alive with victory, their victor doing what they all knew he could do. You turned to me as the ref called the fight, a smile split across your face.

You did It, I mouthed to you, knowing that you would understand, you put a hand to your mouth as though you were blowing a kiss and I wanted to laugh at your antics and at the girl in the front row who assumed it was directed at her. Soon the ref had both of you in the middle of the ring and was raising your hand in the air, you pointed your hand at me and the girl almost fainted but I didn't care, I *couldn't* care because the man standing in the ring was *mine*. I felt pride rush my chest, I wanted to turn to everyone to tell them that '*yes, that man standing there in the middle of the ring is my boyfriend, look at what he did!*' I truly was a teenager jumping up in the air because of what you had accomplished, the anxiety fell from my shoulders because—because you were okay.

Soon you had the trophy in your hands and you were walking out of the ring without looking back. I wanted to run to you, to run my hands up your back and convince myself that you were okay but I couldn't, not yet. Instead, I watched your friends all group together, telling the girl that now was her chance. I don't remember her name; all I remember is that she had red hair and walked up to your door with so much confidence that I wouldn't be surprised if she had never been turned down before. When she knocked on the door, no one answered and instead of running into your arms, she walked away with scornful eyes. I wanted to laugh at her. Once the crowds started to scatter, and the fighters started going home with their teams, your friends left for a party I'm sure you were supposed to be at, and only then did I slowly walk towards your door. I knew that I shouldn't, that it was dangerous, and that I should just wait outside the way we had planned it, but I couldn't stand the idea of waiting another second.

I felt my heartbeat against my chest as I knocked and I enjoyed the risk of it, the way that any second could be the last. You looked through the small window before drawing the blinds and opening the door to usher me in. I stood there, taken aback by the smell of sweat and oil trying to come up with the right thing to say, for what could I *possibly* say to give justice to what I had just witnessed, but before I could you were crashing into me, wrapping your arms around my neck as though you hadn't seen me in a month. All I could do was hold on, taking in every breath, every movement because you were okay and in one piece and you had done it. I ran my hand along your back, making sure you were there and whole. You were truly disgusting, covered in a mixture of sweat and something strong and oily, but somehow, you still smelled like you. It was almost impossible to remember that less than an hour ago you had looked like an untouchable warrior.

"I did it." You said like a child bragging to their parents. I pulled you impossibly closer.

"I'm so proud of you," I whispered, too many emotions running through my chest to make my voice any louder.

You pulled back and I could feel the joy radiating from you, the spark in your bright eyes was so alive. I put a hand to the side of your face, taking in the sight you presented me with, I ran my eyes over your chest, down your side until I reach the spot where the skin was changing to shades of yellow. Ever so lightly I traced a finger over it, unable to take my eyes off of that one horrible spot.

"I'm alright," you said, already knowing the thoughts running through my head.

I nodded while reaching for your neck, pulling you into me for a desperate kiss. I knew the danger of what we were doing, that anyone could walk in at any moment and the game we had been winning would be over. But the danger only made me hold you tighter because in that moment I would have fought God themself to keep what we had. I pulled away slightly.

"That girl who sat Infront of me thought you were in love with her." I mumbled, remembering the way she had squealed when you looked in her direction. My voice was light because you were with me, had *chosen* me. You laughed a real laugh and I thought that I might explode with the things I was feeling.

"Shame, if only she knew who it is that I love." You said the words so softly but meant everyone and it was like the world had stopped for everyone other than us. The violence and pressure constantly trying to drown us, my father's loud voice, and your mother's cold eyes, none of that could exist in the space between you and me because you said you loved me. You, Sebastian Morgan, loved *me*. I played with the hair stuck to the side of your face, letting the moment sink in, wanting to relish in every single second of it because never before had I loved anything the way I loved you while standing there in that stinky dressing room.

"What a lucky guy," I said, moving closer until we were a mere breath away, I felt your nose pressed into my cheek, moving closer by the second. I couldn't get the right words to form in my mouth, couldn't find the right ones to say the things I wanted them to, instead, I closed my eyes and leaned into the feeling of having you so close, feeling your every breath hit my skin.

"That's where you're wrong, it's me who is the lucky one." You whispered before finally closing the distance between us, letting us stay in the world of bliss for a little longer.

That's what I think of when someone brings up the beginning, I want to tell them that once upon a time we knew who we were and thought we understood the rules of the world we lived in. How were two kids supposed to know that our little game had a time limit? How could we ever have known that our time was about to run out?

4

Saturday, September 8th

I don't want to do this today—I don't want to write this *stupid* story anymore or think about the fact that our daughter, who *you* wanted, is going to have absolutely no record of who you are outside whatever the hell it is that I'm writing. I don't think she even understands what's happened, too young to know that death is something coming for us all, the only thing she knows is that *you're not here*. You're not here and no matter how many words I write, regardless of how poetically I can describe your voice—it *can't* bring you back; *it can't make this real*—I can't escape back into history when we were okay, when we were more than just flaky words on an endless page. But I told Dr. Riley I would have something for her tomorrow, something more than the word NO written in a hundred different forms, so screw it, where were we in this godforsaken story?

. . .

Before I could blink we were 18—I was anyways and *finally* I was about to leave behind the town I feared I would never escape from. It's funny how the world changes when you turn 18, as though somehow, I was suddenly an adult even though at school I still needed to ask an adult for permission to use the bathroom. But nonetheless, there were more people than not telling me that I needed to take my life more seriously than I had only hours before. Most of the conversations went the same way; all of them ended with the idea that the only way to be successful was to be a doctor or a lawyer, I remember that my father wanted more than anything for me to go to school in the glorious Salt Lake City because that's where he went, it was also the birthplace of his father and his father before him. All I did was nod my head in agreement because it wasn't worth the fight that would ensue if I told him what I really wanted; that more than anything I wanted to follow you to New York because there was a scholarship sitting on your desk, or that I wanted to study art and photography while you studied the art of war. Back then they weren't ready for my version of reality, they never were, so instead I let them believe that I was nothing more than what they had always believed.

One night, after I had stupidly voiced what I wanted to my dad, I met you at the old junkyard. You know, the place where we would go when we wanted not to be seen, or when we wanted to throw shit at other shit without anyone caring about what we broke. My hands were shaking and my cheek hurt, every step I took away another step from him and a heartbeat closer to you. I think you must have been away for a few days; I don't remember the details anymore but for some reason, you weren't there and I was alone, something which made me realize with complete clarity that I didn't want to be anywhere you couldn't be. I saw you sitting on the edge of a broken tire, your hair tied up in a bun because it had grown to be unruly and long over the course of summer. I wiped my eyes before running up behind you and wrapping my arms so tightly around your neck that we both went tumbling to the ground. In hindsight, it was a horrible idea as there was a huge chance you would have thought I was a criminal and beat the shit out of me, but luckily somehow you knew it was me, and as we tumbled onto the cold dirt your laughter was all-encompassing and real which almost made me forget about the blood I knew stained my father's hand.

"I missed you," I said once we sat back up, you dusted the dirt off my shoulders with a smile. I leaned closer, feeling your breath on my skin as you nudged your nose into mine

"I was gone for five days." You said but I could hear in your voice that you had felt it too.

During those first years in high school, we had created a haven between the two of us—a single safe place from an otherwise unsparing world. In all the books and poetry, people tell stories of the time they finally found God at the bottom of their sock drawer; maybe in the corner of their attic or under the floorboards, and its always at the moment they finally surrender to the constant despair trying to drown them and from their pain, they find their salvation. Well, I like to think it's the same way in which we found each other just before we submitted to the calamity awaiting us on the other end of everything we had always wanted. Through every endless war, we would face, you were always my foxhole to escape the shooting.

"Five days is a lot; entire civilizations have fallen in less," I said back as you draped an arm around my shoulders, content to sit in the mud and watch the stars burn out from above. I leaned into your side and felt your laugher shake through your chest, I needed something real to hang onto.

"Ah, where did you go while I was gone?" You played with a loose string on my sleeve. I smiled, knowing that you asked because you actually wanted to know the answer and not just because you thought it was polite.

"Greece, more specifically the fall of it."

But I didn't want to talk about Greece, I didn't want to talk about Rome or anywhere else in the world because it felt like my own life was about to be written into the pages of history as just another thing destroyed. What I wanted to say was that my dad set me up in an apartment thousands of miles away and that every time I came home too late, he waited for me at the kitchen table to ask a thousand questions that I never had the right answer to. I wanted to scream that it was getting harder and harder every day to keep our game a secret because I knew it was constantly being written into the lines of my face like blasphemous poetry. I wanted to cry because I had absolutely no idea how to fix any of it before it consumed me but—you were smiling. And back then I didn't have it in me to be the reason for that smile to disappear so instead of giving my panic a voice, I pushed my face into the crook of your neck and breathed as though I could ignore the falling cities around me as long as that one thing remained true.

Looking back on it now, I could have saved us a lot of pain if I had just told you the truth, if I had been upfront about my father's eyes baring down my back because it really was only a matter of time before the bomb fell and we were left as discarded casualties. Not that we could have done anything about it, but at least maybe we would have been ready for the explosion.

It couldn't have been more than a month later that thing started to crumble; my dad got my oldest brother to keep an eye on me at all points of the day which made it almost impossible to escape out the window or run from the back door. I thought that if I could just keep it up for a few more months, all I had to do was make it to graduations, and then I would be fine. Either way I was going to be screwed as I had next to nothing to my name and no plan or future endeavors, or really anything that would help us leave, but at the time it felt just like everything would change the day I walked across the stage and threw my cap in the air. But on one Wednesday in February, everything changed for us. it's at this time I feel like I should warn the reader, whether it be my child one day or my therapist tomorrow, but things are about to become not okay very quickly, and I need you to understand that I did everything I could have in order to avoid it, but I couldn't avoid It forever.

On that Wednesday in February, I came home from school in a rush.

I knew if I could get out of the door before my brother got home then I would be free until nightfall where I could very carefully climb into the second-story window. I ran to my room in order to drop off my school stuff and change my shirt, but when I got to my room my father was already in it, sitting on the bed with an expression I'll never forget.

More importantly than what was written on his face was the items placed in his hands; my laptop was open with a picture of the two of us on the screen, the one we took on my birthday when you kissed my cheek, and spread out on the bed was the letters we wrote back and forth because you said it was romantic. *I couldn't breathe* like suddenly every word I could have said got stuck in my throat because he knew, and there was nothing I could do to make him forget it. I carefully put my bag down on the floor because I had to face it. Maybe a part of me wanted him to know, maybe that's why I kept the picture and the letters, maybe I wanted him to know because it was slowly eating me alive having to hide it. Either way, there was nothing I could do but face my choices despite the fact that my hands shook when I took my phone out of my pocket. In one last act of rebellion or maybe it was my last attempt at salvation I sent you a text that I can't remember the contexts of, but it was for sure something close to a confession. I heard the reply on my computer, and then again, and again, but neither I nor my dad looked away from each other. I took a shaking breath.

"That's—he's my best friend," I said, trying to keep him from seeing the sweat roll down my neck or the fact that my heart was beating in my teeth and down my spine. I thought he would be mad, would throw me against the wall—which he did, but before any of that, it was just pure sadness pouring from him. I knew *exactly* what he had seen since my laptop was synced to my phone. Every text message, every photo, every video, the last three years of our lives written out for him to read as though each one was a copy of my guilt and admission. I backed away, taking each step one at a time but I didn't know what to do, I knew my mom and siblings wouldn't help me, I knew that you weren't there to save me, it was only me—me and my father's burning eyes.

We were two enemies standing on opposing sides of a field and he towered over me as he moved closer, my laptop forgotten on the ground. I thought about all the times I had seen you fight and about what you would do if it was you in the situation instead of me.

"It's okay," he started to my surprise, making something in my chest shift with confusion. "We can still fix this, it's not too late to be saved." His voice was nothing but condemning, each word raw but believed. He reached out a hand slowly. "It's not too late, God forgives those who ask for it—" A switch went off, and in the half-second between breaths I decided exactly who I was going to be.

"I *don't* need to be forgiven." I spit quickly before I lost the nerve too, "I'm not broken—" before I could get the words out, I felt his ring cutting across my face, I can still feel the way my skin split under his power but the physical pain was nothing—nothing compared to the feeling sitting in my chest that threaten to drag me to the floor.

"How dare you—" he said and his words were nothing but venom.

"Dad—" I don't remember a lot after that point, or honestly a lot of the days that followed. What I do remember is falling to the floor when his fist connected to the perfect spot on my temple despite my desperate pleas, it was like he didn't see me anymore, didn't see the kid who he raised and fed and held, he didn't see the boy he read fairy tales to when I was sick; instead, all he saw was the things I had done, and the person I loved. Everything spun around me, my ears rung when my face hit the carpet with a painful burn. Life became nothing but a series of moments, pain numbed me to anything other than its own existence. Thinking about it now, I think he would have killed me in my childhood bedroom, but at that moment I didn't care. I couldn't see or hear; I could do nothing but lay there waiting to either die or survive while I mumbled out soft pleas. That is until through some last act of God, you showed up. Of course, I didn't know it was you at the time, all I knew was that someone was yelling, and then my dad was gone and the punching stopped, and then someone had their hands on my face. I couldn't keep my eyes open; everything was too much and too loud. I remember your hand tapping the side of my head

"Hey—focus on me—I'm—now—" You were talking but I couldn't

understand, your voice broke but I couldn't fix it, I wanted to say that I was okay, that things were okay but I *couldn't* speak, instead all I did was close my eyes and give in to the darkness surrounding me.

The next events are still blurry in my brain, all the years in between now and then not making my memory any better, but I woke up in a soft bed. I remember opening my eyes and the feeling was more painful than anything I had ever experienced. I didn't know where I was, or even who I was; all I knew was that my skin was on fire and every breath made my eyes water. As though a wave, the events hit me all at once and left me drowning. I felt your hand tighten around mine and it was the only thing I knew was real. I turned to you and forced my eyes to open as I took in quick, panicked breaths. Your face was wet with tears and laced with fear as you dropped your head onto my chest.

"I didn't—I didn't know what to do—" you said and I could feel the weight of the words hit my ears, my heart beating so fast that I couldn't keep track of it but you were there and you were holding onto anything you could. I looked around at the room, only to see that we weren't in a hospital or somewhere I thought we would be, instead we were in your room. I turned back to you. "I didn't—the hospital knows you and people would ask questions and I didn't know what would happen—and I—I definitely should have brought you there but I—I didn't know what to do—" Your words were so frantic and unsure, each one running off the energy of the last and I had never heard you speak like that, not with that level of desperation in your words that were usually so precise. "You just—I didn't know—" you were crying, I could feel the tears hitting my skin and I think you may have been shaking just as much as me. It was a scene of utter destruction; of two people desperately clinging to the only thing they had left and I closed my eyes to the feeling of it. "I'm sorry—" I brought your hand close to my chest, signaling without words that I wanted you to come closer and you did without hesitation. Soon your arms were carefully placed around me and you were holding on as though I was something incredibly delicate that could break apart in your hands. All these years later, I still remember that moment more than any detail from the week because there was no one left to comfort us; no family, nobody to tell us that we were going to be okay instead it was just you and me, both broken and bruised but still alive.

Suddenly we were so young, so afraid but still—*alive*. It was easy to forget that you were ever afraid of anything.

I said your name over and over again as though a prayer, my fingers dug into the back of your shirt because you were there, and we were together and I had somehow survived the unescapable thing I didn't think I was ever going to see the other side of. You didn't say anything, only placed your lips on my forehead.

As though we hadn't been through enough, the world was not done with us yet. Although I think the next part is something I will leave for tomorrow, there has been enough pain written today and I can't think with our baby crying from down the hall.

5

Monday, September 10th

Today is going to be a short one because I don't want to write it. I saw my therapist and she told me to keep going with this even though every word seems worse than the last. But she doesn't know what I do, she doesn't know the things I've done, or that I don't know how to write them down without admitting that I made the wrong call. Maybe that's why she wants me to keep doing it. Anyways, Maisy has been crying for 14 hours straight and *I don't know what to do*, your father said he would stop by later tonight because I can't—I can't do this anymore—*I can't*.

. . .

After I woke up on your childhood bed, I honestly don't remember the next few days. I found out my family was long gone and that no one knew where they went, you held onto me even tighter than you had before, but really, for a few days, we just existed while trying to heal. Your family was out of town with Christian and for the first time in our entire lives there was nowhere I needed to be; no parents with wondering eyes, nothing but the two of us. I didn't think about my dad, or my mom or siblings because I *couldn't*, I didn't until I was older and finally away from the fray, I realized that we can't deal with trauma while living in a constant state of it. Instead of letting myself fall apart because of my destroyed family, I let myself think of you and simply exist with you because you were there, and they had left me to die.

It was a few days later my head stopped pounding and I could move without wanting to cry. You came into the room with two mugs of tea before putting them down and falling forward onto the bed with a sigh. I laughed while crawling onto your chest, wrapping my arms around your waist tightly

"You comfortable?" You said, all I did was press my lips to the dip in your throat, feeling your laugh vibrate through your entire body. It must have been getting close to dark as you looked at me with tired eyes. "Are you tired?" There was a hint of mischief to your voice. Your hand tangled in my hair as I smiled against your skin.

"I've been asleep for the past four days; I may never sleep again," I said back as your hand pushed me towards your lips and soon my hands found their way to the side of your face, yours roamed the skin of my back and everything happened so fast but also in a timeless progression. It took less than seconds for the kiss to deepen, your hands found their way to my hips while I kissed the side of your jaw.

"You are everything," you said and it was *such* a cliché, but you said it anyway and I thrived under your soft words. My hands ran over your collar bones like they were the steps to an altar, like I was a sinner who needed to confess under the pulse of your breathing. Your hand moved under my shirt as I pushed yours over your head so that there was nothing left between the two of us and your skin was so warm, you were always warm under my cold touch. I don't care that we were cliché and stereotypical, I don't care that we were young and in love and honestly thought we could solve the world based on nothing more, I don't care because now those times when your skin was on mine and your heart beat fast, those are the memories that were scored into my brain like song lyrics and poetry, those are the things I remember more than anything else. I can still feel your fingers run over my back like a ghost when the night is too long.

That night, however, you moved and suddenly I was laying on my back underneath you, with my hands pinned above my head and your lip between my teeth. We were both so caught up in each other, of your lips trailing down my stomach and there was *so* much skin and we were so young—we were both so caught up in each other that didn't hear the door slamming from the kitchen, or the car pulling into the driveway or the feet coming up the stairs, instead, all we did was laugh.

"Sebastian—" Things happened too fast for either of us to understand after that.

One second, we were laughing and your mouth was on mine, and the next you threw yourself to the ground in mortified horror and I knew right then that everything was about to change. I remember your mother standing above us both and I knew there was absolutely no way to convince her that we were doing anything innocent because—well, I think it's self-explanatory. All I could see was my father in her face, with his words and bloody knuckles and abandonment, I couldn't look away from it all and It was the harshest form of self-punishment. I looked at you, but you were in a battle with your mom even though neither of you had moved. I never met her, not really, I didn't know who she was or what she would do. All of a sudden you stood up and moved between me and her as though you knew something I didn't. She didn't say anything, only looked at me as though willing me to disappear.

"Mom," you started, your mind running to find the right words, and I couldn't believe that this was happening again, *how* could this have been happening to us again but it was, and there was nothing I could do to stop it. Sometimes I think that we doomed each other from the very beginning.

"You need to be gone before your father gets here." Her voice was calm and even, and suddenly I couldn't stop looking at the cross around her neck. I watched the muscles in your back tense.

"What—mom please—" your voice was tight and I knew that your features would be contorted in silent agony, that the feeling that washed over your chest would never go away because— you thought that your family loved you; that they would support you no matter what you did and come time they learned—well your dad did, but in that single moment you were being pushed away from everything you had ever known. She looked away and there are tears building in her eyes

"I don't want to hear it, Sebastian. Your dad has been at the hospital with Chris and—" Her voice broke when she said his name, she didn't look at you again. "You need to leave my house." I thought she was beautiful while you threw what you could into a bag, you had her eyes. I threw on my shirt as fast as I could with my shaking hands. "How dare you—" She spit like acid, and you turned to her instantly, stepping into the middle of it as she moved towards me.

"Do not." Your voice was dark in a way that I had never heard and suddenly you were every bit the fighter that I forgot you were. She looked at you as though she didn't know who you were anymore and you never let her see you break. Suddenly you gapped my hand and I held on as tight as I could as we walked away, storming past her down the stairs into the kitchen where we saw your dad helping your younger brother into the house. I saw the way your dads' eyes changed when they saw you—more so when he saw me holding onto your hand. I still feel bad for him because he never wanted it, he would have held onto you and told you that you were enough, and we would have been saved from the horrors that were awaiting us in the real world. But he couldn't do anything but look at us with sad eyes. Your brother just looked confused. I remember more than anything that you leaned down to kiss your brother's forehead and the tears were stuck in your eyes because you wouldn't let them fall. You look your dad in the eyes when you stood back up

"Where are you going?" He asked in a heavy voice. You gave your dad one last tragic look.

"Me and my boyfriend aren't welcome here. We are going to go somewhere that we are." With those final words, you walked away from your family as though you would never see them again.

We walked for a long time before anyone said anything else. I didn't want to ask any questions or open my mouth because, for the first time since I had known you, you didn't say anything. Only walked with your arm around my shoulder because there was no longer any point in hiding it. I didn't ask you, and you didn't ask me but I knew where we were going, the only place we *could* go because there was an empty house a few blocks away with my blood-stained on the carpet.

I'll never forget the first time I went back to that house, it felt like a ghost of the life that had been violently ripped away from me. As soon as we walked in, I could see the blood. We didn't go up to my room, we didn't look at the stairs, because we knew what would await us at the top if we did. I knew that the sight would haunt my waiting hours forever. Instead, I walked you over to the middle of the room as I quickly ran into the spare space and slowly dragged the bedding into the middle of the living room where you still stood staring at the ground. It would have been easier to just sleep in the spare room, but it would have been too real, instead, it was easier to act as though we were just kids playing pretend and things were still okay. I made us a little nest on the ground and pulled you down onto it slowly.

"They kicked me out." You said softly, but your eyes were far away as though you needed to say it in order for it to be real. "I didn't think they would." Finally, you looked at me and there were tears falling, I couldn't stand to see you cry anymore.

"I'm sorry—I'm so sorry," I said, feeling like it was my fault. I still do feel like it was my fault because if I wouldn't have been there, then they wouldn't have known and things would have been different. We were sitting in the skeleton remains of our old life and I wanted to burn the family photos that hung on the walls, I wanted to tear up the art from grade school that still hung on the fridge because—because they were all lies. "I'm sorry that this is happening," I said because I was, God I was so sorry that this happened to you because you deserved so much more. "You should go back, tell them I made you do it, they—they will believe you."

I was so afraid that you would grow to hate me, that you were going to resent me for the rest of your life because I took them away from you. Your eyes moved to mine sharply.

"I'm *not* leaving you." You said without hesitation, as though it wasn't a question. It was never a question for you. "It's not your fault." And now I know that it wasn't, that it wasn't my fault or yours because no matter what, our parents should have loved us and they chose not to, they chose some invisible force over their kids and now that our child is asleep down the hall, I know there is nothing in the world she could do or say that would make me treat her the way the treated us.

That night we were both filled with so much heartbreak that we couldn't breathe; the walls around us became so confining that it felt like a grave. As we lay there together with my head against your chest, I couldn't help the thoughts that formed in my head.

"We are destroying each other," I whispered because I couldn't say it any louder than that, I didn't want to say it at all because what if you agreed? Instead, I felt your hand press tighter against my skin.

"We are. But I would rather feel this destruction than their idea of peace."

That line, that single string of words is something I have never forgotten, something that is tattooed down the side of my arm because in that one moment, on that single bed in the middle of a war; we *still* chose each other, and it was enough.

I think I have written enough for today; the baby is finally sleeping and your dad will be here any moment. Sometimes I can't bare to look at him because—because he looks *so much* like you—sometimes without meaning to I find myself looking at his green eyes and warm smile, at the lines that form on his forehead when he laughs and I think wow—this is what you're going to look like one day when we finally grow up—but then I am hit with the relentless reminder that you, you are never going to grow old like your dad.

I *can't* do this anymore—not today. Maybe tomorrow will be different, maybe it will be easier to breathe when Maisy isn't looking at me as though I'm not nearly enough.

6

Friday, September 14th

Yesterday was a bad day. And no, I *don't* want to talk about it because what is there to talk about when the person I want to tell only exists in this shitty notebook?

Spencer came over last night and took Maisy back to his and Andi's place, which means for the first time since I was 16, I'm truly and utterly alone—other than the sound of your voicemail playing on repeat beside me. It's still *you*, even if it's not real it's just—it's your voice, and your words and it's the only thing I have left. Maybe I'll find solace in these stupid pages or maybe if I look hard enough, I can still find you in the bottom of the bottle laying empty beside me.

I don't remember a lot of what happened after we left your house that night, or maybe I do and I just don't want to stain our story with the things we had to do in order to survive what happened next. We couldn't stay, and it was only a matter of time before word of what happened spread like a virus to every person we had ever known. It felt like a nuclear bomb was about to drop and all we could do was run before we became ground zero. So, where could we go? I was barely 18 and had nothing more than a pile of babysitting cash, you were 19 with nothing more than a few hundred dollars saved from working; We had no family, no ties, we were two astronauts whose tether had been severed, leaving us both floating through space with nothing to hold onto but each other. All we knew, was that we couldn't stay. Do I wish I would have finished high school? Of course I do. There were so many things that I wanted to do in my life; I wanted to go to university and learn about absolutely everything I could. I wanted to take art and philosophy and learn about *why* we strive to exist but I also wanted to learn about the stars and how they die, I wanted to know *everything* and be known for something, but in less than a second all of those choices were no longer ours—or more so, they were no longer *mine*. You still had a scholarship and a future to make whatever you wanted but it felt like mine was collapsing between my fingers.

Looking back, it's the best thing that ever happened to us because it brought us to a new place where we met our real family, the place we lived and breathed and thrived away from the pain of our town. With no other options, we left for the big city I had always dreamed about. Of course, it took exactly three months for you to fail out of your courses, even less for us to run out of our combined funds but regardless, we always figured it out. You found a new gym that was willing to take a chance on you; it helped that your name and reputation was growing, they let you train and paid you to coach their kid's class. I found a job serving and we slowly started to become something close to stable. We still slept on various couches and floors, sometimes a cheap hotel with rats in the walls and stains on the bed, but we made it work because at least the small amount that we had was *ours*, and no one could take it away from us.

I wish I could say that I remembered more from the first few years when we had nothing but I *don't*. they were busy and difficult and something that neither of us wanted to remember the details of.

But now that I sit alone in our beautiful home, surrounded by art and all the things we bought because we simply wanted them, I would give *all* of it up if it meant I could be 19 and cramped beside you on a single mattress in some stranger's basement again.

But my therapist doesn't want to hear about the small stuff like how we made money, or the people we met, or the horrible things we drank when we wanted to laugh again. No, what she wants to hear is the real things, the things that brought us to where we are now. I think you would agree that the year I turned 23 was the year something fundamentally changed in the tight balance we had miraculously created.

The first thing I remember from that time in our lives was walking down the street near our new tiny apartment to grab a coffee from the independent place I worked, even when not working we always went there to see a girl named Sam, and for that period of our lives, she was one of the most important people in the story. She was the one who got me a lifesaving job and let us crash on her couch for months until we had a new plan. I heard the familiar bell ring above my head as I walked through the door.

"Collin!" she said, her smile bright and alive and hers. Alive is the best way that I can, and could describe her; something about the set of her shoulders and arch of her back, maybe it's her dark eyes or playful smile, she is just *alive* no matter how old we get, or how many things changed, she has always been bright, it's impossible not to feel lighter the second she enters a room. She looked at me over the counter, her eyes searching my face for something I don't remember,

"Wheres Seb these days? It's been forever since he graced us with his presents."

"We are actually both leaving tomorrow for his fight, he's next to killing himself trying to train." I always hated when you had to fight because you became someone else; someone sharper and focused, you stopped talking about random things and smiling, your loud laugh became rare, somehow you turned into a *thing*. A thing that was able to endure the constant punishment you put yourself through.

"Tell him that we are all rooting for him." There was something else in her face, maybe it was worry or fear or a mix of both. I wanted to tell her that you came home at night so tired that you could barely move, that only a few days ago you had sat by the door and silently cried because your body was physically unable to do anything else, or that you hadn't eaten in days making your eyes sink and skin pale, but I didn't tell her any of it because it was something only meant for me to see. Because it was something you didn't let yourself show to anyone else. She handed me a coffee that I didn't order. "Are you guys going home for Easter?"

I didn't know what to say to her because the idea of home was still too fresh and something I didn't let myself think of because I knew I wouldn't be able to control whatever emotions came falling from me if I did. I wanted to go home, I wanted to run to my mother and have fun with my brothers, or sister who was still so young, but I couldn't. And I couldn't let myself think that I could for even a moment, instead, I just shook my head with a sad smile.

"We are home. I'll see you later Sam." I said, suddenly needing to be away from anyone who knew I had been somewhere before the city had caught me. She waved as I walked through the door.

I don't think I went straight home. instead, I walked around our neighborhood in search of places to do my next shoot. I had been working part-time as a photographer, doing sort of modern city-portrait-things and slowly my clients were bubbling in. Obviously looking back now it was nothing compared to what would eventually happen, but at the time I thought I was busy. I watched kids dance on the side of the road to a beat made up in their heads and I watched as teenagers spoke in soft voices on the steps of tall buildings, I saw myself in the people begging by the side of the road. Before I could spiral too deep into my own thoughts, I remember my phone ringing because I almost got hit by a biker when I stopped walking to answer it.

"Hey, I'm gonna get take out on my way home," you said and I had to laugh because your voice was heavy and wet, as though you had been running and couldn't find any breath left to speak. I can still picture what you would have looked like that day; all sweaty and gross while leaning over a railing in order to not fall over. I shook my head in amusement while following the flow of people back home.

"Please," I said simply because you already knew what I would eat, although my insides felt like a rolling storm when I thought of what we had to do the next day. I still hated watching you fight, especially at events like these where people regularly got severely injured or worse. I can't even imagine what I would have done if something—I just always hated watching you fight.

"Alright, I'll see you soon." Then you hung up the phone and left me alone with my spinning thoughts. I'm sure there's more I could say about that night, but really anything else that happened after that point is irrelevant, especially because I know everyone wants to know what happens next. What happens next, is that I do something absolutely horrible.

I woke up with anxiety racing down my back and around my neck, like the air had wrapped cold hands around my throat and was pressing down hard. You were already up rushing around the place pulling stuff into bags and making coffee, I didn't know if you were just nervous and couldn't sit still or whether you knew that anything productive that day was going to have to be done by you. Either way, by the time I got up, you were ready to go. I just smiled and nodded when you threw me clothes. We weren't going by ourselves, even though I had said it would be better to fly, you insisted that we drove down with the rest of your team in the old and shaky van your coach had acquired, and I couldn't say no because I knew it was important for you. Even though the idea of sitting in a van with your team for hours on end was like a realm of hell for me. Despite that, I didn't say anything as we loaded into the van, not when your coach looked at me with judgment or when your teammates made remarks when I walked by them. Even now, that sport is not the embodiment of open-mindedness, let alone back then, and had you been anyone else I'm sure there would have been a problem but right from the first day your feet touched the mats you told them who you were because you were unwilling to be back in the same situation we had just barely escaped from. After you threw one punch it was apparent that they needed you and you knew it, which meant you got to bring me with you wherever you went because there was absolutely nothing anyone could do to stop you. We sat down at the back; it was too early for you to talk to anyone yet. Instead, you put an arm around my shoulder as though the whole van wasn't watching our every move.

"I'll be okay." You said softly as you rested your head against mine. I moved closer.

"It's alright if you lose, we will be alright," I said because I knew it felt like the entire world was resting on nothing but this one single fight; like your entire life had built up to that moment and if you made it, then it would justify every sacrifice you'd ever made to end up there; maybe you were trying to find something to justify walking away from your brother, maybe you thought if you could make it big then it would justify your parents walking away from you. Either way, I said the words because I knew what it was like to fail, and no matter whose hand was raised in the air at the end of the night as long as you were whole and alive and *you*, then it didn't matter. We could figure it out. But you didn't see it that way, you never did because you were being held ransom to a sport that screamed it was everything you were allowed to be.

You didn't respond to me, only looked straight ahead to your coach who was driving the van.

"Yea." You put your headphones on after that and closed your eyes. A man named Jarrad, someone who would play a part in our undoing, looked at me with wild eyes—maybe it was hate, but now I think it was just pure jealousy at the fact I knew who I was. Maybe you weren't sleeping because I remember you pulling me closer.

To be honest, the rest of the drive just blurs together, I was tired and stressed and too scared to let myself think of the ticking time that was bringing us closer and closer to the moment I was dreading the most. I wish I could tell you more about it, only so that there is more time until things go wrong, as though if I write things down differently this time then I could change our history altogether. But I honestly have nothing to say about that drive other than the fact that it was uncomfortable, hot, and anxiety-inducing. All too soon we were pulling into the parking lot and I was watching your teammates pile out of the vehicle into the parking lot.

"Ready?" You said against the shell of my ear and I took a breath because I was as ready as I was ever going to be.

7

Who Cares What Day it is.

Sometimes I feel like I'm nothing more than a standing collection of memories. As though I'm no longer a person but instead a crumbling monument to every beautiful thing I've ever lost.

How can I be anything else when your tattoo burns the inside of my skin; when your pendent hangs around my neck and your old clothes are still next to mine in the closet—nothing I've ever owned has ever truly been *mine*, every single part of me has *always* been laced and entangled with the meaning of you. So how can I possibly be a real person when everything I know about myself fades deeper into history by the second? I don't want to write this anymore; I can't look at all my mistakes spewing out onto these pages line by line as though it's just some story that I get to one day walk away from. This is the rest of my life and I—I don't even know how to want it.

. . .

The hotel that the event was being staged at was beautiful, especially for people like you and me who came from nothing. It was exactly the way fancy resorts look on TV; with tall windows and palm trees near the entryway and a chandelier hanging in the lobby. You wrapped an arm around my shoulders as we walked through the doors, and the doorway alone was bigger than our entire apartment. I looked around the room at every detail.

"Are you sure we are in the right place?" I whispered into your side because this seemed too nice for people like us. But when I looked to you, your eyes were bright and certain.

"This. *This* is the kind of place we belong." Belonging was written on your face in every line. Finally, you were standing in a room with the best of the best and being given the chance to prove yourself amongst them; a chance to belong to something other than the two of us again and I wanted you too, god I felt lucky to even stand beside you because you still screamed confidence and knowledge and that same stupid safe arrogance, and it was intoxicating. I smiled instead of giving a voice to the doubts running through my head.

Your coach checked us both into our rooms, me being the only reason you got one to yourself instead of sharing with five other people. I honestly can't remember his name right now, something like Dave or Rob, something stern and strong, but really the name doesn't change anything, maybe that's why I've forgotten it. I feel like it was Rob, so let's go with that. Rob looked at us both before handing over the key. I was waiting for his snide remarks, he thought I was a distraction and had said that much to my face but he didn't have to like me, even in the years that followed he never warmed up to my ongoing presence in his gym, not even when he hired me to photograph his fights; instead, we created a mutual tolerance of each other.

"Be down for pads in ten minutes." You nodded your head with a smirk, both of us caught how the word *alone* was hanging off the tip of his tongue, but you were untouchable, especially for that weekend. It's not often that you were nervous, always level headed and calm, its why we worked so well; we were like war in peace sleeping in a single bed, I would do the negotiating while you fought the battles, but at that moment, you were just as nervous as me.

I knew it because when we finally got to our room, instead of sitting down as I did, you decided that you needed to look at and touch every single object that wasn't bolted to the floor. I watched as you bounced on the heels of your feet the second you stopped.

"Babe please, sit down you're making me dizzy." Slowly you did, coming over to sit down beside me with a sigh of impatience. I put a hand to your shaking leg. "Just take a breath," I said and you did, slowly letting it out once a few seconds had gone by.

"I just want to get it done and over with. I want to get in there and do exactly what I've been trained to do." The ring was always your safe place; the gym was like a hiding place where you could hold up the world which always seemed to fall apart above you. Sometimes you reminded me of a Greek hero; back then you were Atlas with how you carried the weight of the world on your shoulders every day without ever complaining, but now I think Achilles. Young, beautiful, and fated to die before he had a chance to live, and I'm just the poet destined to write about it once it's over instead of being the hero to change things while they could. That night, whether Achilles or Atlas or any other godly being, you were filled with the all too human feeling of waiting.

"Go hit pads, it will chill you out." I laid back on the bed, feeling the soft blanket beneath me; I was exhausted.

"You coming?" You asked while grabbing your gear from our single suitcase. The carry-on was for your gloves and protective gear and we didn't have enough money to pay for more baggage. I sighed. Really it would have been fun to go with you that night, I wish more than anything now that I would have just gone because then no one would have been in our room to answer the phone, we both would have been away and it would have been no one's fault but fate. But no, I stayed behind that night even though I usually went, but I was tired and didn't want to fight with your coach anymore. It was your weekend, not mine.

"No one wants me there. it's easier to stay here." For once you didn't try to argue with me or give me some long explanation as to why I should be with you, instead you nodded your head because I was right.

"You can come with me if you want to." You added, as though trying to make me realize that there was no line you wouldn't cross; nowhere you could go that I wasn't allowed to follow but not everything in our lives had to be a war; everyone didn't always have to pick the other side and leave us defenseless but fighting none the less. This was one of those times.

"Go and get some energy out. I'll meet you in the lobby before weigh-ins." You nodded with a small smile before walking over to where I sat. We looked at each other for a split second and it was just us. It was always you and me fighting this invisible monster that neither of us could see. You kissed my forehead while I smiled, loosely grabbing the fabric of your hoodie to keep you close.

"Love you," you said while basically pouncing out the door. I let myself sit with my eyes shut for a while afterward, letting the feeling of your lips on mine linger long after you left. I laid back down before the bliss wore off. It's at this point I made my first mistake.

I remember this moment like a scar because I was given a choice and I know a lot of people would have made the same one as me, but it doesn't change the fact that I almost took something irreplaceable away from you. I woke up to the sound of your phone ringing beside me. You never brought it to the gym for this exact reason. I reached for it slowly although I was still half asleep.

"Hello?" I asked, thinking it was Sam or someone else from the city.

"Sebastian—it's Hannah—it's your mother," I choked on my own breath because—because it was your *mom*. "Something happened and you—we need you to come home." Her voice was tired and worn as though she hadn't slept in days.

A part of me wanted to scream at her because it was your mom; your mom who never called or emailed, never tried to find out where you went or if you were even still alive, she just let you walk away and never, *ever* thought to make sure you were okay in the world. I don't understand how any parent could care so little about something they had created. I'll never forget the first time your birthday came and went without a word from her or the first time you were in the hospital and the only thing you wanted was your family but there was no number to call but mine. I wanted to hang up the phone because how dare she call five years later, after *everything* she had put you through? I was the one who put you back together after she left you in millions of scattered pieces and I couldn't do it again. But I didn't say any of that because I could hear her crying from the other end of the phone.

"What happened?" I asked, I knew I should have told her that it wasn't you but I couldn't, I had to know what was so important she decided to reach out. I wish I would have run down the stairs and burst into the training room to tell you that your mom was on the phone because you deserved to know. But I didn't. And I think about that choice every day.

"It's Christian—it's bad and he, he asked for you." Her voice broke on his name. "What I mean is—you need to come say goodbye." I almost dropped the phone because—*Christian.*

The child who had been fighting since the day he was born; the reason that you fought so hard to succeed and the only reason you would ever go back. The boy you would die for what dying and you weren't there to hold his hand. I took a deep breath while closing my eyes tightly, as though I could escape reality for a moment.

"Hannah, I'm not your son. But I promise I'll pass on the message." I hung up before I could hear her cry anymore and all I could do was stare at the phone. It felt like a rubber band was about to contort my lungs into nothing but pin-sized holes; the grief building in the pit of my stomach for someone I never even knew was heavy and real but it wasn't my grief—it was *yours.*

Everything in our life was about to change and there was a piece of me desperately trying to hold onto the sweet moment of peace we had found. But I couldn't change this, and this was going to change you. It was going to change the way you looked at yourself in the mirror, it was going to change the way you looked at me because it was my fault that you left him in the first place. At least that's what I thought back then, now I know it was nothing but selfishness that kept me from telling you the moment I found out; I wanted you like you were, I wanted you safe and happy and *mine*. I think I was afraid that if you went back to that town, it would hold you forever. I should have told you and I was going to tell you, but then I looked at the clock and remembered the fight and the rules meeting and that you were waiting for me, and I realized that you were stuck living in a world that didn't exist anymore, your ignorance to reality kept you in a moment when your brother was still alright. I couldn't take it away from you, not right before you got into the ring. I could live with you hating me, but I couldn't live with the idea of you being seriously hurt because I opened my mouth.

I don't think I'll continue on with this tonight, as I don't think I deserve to talk about the good stuff that followed on the same page that I confessed. I have to pick up our daughter tomorrow and a part of me wishes more than anything that I didn't. I don't know how to do this; *I don't know how to do this* and I don't *want* to do it because you're not here. It was supposed to be you and I remember? You and me and all our history and pain and wars, you and me in this foxhole together while the rest of the world fought each other but then—but then you had to go and *die*. Now the foxhole is locked and I am stuck in the middle of the crossfire without a way to surrender. How can I look after an entire person when I can't get out of bed? How can I look her in the eye and tell her ill protect her when every morning I wake up waiting for you to protect me? I don't know how to do this; I don't even know how to try.

8

Sunday, September 23th

A few days ago, Spencer said that he was going to take Maisy to see your dad until Wednesday. This was decided a few days after I stopped answering the phone, or maybe when he showed up and I was still in the same position I had been in the last time he saw me as though my bones had calcified and morphed into the shape of your indent on the left side of our bed.

51 days ago, you laid there beside me; you took deep breaths and laughed and put your hands around my torso when you were cold. 51 days ago, we laughed when Maisy cried from down the hall and argued over who got to pick her up because you couldn't stay away from her for more than a minute. 51 days ago, I knew who we were, now I'm trying to find the pieces of myself scattered through the pages of this book.

. . .

After I got the phone call, I didn't have much time before I had to go to the rules meeting and watch you step on the scale in front of hundreds of people. In my personal opinion, it was the most messed up part of the sport; you got on a scale, wearing little to no clothing in your most vulnerable state and waited for it to tell you whether or not you were enough.

That night I wiped my eyes and put on your sweater and left, I left the phone plugged into the wall. That hotel was larger than I expected it to be, the space seeming so much bigger when I was forced to navigate it by myself because everyone there looked so important, so intimidating and regal. They could eat me alive; my shield of untouchability was gone leaving me exposed to whatever horrors that would come upon me. The only thing that kept me from falling subject to the disorder was your last name written in bold letters across my back, but it felt like a status I didn't deserve, not when the only thing I had done to earn it was asking you for a pencil all those years ago. It felt like everyone I passed was staring at me by the time I found my way to the ballroom, I wanted to cry when I saw you standing with your team, a smile gracing your face. It was supposed to be your big weekend, the moment that was destined to change your life, and in a way, it did, just not in the way we thought it would.

You starting jogging towards me as though we had been separated for months and not hours. You always greeted me like that, every single time no matter how long we had been apart you always acted as though it was the first time. I held onto you tighter than I had any right to at that moment, pushing my face tightly against your chest as though I could stop what was about to happen. You laughed as you ran a hand lightly through my hair.

"Miss me?" You joked while pulling away, I grabbed the front of your jacket but I couldn't look you in the eyes

"Always." And it was true, it was true then and it's true now. You put an arm around my shoulder before walking towards our seats. I really wasn't supposed to be there; these meetings were strictly for coaches and fighters but there I was anyways as though I belonged. How did they know I wasn't a coach? We sat down and the man started talking about the rules of the fights but I couldn't pay attention, all I could think about was the fact that I *needed* to tell you. I thought I could keep it to myself but I couldn't, I couldn't look at you without seeing your mom and brother. Maybe things would have been different if I would have kept my mouth shut till afterward. My hands were shaking as you walked up to the scale. I knew it was going to be close, I had watched you eat next to nothing for days, I prayed to God that you could have just one more moment of joy before I had to take it away. If nothing else, no matter if you made weight or not, I wouldn't have to feel you tremble in my arms from malnutrition again. I smiled despite my internal conflict, something I did a lot back then. The crowd went silent while we all waited in anticipation.

"160.0." The announcer said over the speakers and I wanted to cheer out from the pure relief I felt. I laughed as you played to the crowd, raising your hands in the air as though you had already won because you made it. And sometimes those weigh-ins felt like a bigger victory than the fight ever did. I push my face into your shoulder when you sat back down beside me, wrapping my fingers around the fabric of your hoodie as you placed a kiss on my forehead.

"You did it," I said and I felt like I was going to explode with the mix of emotions running around in my head; happy that you made it, guilty that you weren't already on the first flight home, horrified of what you would do when you found out I had been keeping it from you for hours. The rest of the evening went by surprisingly ordinary.

I won't bore Dr. Riley with the specifics of rules meetings because they really might be the most boring things in the world, but the entire time I kept waiting for a pause, for a moment when I could steal you away and spill my guts about what I knew and wait for your world to come crashing down around us. But the time never came. Before I could do anything, we were all standing outside the hotel laughing about something I don't remember, probably the fights or the food, cheering about the things that were promised to happen in the following days.

"let's take a look at what's going on down the road," Jarrad said while taking control of the group. I don't remember most of the people other than a tall man named Jax who had kind eyes.

He is actually coming over tonight. The group of fighters started walking in the direction Jarred had pointed and I wanted to scream in frustration because NO, now was *not* the time for laughing and smiling and walking around downtown, I wanted to rip out my hair and rake my nails up my arm because it felt like my skin was crawling with all the things I hadn't had a chance to say. You smiled as though waiting to see if I wanted to go, I smiled back and started walking, holding your hand tightly as I did.

The things we saw that night in Orlando, are to this day, some of the most amazing things I've ever seen. Maybe one day when she's older, I'll bring Maisy there too. We walked with stringed lights hanging above us and a band playing in the background. It was warm and inviting and it felt a lot like home with the constant activity even though it was getting close to midnight. We stumbled across a night market and I wanted to cry because it was something straight out of a movie; something that didn't really happen in the real world like a dream and then you were kissing me right in the middle of all of it as though I was the main character.

But I couldn't even enjoy it. I couldn't laugh or let myself believe that this was the life we had fought so hard to make because under it I knew I was keeping the real world hidden away. You pulled back and we both watched as Jarred ran towards a milkshake stand. You looked at me with something weird in your eyes.

"Are you okay?" you asked, gripping both my arms to keep me from turning away. That was it, that was the moment I had been waiting all night for. I looked at the ground.

"Yea, everything's great. Go have fun." I couldn't do it. Not when everyone was dancing and jumping and laughing, not when the moment was so pure and sweet. There was about to be so much darkness in your world, I couldn't take away a single moment of light.

I followed behind you guys slowly, taking a moment to myself to look at the sights and the people walking by me. It seemed crazy that I was standing there at all; when I thought of the last five years in the city and the things that happened before, I couldn't find the right words to describe how grateful I felt to be standing there at all; to have you kiss me in the middle of the street and to have a place to call home and friends who actually knew us. It was everything I had ever wanted. I moved to sit on the steps of the milkshake shack, looking above at the dancing lights.

"You are going to love this." You said while coming to sit on my left. You handed me a cup. I took a sip of the peanut butter ice cream situation and really, it was magical. But what was even better was watching the childish amazement on your face after you took a bite of the burger you had been dreaming about for weeks. To be honest, I think you may have been more excited to eat than to fight.

"Is it absolutely everything you thought it would be?" I asked with a tease, you just nodded your head while taking another bite.

"Hey, remember to breathe over there," Jarrad added while coming to sit on my right, seeming to be taking the same joy from watching you as I was. I almost left him out of this story completely, but then I realized if Maisy ever read this, I would want her to know what a bad man looks like. I wouldn't want her to be afraid to talk about the things that scare her so neither will I. We both watched as you ate like a child who had been deprived of food for months on end. Not even your mother could stop me from laughing.

"I dare you guys to go on that," Jarred said while pointing to the giant two-hundred-foot swing ride that towered above us, even looking at it made me want to throw up. You shook your head.

"Nah, C isn't big on heights." Jarrad looked to me with a challenge, his eyes seeming to scream nothing but the fact that all I ever did was hold you back.

"Come on, don't you want to have a little fun?" he said directly to me this time, but there was something dark in his voice, something unplaceable and wrong. You seemed to hear it because you stopped eating your precious burger to look at him.

"I can do it," I said before you could say anything more. I wanted to fit in, I *would* be more than just a weight tied to your back. You just looked at me as though I had four eyes instead of two.

"What? You don't have to, Jarrad, leave it alone." I clenched my jaw.

"No, I'm sure. Let's do it." You smiled at me and it was real if not surprised. I would be one of you, maybe not in the ring, but just this once I would be the same as you. I wanted to belong even half as much as you dared to.

Of course, it took me all of five seconds to regret every single decision that had brought me to that point because I was strapping into a flying death trap. Nothing until the last few months has ever made me feel that afraid before and for good measure. But it was too late to back down, the seat belt was tightened and the gears were turning and I was committed to my worst decision. I couldn't help but look at the very thin chain connecting us to the main structure.

"You have nothing to prove to them." You said and your voice was so full of understanding and confusion as though you couldn't understand why I would change anything about myself in order to fit someone else's agenda. My hands shook as they gripped the restraints tighter. You put a hand on top of mine.

"Maybe you should have left this to us." Jarred said from the seat in front of me as though he was afraid of nothing at all.

"I'm fine." I gritted between my teeth but I wasn't, I was so far from fine that I couldn't even see it anymore. My anxiety ran up my neck like a whisper, finding its way into my chest making each breath more constricted than the next. If I was standing up, I think I would have passed out, but the *extreme* nausea shooting through my chest was nothing compared to the guilt resting on my shoulders. You didn't say anything else, only shook your head like a disappointed parent. From the day we met until, the day you—something that stayed the same was the way you never changed yourself for someone else; not your parents or coaches or friends, no matter who it was, you always gave them *exactly* who you are and never anything else. It confused you when people played pretend.

I stopped breathing when the ride started, the two of us going around and around in circles as we got higher and higher. I wish I could say that somehow the higher we got the freer I felt, or that despite my fear in the aftermath of it all I was glad I did it—I mean, I'm glad I got to hear you laugh and smile and throw your hands to the air like a child, and I'll never regret one moment with you, but if I had to pick five of those moments that weren't my favorite, that one would without a doubt be on the top. You grabbed my hand tightly.

"Remember the time we went to the beach? We sat behind that horribly smelling bush so that people wouldn't notice us." Your voice was strong, as though we were in the car or back in the hotel room instead of on a death-defying ride. I closed my eyes, unable to keep them open any longer without losing my grip.

"Yea—we drank diet coke out of Champaign glasses." You didn't comment on the shakiness of my voice, only grabbed my hand tighter.

"That was a fun day. I realized I loved you on that beach." We were spinning even faster but I tried to listen. "The sun was down so we were walking around since everyone else was gone, and you found a little crab too far away from the water—I think it was in a sandcastle left by some kid but you picked it up quickly and ran to the water," I wanted to laugh at the memory, how naive and young we had both been. "You even flipped over some rocks until you found more of them, you said that you didn't want him to be alone. As we stood in the freezing water, I knew I loved you." I pushed my face into your shoulder, smiling at the memory.

I don't remember there being one distinct moment where I realized I loved you; Instead, I think it was *everything*. It wasn't like on TV when the main characters have these epiphany moments where they realize they are in love because loving you, loving you became every small thing we ever did. It was the way we went grocery shopping, and how you knew my drink order no matter what coffee shop we went to; it was how you started keeping a sweater in the back of your car because I always got cold or the way you always had a pack of gum in your pocket in case, I had anxiety. It was the little mundane things that proved how interlocked our lives had become because really—being loved is simply being *known*. But, if I had to put a finger on one single moment, it would be when I walked home one night and got hit in the face with just how far I was willing to go in order to protect what we had created. It terrified me because I found myself thinking of the future and you as synonymous with each other; It was indescribable and irreplaceable; every part of my life had been tangled with yours and there was no way I would be able to untangle it even if I wanted to.

"Such a sap."

I gripped the fabric of your shirt tighter as the people in front of us shouted out with joy. There was something magical about screaming into the night air with no one around to judge you but the moon, in another life I would have had my hands towards the sky and had nothing to fear. I would have been invincible, but in this life, I was quite certain we were about to fall to our deaths.

"You're doing great. I promise your perfectly safe, I got you." You said louder this time so that I could hear you over the noises around us. To be honest, it gives me anxiety just thinking about that night, it makes my skin crawl and chest fill with led because it really was one of the worse experiences I had faced up to that point in my life. For some reason, when I heard a man named Damon yell out in joy, I had this insane notion that I could suddenly be brave like them. Slowly I moved my head away from your shoulder, as though I was about to look at Medusa, and opened my eyes. I looked at the people on the ground and they looked like ants, I thought I was going to throw up. The only thing that could make our situation worse would be me throwing up. You draped an arm around my shoulders, pulling me as close to yourself as you possibly could.

"Oh god," I said quietly, feeling both embarrassed and thankful that I could feel us slowing down. Actually, I think I was far too afraid to feel embarrassed; I was just thankful we didn't die.

"It's almost over." You said while placing a kiss on the top of my head. Even when I did stupid things you never got mad or frustrated, only went along and made sure I was still in one piece after it was over. Maybe it came from growing up with a younger brother who constantly needed you.

"I'm sorry," I said because I couldn't stop myself, I'm still not sure what I was apologizing for. Whether it was for ruining your fun, or your life.

"Nothing to be sorry for." You laughed but there was *so* much to be sorry for. That ride seemed to go on for another three hours even though I'm sure it was only ten more seconds. I already knew that I was never going to hear the end of this, that the second we were back on the ground your team was going to rip me a new one for being such a wimp, but I didn't care. At least we would be on the ground. "Told you that it would be okay!" You said with a smile once I lifted my head to realize my feet could touch. The whole experience felt as though it had taken years off my life span, but I don't think I'm that lucky.

"I think I'll just watch next time," I stated with absolute certainty. Maybe one day I'll go there with Maisy and ride It again with her, I'm not sure anything can scare me anymore.

The second the ride stopped I was detangling myself from the seat and walking over to the bench in order to gather my thoughts, I couldn't breathe. My legs were shaking too much to stand. I felt your hand on my shoulder but didn't open my eyes, instead, I focused on myself and the things I had to do in order to stay in one piece. I heard Jarrad's laughter before I noticed him in our space.

"Too much for you yea?" He teased as he punched my shoulder "playfully". You moved to stand more in front of me.

"Leave him alone." Your voice was still light and fun but it hinted at something deeper, anyone else would have backed down instantly. Jarred didn't, instead he raked his eyes up and down as though sizing up an opponent. Maybe things would have been different if you two fought that day instead of a year down the line.

"What, he can't take a joke?" The rest of the team looked at each other as though deciding whether to laugh or walk away. You could take a joke and so could I but, at the moment, it wasn't funny; it was embarrassing and only said in order to make me feel small and insignificant compared to the rest of them. Everyone knew I was off-limits; you would tolerate a lot, but not that.

"I said, leave him alone." That was the end of the conversation. Everyone nodded along, not wanting to be on your bad side because they all knew that Jarred was being a dick just because he could. You gave me a hand and I took it, unable to look any of them in the eye because once again I was a little kid who couldn't speak for themselves. Thinking back on it I should have said something, but I couldn't. I was so busy thinking about the ride and your mom and everything we still had to deal with that Jarrad's sharp words didn't even cut through my first line of defense. When you turned to look at me your face was soft, all the hard edges had been replaced.

"Want to ditch this whole thing?" I nodded my head but I didn't want to, not really because the second we were truly alone I was going to have to tell you what I knew. It had been five hours already and every second felt like another mark on my own grave. You turned to your team with a wave. "We are gonna go, have fun guys." Your arm moved around my shoulder as we walked away, hearing someone whistle behind us.

We formed a comfortable silence that automatically engulfs two people who have been around each other more of their life than not. I think we were probably almost at the hotel by the time you sighed.

"Want to tell me why you, someone deathly afraid of heights, thought *that* was a good idea?" The embarrassment ran up my back because it was you, not your teammate or coach, it was you confronting me and I knew it was stupid.

"I wanted to be like you guys," I said quietly and you couldn't get it. You had never tried to fit in or worked hard in order to be seen, all you ever had to do was exist for people to love you.

"I don't want you to be like them." You said it as though it was obvious instead of something I could never truly believe. You didn't look at me, only at the people around us.

"I just wanted to fit in with you guys and your world, and yea—maybe I just thought that was the way in."

"But you don't have to fit in with that world C," You stopped walking and moved us out of the direct line of traffic so that we had a minute to ourselves. What you said next is something that sums up everything anyone ever needs to know about us or the people we used to be. You looked me in the eye and said; "It's them who have to find a way to fit into *ours*."

That's it, that's who we were. Both of us were against the army, huddled underground in our little fox hole praying for the shooting to stop. Everyone else outside the two of us was automatically a stranger who needed to find a way to belong with us because you and I weren't going anywhere. You kissed me slowly before moving away as though the kiss was nothing but a seal to an indirect promise. I held your hand tighter.

"What did you think about the milkshake?" You asked as though to lighten the mood somehow

"It was good." My mind was already back in the hotel room as I ran through the conversation we had to have because I had no idea where to start.

I wish I would have been in the moment more; I wish I would have told you that the milkshake was the best thing I'd ever tasted and danced with you to the sound of the band. I wish we would have walked around all night long because it was the last night like that we would have for ages and if I could go back, I would have taken in every single second of it to keep close when things got too difficult to breathe. But I didn't, instead, I was stuck in my head already grieving the loss of you as though you had already left.

"Just good? I think what you're *trying* to say is that it was earth-shatteringly amazing." You were trying to make me laugh; making each word more dramatic than it had to be in order to make the storm cloud disappear from my chest. But even you couldn't make it better and it's something that haunts me every day because *god* I wish I would have just laughed with you. You must have noticed my change in attitude because you didn't try to talk again, instead you gripped my hand deathly tight as though you could feel me about to float away.

By the time we got back to the hotel, I could barely breathe, suddenly the only thing I knew how to say was my confession so I didn't speak. Not until we were safe in our room away from the prying eyes of the world. You knew something was wrong because you sat down on the bed and started bouncing your leg up and down. I paced around the room as I tried to find the right words to say; the room filled with enough energy to kill us both. You grabbed my hand to make me stand in front of you.

"What's going on Collin?" Your voice was so quiet and suddenly you weren't a fighter, you were just a boy who was afraid of the next thing I was going to say. I looked at you and had to stop the tears from coming to my eyes at the pure fear written across your face.

"I—I have to tell you something," I said and the words were desperate, as though I was already asking you to stay.

"If you are going to break up with me, just stop because it's not happening—" I kissed you before your line could continue because I couldn't hear you say it. I couldn't hear the panic in your voice at the thought of me leaving you as though there was any world where I could. I moved away but left my forehead resting against yours. I kissed you as though I was never going to kiss you again

"I promise I'm not," I saw you take a breath as I backed away, I knew that your mind could change, that our entire life was about to change and you didn't know it yet.

"You're scaring me."

"Nothing scares you." I was trying to delay the inevitable a little longer, even now as I write this, I am trying to put it off because I hate this part of the story. You didn't laugh.

"You have always scared me." There was no hesitation to your voice, instead, the words were certain and raw. I took a deep breath.

"No matter what, I love you." It felt like my final words, like it was the last thing I would say before I died or you walked out of my life forever. Of course, it was stupid to think you would leave, of course, you would stay but I was *so* afraid that you were going to get mad and leave like everyone else always did. I wiped away a tear that started falling down my cheek.

"I love you too." I dropped your hand and continued pacing around the room, the motion helping me to collect my thoughts

"Seb—your mom called today." I held my breath and waited for the bomb to destroy us. I was waiting for you to move, to react or for your face to change but it didn't, instead, you just looked at me with confusion.

"What?" Your voice wasn't yours; it was controlled yet more vulnerable than you had been in years.

"Your mother called this afternoon while you were hitting pads." I moved to sit down on the floor in front of you as though supplementing at the feet of a king. I was close, but still not close enough to touch. You looked at me, and I'll never be able to forget what your face looked like, I don't even want to describe it because it was something meant for no one but me.

"What—what did she say?"

You had been waiting five years for that one call and you missed it. She never phoned back. Your voice was tight as though you were trying to hide every ounce of emotion. I looked at the ground, not able to meet your eyes because there were tears forming and I couldn't see it as I choked on the words that would break your heart. I just wanted things to stay the same, for you to stay mine and for the world to stop ending. "Andrew—what did she say?" I looked up because you said my first name. Since I met you, I think I've heard you say my real name four times; one was the first day we met, the second time was that night in the hotel room, the third was when I got really sick in the hospital and you were more afraid than I think you'd ever been, and the last time was the first time we held our daughter. This was by far the worst.

"It's Christian—" I spit out, the words burning my throat. I saw your jaw clench.

"What?"

"She said Christian—Christian is dying and you need, you need to go say goodbye." Once the words had been said I couldn't take them back. I couldn't take them back and it felt like I had jumped off a cliff and halfway down started regretting my fall. I watched motionless as tears fell from your eyes.

"Christian—" Your voice broke on his name. The person you had cried over, had walked away from and left there because your family had given you no choice. You always wanted to call him, to reach out and give him the choice to know you or not, but you never did. Instead, you let him go, maybe it was easier for you to have no reminders of the past, other than the man who slept beside you each night. You left him, because of me.

"I'm so—so sorry," I said, wanting to reach out and touch you but I knew it would not be wanted. I searched your eyes for something—for *anything* to give me some sort of sign that you were okay or not or just stuck somewhere in between. Before I could move you were up and walking around the space, right past me as though I wasn't there. I watched as you ran a hand through your hair.

"Why didn't you tell me? I hit pads this afternoon, what if—" You never raised your voice when you were mad, instead you just calmly stated the facts and your feelings and it was always worse the yelling. Hearing your voice break on his name and watching the betrayal form in your eyes when you looked at me was *so* much worse than yelling would ever be. I always wished you would have yelled. I wanted to drown under the guilt that passed through me.

"Because I didn't know how—I wanted you to focus on the fight cause you could get hurt—" My reasons didn't make sense, I knew It; nothing I said could justify what I had done in keeping that from you. I couldn't bare the idea of you being hurt because of me, in my own horrible way I thought I was protecting you.

"That's not your choice—*you should have told me.*"

Your face broke my heart—I felt like I had cheated or done some horribly unforgivable crime, I deserved the pain you made me feel in that moment. I feel bad saying it like that, because the pain was yours, not mine.

"I'm sorry." I pleaded, still sitting on the floor and I couldn't tell if the tears in your eyes were because of your brother or me.

"We are supposed to be a team C, you and me, *always*—how could you keep this from me." I knew I was wrong; I could have taken away your chance to say goodbye. I didn't realize that fact until that very moment, that I could have been the reason you didn't get to say goodbye to him. You seemed to realize it too. "I have to call them—" You could barely speak and I wanted to take it all away, somehow, I wanted to fix it or change things but I couldn't. You grabbed your phone from the counter no longer thinking about the past or the barriers between you and them because it didn't matter. None of it mattered because your brother needed you and you *would* be there. I tried to find something to say but before I could you turned to look at me, and your eyes were on fire. "I can't—I can't look at you right now." You left and slammed the door behind you.

I need to stop here for tonight because—because my heart is racing so fast, I can feel it in my teeth. *Everything* hurts, every breath shakes and every heartbeat tears me apart because *you're not here.* I write these words and am going through hell in order to show some proof that we existed, as though someone is going to read them other than my therapist but they won't, they won't because it doesn't mean anything—*nothing means anything.* I can't describe the feeling coursing through my body right now but it leaves me paralyzed and unable to breathe a word other than your name, or speak because everything comes back to you, every song, every word, every time I eat or drink or just exist—*every time* I see our child or your friends, every time someone asks me if I'm alright or says they are sorry it comes back to *YOU*. You and your history and your life and your heart that stopped. How can I possibly be expected to survive without it when you never showed me how?

Everyone keeps saying that things are going to get better, but I don't think anything will ever be okay again. Maybe I'll finish this off tomorrow, maybe I won't.

It doesn't matter anyway.

9

Friday, September 28th

Jax is making me write this. And I mean he is *literally* sitting on the ground in front of me making me keep going with this godforsaken book. That's all I have to say about my life currently because I've said everything else I can possibly say. I wasn't going to continue with this; I put the book in the trash and threw out all the pens and was ready to lay in bed until I died, but then Jax showed up a few days ago and found out, and he hasn't left since. Maisy is in her room sleeping and Jax makes sure she's alright because we all know I can't do it. Let's just get this story done with.

The night that you walked out was rough.

I wish I could hide the truth and say that it wasn't, that I understood what I had done and was ready to face the consequences of it. But I wasn't.

Instead, I sat on the floor and waited for you to come back but you didn't. In all the years we had been together, we had never fought like that; sure, we had disagreements and got mad, I yelled and you took a walk but nothing had ever felt as real as that did, nothing felt like the way you looked at me before shutting the door. I didn't know what to do, how to move or breathe because you left, and I couldn't stop it, I couldn't make you stay or be mad because it was *my* fault. It was like someone had hollowed out my chest and then taken a knife and ran it through my lungs until there was nothing left but a slow beating heart. Of course, that was before I understood the real meaning of pain. You were gone and I had no idea where you were; whether you were sleeping on Jax couch, or on a plane to a home that never wanted you, or if you were out in the city trying to clear your head. I had no idea where you were and it was killing me. I cried that night while I watched the door. I watched it until I could imagine you walking through it as though if I willed it hard enough, I could make it happened. I wanted to scream, to plead with God to forgive me, or for me to be able to forgive myself for what I had done but then the alarm was going off and I realized it was the day of your fight, and I wasn't there.

Usually, I stayed with you backstage, I helped rub your legs down with Thai oil and helped you warm-up, I was right there in the middle of all of it every single time and now that it was the biggest fight of your life, I wasn't there. I wanted you to know that I was still there, that even if you hated me, I was still there and I couldn't just sit in that room and miss it. Instead, I wiped my raw eyes and threw on some off-brand hoodie, I pulled up the hood to hide my appearance.

The walk to the ballroom that day was different than the night before; your name wasn't on my back and I was walking alone with tear tracks down my face. I felt so small and insignificant, as though the people around me were going to eat me alive if I looked at them the wrong way. I knew better than to try and find you; I actually made every effort to avoid anywhere you would be because I couldn't handle seeing your face, I knew that you wouldn't be able to handle seeing mine. But I needed to know if you were there or if I should call to make sure your plane landed.

I walked up to the board of set fights where everyone had to sign in and tried to keep to myself as much as possible. I looked at the hundreds of names and there it was, your name written on the top because I had no doubt you had been the first person there. I didn't know what to do now that I wasn't with you and there was a nervous energy wrapping around my throat that I hadn't felt in a long time, not since that first day I watched you fight. I slowly walked into the ballroom and found a seat near the back because I didn't want to get in your head more than I was. Everything felt wrong; I couldn't keep my hands from shaking against my legs. I looked and saw other members of your team sitting in the front row.

The fights seemed to go on forever, each one drawing out until the very last round. I wanted to see you, I scanned my eyes around the room trying to find a flash of gold hair and green eyes, just to tell myself that you were okay but I couldn't find you, a part of me didn't believe you were there. I wanted to get down on my knees and beg you not to step into the ring because everything was wrong with it. By the time your fight got called, I had chewed all my nails down to nothing and I couldn't sit still. There was no walk-out or announcement before your fight, only your name being called in a robotic voice to a crowd of strangers. There was an overwhelming sense of wrongness to the entire event, every second of it was off from the very beginning. I watched your opponent walk to the ring, I don't remember his name so for now, I'll call him Jordan—I watched as Jordan walked to the ring with pure focus and determination, he was in for the fight of his life and was willing to go the distance. When your name was called, the sight was somehow worse than I thought it would be. For lack of better words my love, you looked horrible, and I couldn't look away because you looked as bad as I felt. Your eyes were dark and red, so far away from the ring you were walking into that I don't know if you had even registered the fact that the fight was starting. You were the sight of pure heartbreak; of tears falling and hearts breaking and I couldn't take it away or make it stop. *RUN* I wanted to scream, *RUN NOW* because it was *wrong*, the way you walked and held yourself, you had already given up and everyone could see it, worst of all, Jordan could see it. For the first time since I watched you fight all those years ago, I was filled with pure fear when I heard the bell ring.

You had lost before you threw the first punch and we knew it. Your coach could see it as he yelled at you desperately, your team knew it as you let Jordan throw shots that never should have landed, shots that on any other day never would have gotten anywhere near you but they did. You threw a jab out every now and then but it was as though you were just going through the motions, your heart both halfway across the country and right across the room. It was like the confidence you always carried had been eaten away before our very eyes and I couldn't stop it. I watched helplessly as Jordan pushed you into the corner, throwing knees that made you gasp.

"Put your hands up!" I yelled louder than the people around me, I could feel tears run to my eyes because I had never felt so *helpless*. You were going to get hurt and there was nothing I could do—I couldn't save you even though I would have done anything to. I didn't realize I was standing up, only that soon I was walking closer to the ring but not close enough for your team to realize it was me, or if they did, they didn't act on it. I watched you throw a body shot that made Jordan stumble back. "Go!!!" I screamed, half hoping you couldn't hear me but also praying you did. I watched as your coach looked at me with pure acid, and maybe it was because you told him what happened or maybe he knew all along that I was just going to mess everything up. Either way, when the bell rang, I looked away and walked back to my seat while running a hand through my hair.

"What is that kid doing? It's like he gave up." The man sitting beside me said, I turn to him with eyes of glass. "He is about to throw his life away for no reason." The man beside him nodded his head in agreement.

"It's a shame, he is making every wrong move, was he really trained for this?"

I couldn't hold down the anger growing in my chest anymore, instead of tears I wanted to punch him in the face because he had no idea who you were or what had happened.

"Hey, until I see you standing in the ring fighting for your life like he is, stop talking shit about things you can't possibly understand, you don't know who he is or what's going on in his life so just shut the hell up." I wanted to say so much more, I wanted to punch him and tell him that he had no right to judge you because your brother was dying and your estranged mother called you and your boyfriend had hidden it all. I turned away before he could say anything in response because I didn't want to hear it. I didn't care because I was mad and just wanted things to be okay again.

When I looked back at the ring, you were already looking at me and it took every ounce of strength that I had left not to run closer. Instead, I took a breath and nodded my head, forcing myself not to watch the blood run down your face. We shared a thousand words in that one glance.

Your coach moved to block me because he was desperately trying to get your mind back in the game you still had to play but it was to no avail, your mind wasn't going to come back to the fight because the fight wasn't real; it was a sport, not your life and we both felt it. I brought a hand to my mouth as the second bell rang. It seemed impossible that only a few hours before the world was different; you were set to win and everything was going to be okay. Now you were standing in a fight against yourself and there would be no winner. This time when the round started, you threw the first punch, and the second and the third. I heard your coach yell in triumph.

"Go!" I yelled but it's like my small words broke the spell because Jordan's next shot landed perfectly to your ribs, leaving you gasping desperately for breath and I could see the next shot before it happened.

I had watched enough fights to know how things worked and to notice the devastation that Jordan's next shot was going to bring and I couldn't look away. You saw it too late, something that never would have happened if you were focused but before you could move or put your hands up, the punch was thrown and for the first time in my life I was watching you fall to the canvas.

It was as though time stopped while you laid there unmoving, maybe you didn't want to face the crowd that was roaring in surprise or you couldn't bear to see your coach walking away but none of it mattered because this was more than a stupid fight. You were *hurt* and it was like my worst nightmare being presented in front of my eyes. I didn't know that I was moving until I was standing as close to the ring as security would let me and even then, I fought against him because all I could see was you.

"Seb—get up," I said desperately and the ref was standing above you but I didn't care, I only watched as you turned your head to face me and you were *so* broken—so broken and your face was so sad and I wanted to hold you while you screamed at the world for what it kept doing to you but I couldn't get within five feet. I needed to know you were okay but for the first time, I questioned whether or not I was truly your salvation.

I could barely see over the panic growing in my chest, everything I had suddenly was thrown into searching your face for something to hold onto. Slowly, with the help of your coach, I watched as you tried to get up, stumbling over to your chair with unseeing eyes and there was nothing I could do but slowly walk back to my seat with my heart beating a hundred miles per second. The walls felt as though they were closing around me, the floor seemed to fall away as I stumbled to my seat. The two men from earlier watched me as though I somehow owed them an explanation for what they had seen but I didn't owe them anything. I flipped them off as I stumbled towards the door because I needed to talk to you, to see you; to touch you and beg you to forgive me and I couldn't do it in that ballroom.

I don't remember walking up to our room, my mind couldn't stop seeing the sight of your bloody face and limp body and I couldn't breathe, my head spinning as though I was about to faint because I couldn't grasp onto anything solid. I was on the floor of our room gripping onto the carpet as though it could hold me to earth as my body trembled and I don't remember a lot of this from the moment it happened, a lot of it is how my mind filled in the holes of it all because my mind didn't feel like mine anymore. It was every fear and nightmare I had about you fighting all coming true and I just wanted it to all be over, I wanted the aching in my chest to stop and for my limbs to stop trembling and for my mind to let me go but it didn't, instead it held its hands around my throat and all I could hear was my heart racing in my ears. You were hurt and I wasn't there, *I wasn't there* and all I could do was curl in on myself while waiting for something to happen that would either kill me or let me breathe.

Eventually, I was sitting against the side of the bed, silent tears stained on my face as I watched the door, but hours passed with nothing. My brain was too tired and strained to think anymore. But of course, you came back at some point, maybe it was only an hour later or maybe it was six, time didn't exist in that room.

I watched the door open and I felt both nothing and everything at the same time, like a part of me wasn't sure whether you were real or only in my head. You didn't say anything as you stood in the doorway with a bandage across your forehead and bruises under your eyes. There were so many things that we both needed to say but neither of us could find the words to say it, you only shut the door and turned on a lamp. I hadn't realized how dark it was. When you came closer the sight of you made me want to throw up; your eyes were bloodshot and glassy, your skin torn and bruised and it was like a horribly distorted version of the person you had been before. You didn't say anything as you walked over to where I sat on the ground and I thought you would yell, that you would do something but instead to my surprise, you collapsed into my arms. I didn't move as you let your long limbs fold in order to fit on my lap and I didn't know what to do as you pushed your face against the side of my neck. A part of me was afraid that if I moved even an inch it would break the spell and you would leave again but I couldn't help it. Before I could think twice my arms were wrapped around your trembling form tighter than I had ever held onto you because you were *mine,* and you were whole and alive and I was *so afraid.* It was a moment of complete surrender even though the war was still being fought. You gripped onto the front of my sweater tightly as I heard you take a shaking breath.

"I'm so mad at you," You mumbled and there was no hint of a joke in your words, just raw, honest truth but your voice was so small. I rocked us back and forth slightly as though it could make the heavy feeling in my chest go away, I gripped my hands into the back of your shirt as though it would make you stay. "I almost didn't come back tonight." The words hurt something because I couldn't have imagined just waiting alone for another night while you slept broken and in pain on someone's floor. I pushed my face into your hair, smelling oil and sweat and you.

"Then why did you?"

I remember in that moment I became aware that I wanted to remember absolutely everything; the way it felt to have your fingers digging into my back and your hair brushing against the skin of my face, your smell and weight, and everything I could possibly think of because I never wanted to forget a second of it.

Jax tells me about the day he could no longer remember his mother's voice and the idea of that—of somehow living the *rest of my life* without you, *I can't*—suddenly you're just gone—

That night, I wanted to remember everything.

You moved against me so that we were looking at each other for the first time, the motion startled me from my thoughts and all I wanted to do was to run my fingers over your cheek.

"Because as mad as I am—you're the only person I'm allowed to be mad with." I didn't say anything, only let you finish. "I don't know how to be mad at you because—we just don't do it; I don't know how to do this." You took a shaking breath, "What you did was messed up but—my little brother is *dying* and I just—I just let down every single person—" I had never seen you so unsure, your words fragile and shaking and I wanted to wipe away the tears that started to fall. "My family, my team, my coach, you—I let them all down—and I'm in pain and I just, everything is falling apart right now and you are the only person who lets me be mad—" you took my hand and placed it against your face as though you knew I was too afraid to do it. I moved my other one to your neck without needing to be told. "—I just, I need—" I didn't need you to finish, I knew what you were going to say because I needed you too.

I pulled you tightly against my chest and ran a hand through your hair because you needed me and you were holding onto me as though you would float away if you let go. I pushed my face roughly into the side of your neck, I needed to be as close as possible.

"I'm sorry—" I started but failed because I couldn't keep my voice from breaking. "I'm sorry that this is happening, that I was a dick and didn't tell you I just—I thought I was doing the right thing but your right, it wasn't my decision to make and I'm so sorry." You were alive and in my arms; I couldn't have lived with myself if something had happened. It's hard to put into words exactly what we felt in that moment. I suddenly picked up a word you said earlier and I pulled away, moving both hands to your face so that you had to look at me.

"Seb—you could never let me down," my voice was stronger than it had been all day. "I don't care that you lost, what matters is that you are still okay and in one piece because—" I pushed my nose into yours. "We will figure this out—*you* will figure this out because you are the strongest person I've ever met, so *please* don't say that you let me down because it's me who messed this up." You looked at me with wet eyes. "But I promise that I'm going to do everything in my power to never let you down again." You didn't respond, only closed the distance between us in the most desperate form of confession I have ever felt.

"Just stay with me," I murmured against your lips, feeling every single word down to my core.

"Always. Even when you mess up." I wanted time to stop, I wanted to stay in that single moment with you forever but all too soon you were pulling away. You stood up slowly and offered me a hand. I took it and before I knew it, we were laying under the covers of the unused bed and your head was resting on my chest, for a moment I could believe that things might just be okay.

I would give *anything* to fight with you again—for you to scream and say It's my fault, swear that you've had enough and you hate me just *please—please don't be dead anymore.*

The morning came faster than it had any right to, before I could grasp the night it was already being pulled away from us. You were already awake by the time I opened my eyes and when I moved to look at you sitting against the headrest, your eyes were a lifetime away.

"I have to go back." You said with something forced and sad. It wasn't supposed to be a question because *of course* you had to go, but when you said the words, it was as though you were waiting for me to tell you that it was okay. I put a hand on your knee.

"I know," I said as gently as possible as though you would break if I spoke them too loudly. Never before had I thought of you as something breakable, but that morning with your bloodshot eyes you were just as breakable as me. You placed a hand over mine tightly.

"You can come with me." I smiled because, for the first time, I couldn't. Although you looked at me as though ready to break down the walls of hell if it meant that I could. You would have found a way to make it happen if I said yes and I did end up there for a while at the end, but you needed to see your family without me. It was something only you could do.

"You know that I have to stay." You leaned towards me and I caught you, moving my face closer to yours.

"I know." Neither of us said anything for a moment. I didn't know what to do because, for the first time since I was 16, I was going to be alone, truly alone in a city I didn't know how to navigate without you. In the long run, it was probably the best thing that ever happened to us because it made me grow up, but at the time it felt like the world was ending and I couldn't do anything about it.

"What did your mom say?"

"Nothing, she acted as though she didn't know me—like I was just some random stranger from the side of the road." I let you drape an arm around my shoulders as I moved impossibly closer to your side.

"You are, they don't know you anymore."

"How am I supposed to just walk in and face them now?" I understood your fear, I couldn't imagine what I would do if I had to walk into my parents' house, I still don't know what I would do or what I would say, and I had nothing that I could say to make it seem easier for you. You sighed beside me. "What if they ask about you? I'm not going to lie about who I am."

I had thought about that and a part of me wanted to tell you that things would be easier if you did. If you just told them you met a nice girl and had a wonderful life It might keep the peace a little longer than you would get otherwise. But I couldn't. They would ask, not only because the last time they saw you were with me, but because our stories were interwoven together in every breath; the necklace around your neck and the three tattooed dots running up your finger, the clothes you wore and the way you spoke, it was *us*. I didn't know if they would recognize the new version of you. I placed a kiss on your shoulder.

"Just try to remember why you are there; it's not about you or them, it's about Christian." You just nodded your head because I was right. You placed a kiss on my forehead

"If you never hear from me again it's because I'm locked in their basement." I didn't laugh because although I was fairly certain that they wouldn't lock you in the basement, I couldn't stop the fear from running through my chest at the idea of you not coming back. What if things were easier there, what If Christian was alright but you couldn't leave him again? I closed my eyes tightly against your chest.

"let's just not joke about it yet." You nodded. "When's your flight?" I didn't need to ask if you had one because I knew your mom had booked one the second you picked up the phone.

"3, when are you going home?" I caught the way you made sure that I knew home, still meant New York.

"Everyone is leaving tomorrow morning." If we had the money, I would have gotten on the first flight back because the idea of having to sit in that van alone with your team made me want to throw up.

"Are you sure you're okay if I leave?" You would have stayed if I asked you to; You would have missed your flight and done whatever I asked and I loved you for it.

"Of course, your family needs you." You stood up but offered me a hand. I took it and soon I was standing with your arms around my neck and my face pushed tightly under yours. I didn't want to let you go.

"I'm gonna come back, I promise." You said into the shell of my ear and I could feel your breath hitting my skin. I gripped onto your back tighter.

"I know." For a moment I didn't, but I'd be damned if I let you know it.

I don't remember much of that morning, maybe it's because the anxiety of having to leave there without you was blinding me to everything else, or maybe it's just that nothing exciting happened, maybe we were both too afraid of the future to speak. All I wanted was for time to stop or for some god to have even a sliver of mercy for us, but they never did. Of course, no cosmic force has ever had mercy on its forsaken. Before I could catch up, we were driving to the airport in your coach's rented car and it was like our fear was weighing down our tongues, leaving us both prisoners to the silence. That is until you moved a hand from the steering wheel and placed it on my shaking knee.

"It's going to be good; they are going to be so happy to see you," I said when you said nothing. You didn't say anything, never one for saying more than you had too especially when you were nervous. I wanted to make you laugh one more time, I wanted to see you smile and your eyes crinkle because I didn't know when I would see you smile again—I didn't know when I would see *you* again. "God, I'm going to have to learn how to use the oven."

You smiled but it was sad. I hated it, I hated everything about everything that was going on because it all felt wrong, but I didn't want you to know that. I just held your hand tighter as you drove closer to the airport.

Soon we were checking you in and I watched as you handed over your luggage that was only supposed to last a weekend. What was I going to do? It felt like I was stepping onto a tight rope for the first time with no net to catch me when I inevitably fell. We both looked at the hallway where you needed to go and we knew I couldn't follow. I took a deep breath as we stepped away from the crowd. Before I could do anything your arms were around my middle and I had no choice but to wrap my own around your neck because I never wanted to let go. You pushed your face in my hair.

"I'm coming back." You said and I could feel you shaking but all I could do was hold on tighter.

"I know."

You weren't just going home, you were going home to a place that didn't want you, to parents who tried to erase you and a brother who no longer knew you. And you were going alone. "Call me when you land."

"Of course," you moved back and I tried to memorize every detail. Even the bruises and dried blood. "I love you." You said and the words were so certain, so real and heavy and then you were kissing me in the middle of the airport, something that only five years earlier I never could have imagined but there we were like kids in love for the first time having to say goodbye. But you had to go, and your flight was waiting for you. You moved away first, "Try not to miss me too much." You laughed as you detangled yourself from me, then you picked up your backpack and smiled, if I was afraid, I knew it was nothing to how you were feeling.

"I love you too," I said as you started to walk away, you kept your eyes on me as you walked backward, placing a kiss on the necklace that hung around your neck. I don't think it was the idea of leaving that left us so torn up, it was the uncertainty of what would happen next; it was the realization that you didn't have a plane ticket home because we couldn't be certain of when it would be. I watched until you turned the corner, leaving me truly alone for the first time since I was a child.

I can barely see any more over the sound of Jax's breathing, the small sound piercing the rest of my senses but he *won't leave* no matter how badly I want him to. And maybe it's not the worst thing ever. He watches the baby and brings me food, and the empty apartment seems less like a coffin when there is someone else in it.

Or maybe it's just easier to go down with the ship when there is someone else on it.

I0

The next one.

I'm not sure that Jax is ever going to leave.

It's been a few days since you and I last talked but it feels like a lot has happened since.

Jax moved a bed into Maisy's room because he thought it would help if I didn't have to worry about the crying baby who I still can't face, or maybe he misses you and she is as close as he can get. It doesn't matter that you and her shared no blood, she was yours the second she came into the world. The two of you became as tangled as you and me and suddenly our foxhole grew room for another survivor. Maybe Jax is just trying to do well by you; by me and her because a part of him feels just as lost now that your gone—either way, he seems to be here to stay and I don't know how to feel about it. I like the silence because it lets me exist without having to be anyone else. I don't have to be the grieving spouse or the unworthy father, I just get to be *me*; a man losing his entire world without any ability to grasp it. Maybe as long as I keep writing to you, I can pretend as though you are simply away for a fight.

Jax is sitting in front of me because I have therapy tomorrow and still have nothing but an empty page.

The first few days of you being gone were some of the strangest days of my young life. It was different than anything we had gone through before, and it was different from when you left the second time once we were older, this was like I was being exposed to the real world for the first time in my life. As soon as I got on the van to head back to the city it became clear just how much everyone held their tongue while you were around and now that you were gone, now that I was *alone*, no one was holding back their shots anymore. The only thing that stopped me from being completely demolished was Jax. He sat beside me the whole time like a shield, as though as long as he was sitting there, I was still untouchable and a part of me felt like it. At least I had one friend behind enemy lines. I don't remember anything else about the drive, only that Jax kept trying to make small talk, and the sound his ring made as it hit the window. I couldn't stop the anxiety forming in my chest but it was for you, for the things you were going to have to endure in order to be with your brother and I wanted to take you away from it but I couldn't. All I could do was sit in a hot bus and watch the world go by.

When I got back to our place it felt indescribable, something I don't know how to put into words but it was just wrong and weird and suddenly so much bigger than it had been before. I don't really know what I did for the first few days, most likely I just lied around and felt sorry for myself, maybe I watched endless amounts of TV and ordered take-out because I had absolutely no responsibilities. I went to work and talked to Sam, but for a while life just continued on in this weird alternate reality without you. On one of the first few days—maybe the third, you phoned me and for some reason, I remember every word from that conversation. I was sitting on the couch watching some videos on my phone when you called and it felt like the world was normal again.

"Hey."

"Hi, miss me yet?" You asked and I let out a breath because your voice was still *yours*. It was different for both of us during those days; you were going somewhere, you had things to do and things to deal with and people who wanted to see you, whereas I was just sitting at home on my own, trying to figure out who I might possibly be.

"Nope, I've already moved in with Jax." I heard your dramatic gasp while I laid down.

"I knew it. Well, I'm sure you two will be very happy together." I watched the traffic outside. "My family really is just a bunch of dicks, save for my brother and dad." I laughed.

"So really you mean your mom is a dick and your dad and brother are chill." I couldn't even imagine how awkward it would have been when you first got there. "Maybe don't tell her that though."

"Why? They are acting as though I'm just some stranger who is imposing on a family emergency and I told them that much, I'm not 16 anymore." I knew that you weren't laughing anymore, you were alone behind enemy lines but I also knew that you were right; you weren't a teenager whose life depended on their acceptance anymore. You had your own life, a life you had created from nothing and no matter how badly anyone wanted to, they could never take that away from you.

"What did she say to that?"

"Nothing, she just walked away silently." I closed my eyes and thought of your voice, it sounded tired and worn already. "Like, they are the people who raised me, who fed me and loved me and they act as though we have never met, it's just weird."

"It's their loss," I said because I didn't know what else to say. Silence fell as I gathered the courage to say what I wanted to ask. "How is Christian?"

"I finally saw him today,"

In my head Christian was still a child of nearly ten; all round eyes and sunken cheeks, but he was almost 16 now, he was the same age that I was when this whole story started and that realization hit me harder than anything else.

"I'm sure he was so happy to see you."

"He was. I was so nervous but when I saw him it was just—he is so much older now C, he's taller than you and he's so different, yet he's still Christian and when I walked in the room he started crying and then I was crying because—I missed it all," I could basically see your eyebrows draw together as you found the right things to say. "He was hooked up to so many tubes and machines but I just held onto him—they never told him why I left." You sounded in pain, as though each word burned your throat to say because deep down you were still the same kid who was discovering that family might only mean blood. "And when I told him, he laughed." I heard you laugh as though in disbelief and so I followed, maybe we laughed because there were thousands of other words to be said yet they were all too heavy to be spoken.

"That sounds like Christian," I said even though I didn't really know who he was, but I imagined that a kid who had been through as much as him, wouldn't care about such mundane things.

"Yea, it was good. I just wish that my mom would have the same reaction." You sighed in the same way you always did when you wanted to change the subject. "What on earth are you going to do while I'm gone?"

"Wait for you to come back," I responded dramatically while looking around the place. "This gives me a chance to clean up your junk."

"It's not junk, it's perfectly organized." I looked at the chairs with piles of clothes on them and random objects that had collected in every corner you could find space in. It's like you had an affinity for closets as every piece of clothing you had was laying on the floor or on chairs and tables.

"For a toddler." I heard the door open on your side of the phone, and then someone was talking in the background.

"Don't lie, *Collin*, you love it."

"Your mom is standing behind you, isn't she?"

"Of course I miss you babe, literally all I do is think about you." I ran a hand over my face, imagining your mom's reaction.

"I'm going to buy a turtle and name it Fred if you don't say no right now."

"You're the best, I can't wait to see you again."

"Alright have fun with your mom, and call me tomorrow?"

"Absolutely, I love you." The extreme stress on the words made me laugh because we didn't say those words very much, only in extreme situations, and apparently when you wanted your mom to know that you were still very much with me. You were an idiot.

"Sure, love you too."

I hung up the phone before I could hear your mom's reaction but I'm sure it was comical. It was weird to be alone because I didn't realize how used to your presence I had become. I waited to hear your laugh from down the hall or to hear the soft sound of your breathing when I woke up, so many little things that I hadn't realized I was looking for until you were gone.

The worst part of every day is waking up—because for a moment it's *so* easy for my brain to think that your still there, that you're breathing down the hallway in the kitchen instead of— I don't sleep in our room anymore.

But that night I did.

There is not much to report on for a while, I just existed in my pre-ferred solitude but then Sam got tired of my absence in her social life and that's when things changed. Maybe it was the moment everything changed for us, the moment that set us down the path that I am on now. Either way, at the time it just seemed annoying. She showed up unan-nounced one Wednesday evening and I regretted more than anything that we gave her a key.

"Get your ass in the shower, put on some nice clothes, and meet me downstairs in an hour." I just looked at her while I sat at my computer editing some photos I had done recently for a couple.

"I think I'm good." She sat down beside me and closed my computer despite my protests.

"I know you miss him and you're going through some stuff but this—this is just sad so you're going to come with me to a party." She pulled me out of the chair like my mom used to do when I was running late for school. It became apparent really fast that I was not going to have a choice. "If you don't get up, I am going to bring them all over here to witness you in all your glory." And I knew that she would.

That is how I found myself sitting alone at a party a few hours later, in a room of people that I didn't know, talking about things that I didn't understand. Sam's friends were a lot, all of them either so posh and high-end that I didn't want to breathe near them in fear of ruining something and the other half of them worked at the same café that she did. In between those two groups was me. I was okay to sit in the corner and watch them all interact as though I was a scientist trying to understand how young people worked.

"I'm not into parties either," someone sat beside me and when I turned my head, I was met with piercing blue eyes. I know in every book and movie the main character *always* has "bright" blue eyes; it's become an overused phrase but his eyes really were bright. They were bright and alive and something I couldn't look away from because it seemed so unnatural. "I'm Spencer." He held out a hand and I shook it with a smile, who still shook hands?

"Collin." I watched as he took a sip of his drink and I can't say enough how inhuman this man looked, his olive skin made his features sharp and focused, his hair was dark and long and it was beautiful and expensive and something uniquely him. If only I had known at the moment that he would turn into one of my best friends, that he would be in my child's life, and that we were about to go through something unforgettable together.

"So how did you end up here?" He asked, trying to make conversation and I didn't know what to say.

"Sam—she's a good friend of mine and basically dragged me out of my apartment." It was oddly nice to talk to people outside of you and Sam, someone who didn't know my history or life, someone who was real and in front of me and not looking at me through a screen. He laughed at my words.

"Yea, that sounds exactly like something she would do." We both turned to watch her spin around the room.

"What about you?" I asked, not ready to let the conversation go yet.

"As embarrassing as they are, these are my people, I go wherever they go."

He spoke which such pride in his voice as he looked at the group of them, as though they were less friends and more like family and I remembered for a moment what it was like to have that. Before we went to war and decided that the only people we could trust were each other. Could I have it again? Spencer looked at me with a question.

"What about you? We all have people." His bluntness reminded me of you, in the way that he didn't seem to care about personal boundaries or private questions. The tattoo on the inside of my wrist seemed to burn when I thought of you.

"Nah, not really. It's been me and my boyfriend for as long as I can remember, but he went home so now I'm just kinda waiting for him to come back." It was the first time that I had said it out loud and it sounded much more pathetic than I realized. Was I anyone on my own anymore? Spencer looked at me with something I recognized as he shook his head.

"Sounds like you need a new group then." He stood up and offered me a hand which I took with hesitation. Both of us walked across the room towards a glowing group of people.

"You guys, I'd like you to meet Collin."

I'll spare you the details of who they were, but it was easier than I thought to fall into a new normal after that. As though I was a character in a YA book, I became one of them, and it was a whirlwind of excitement because they were just as crazy as Spencer had made them sound. His crew was made up of a twenty-something-year-old kid named Ryan who dreamed of being a star, a bright blue-haired girl named Racer who I remember had a tongue piercing, Amos, who was pretty much exactly the type of person my parents were afraid of, yet who was the nicest person I've ever met, and Andi who I found out was dating Spencer. Some of them had money like Ryan and Spencer and some came from nothing, but it didn't matter to them. It was a group of equals who just enjoyed each other's company and it was the first time I had ever been a part of something like that, or known other people who were like you and me. On the weekends they drove to the ocean and went swimming in March, they would drive out of town until they could see the stars, or we would find an old building and camp out. It was the first time that

I had truly experienced what the world was like for someone who had everything, and the number of things that could be done when money or price was no object. It was crazy for someone who lived on the bare minimum to see what these people did.

One day Spencer and I were sitting on the couch and he just stared at me for at least ten minutes.

"What?" I said while taking a bite of my sandwich

"Let's go shopping." I looked down at whatever I had been wearing, I'm sure it was more worn than acceptable and yours from when we were teenagers. Clothes were just things that we didn't have the extra money for. Clothes were worn until they couldn't be worn any longer and that is just how we lived. I played with the frayed edges from where I bit the sleeves when I was younger and anxious.

"What's wrong with this?" I asked and he just shook his head.

"Nothing, nothing is wrong with it if you were 16, but you're an adult who is trying to make it in the world, and that," he pointed to the holes. "Is not going to look very professional to agencies." He had a point. I was still trying to get picked up for photography back then and had yet to make it. I didn't argue with him as he pulled on a coat and opened the door, leaving me once again no choice but to follow him through it.

To say it was an experience does not do shopping with Spencer justice. Money is no object, and it never had been for him so if he saw something he wanted, then he bought it. It was unreal but so fun.

It was like an 80s movie where the main character gets a makeover, that's how I felt as he threw a hundred things at my face for me to try on. I let myself have fun, I let myself enjoy the attention and pretend that I could afford anything I could ever want. We spent hours acting like kids in expensive stores, like two kids playing dress-up, and to this day Its still one of my favorite days because I just felt light and young and alive and it was the first time, I didn't stress about you or your family, and instead just existed with someone else. We went to so many clubs that night and drank way more than we should have but to be around him was to be free. When I looked at him I didn't see the fear of rejection or embarrassment, he was himself and it was impossible not to be the same when his eyes were on me. I don't remember the details of it all due to the alcohol, but I remember what it felt like; it was like sticking my head above the constant waves attached to us both. I would give it all away to be drowning with you again.

When I got home the next day after sleeping who knows where the first thing I did was call you as I put down the many bags of clothes Spencer had insisted on paying for. You almost felt like a ghost that was always attached to me, always there holding my hand no matter where else I went. At that point, I think you had been gone for almost three, maybe four weeks and it was both easier and harder to think about you.

"Hey love," I said when I saw your face on the screen, we had started facetiming instead of calling because it was closer to real life. Your eyes were dark and tired, my good mood was instantly replaced by the normal worry. "What's wrong?" I asked, automatically thinking the worst.

"I hate this place." It felt like someone was pulling on my chest, I could physically feel my heartbreak for you.

"How is he doing?" I asked instead of asking how much longer you would be gone. It was as though I was living two different lives; in New York, I was loud and fun, I was a budding photographer who hung out with people who knew who they were and lived every day as though it was their last, but at home, with you, I was just Collin; someone who came from a broken family and was waiting to pick up your pieces when you finally broke too. I didn't know how to make both sides of my life into one because this is who we had always been, I didn't know how to tell you that maybe our world didn't always have to be just the two of us.

"Yea—shouldn't be long." It's all you could say before I saw you set your jaw as though not to break. You wouldn't meet my eyes

"And how are you?" I asked, noticing the way your fists were balled into the fabric of your shirt.

"I miss you." It was easier than saying that you couldn't breathe. I wanted to say something to fix it, to make you laugh or smile but I couldn't find the words.

"One or two?" I said, it was something we had started the week before where if one of us was upset we could pick either one, which was that we wanted to talk about it, or two, which meant that we wanted to be distracted. You smiled as you finally met my eyes.

"Two." You shifted so that you were lying down.

"I just had the craziest 24 hours, and I'm pretty sure Spencer spent as much money that we do on rent, on clothes alone." You laughed a little but it was enough.

"And how was it?"

"Actually, it was kinda awesome. My god, if my family saw some of this stuff, they would surely die of a heart attack."

It was true but it made you laugh harder. I went through the bags of clothes with you, showing you the craziest things like leather pants and the boots which gave me an extra inch of height, all of them expensive and surreal because I was holding the pieces of the person I had always wanted to be, all I had to do was grab them.

"What do you think?" I asked after I had gone through it all, I was a little bit nervous at the idea of bringing that life into this one. And I knew you would answer honestly

"It's definitely not my area," I gave you a look. "But god, I'm sure it looks good on you." Your acceptance was the last piece I didn't know I needed.

"Your right, it does." I took a deep breath for the first time since I picked up the phone.

"It took three weeks, but my parents asked about you today."

"They haven't asked before this?"

"Well, my theory is that because I didn't walk in wearing a rainbow, they assumed all was good," There was something like venom in every word you spoke.

"What did they ask?" I said instead of commenting on what you had said before. It was important to keep you on topic sometimes.

"I don't think they meant to ask about you, but they asked about my tattoo." I looked down at my own finger and the three dots that ran up the side of it from the time Sam had a tattoo gun and thought it would be cute.

"What did you say?" I was almost too scared to ask.

"The truth, I said that my boyfriend has one too." I ran a hand over my face because sometimes It felt like you were the one always dropping the grenade. I understood that you didn't want to lie or hide or be anything other than who you were, but there was a time for that and maybe your brother dying wasn't the best time to antagonize them.

"You could have just lied." You were making things so much harder for yourself.

"I won't. And what, what should I have said then? That yea no actually I've been dating this beautiful girl with brown hair and we go to church every Sunday and—what was I supposed to say to them?" I could hear It in your voice that you had hit your limit. You were exhausted and sad and alone and didn't know what to do anymore.

"Hey, it's okay," I said as you took a few breaths. "What did she say?"

"She threw a bible at my head and then walked away." I couldn't help but laugh, not because it was funny but because I just wasn't expecting it. My laughter made you laugh and soon we were both in tears.

"I'm sorry," I said once we had settled down,

"It sucks being here without you."

A part of me felt incredibly guilty that I was living life here without you, that I had fun and partied and did things while you were stuck in that place.

"But can you imagine if I was there? She most likely would have had the church there to perform an exorcism." You smiled because I was right.

"That's true yea," We didn't say anything for a moment. "Hey, could you maybe run by the gym tomorrow and grab my stuff?"

I didn't ask why; I couldn't bare to hear you tell me why when it felt like things were falling apart faster than I could fix them. Instead, I just smiled and nodded my head.

"Of course."

"Thank you." I saw someone open the door behind you before

quickly shutting it again, as though the sight they saw had burned them. You looked back at me.

"I should go."

"You should go."

"I'll call you tomorrow"

"Okay," Neither of us made a move to hang up, but then there were sounds on your side of the screen and suddenly you were gone and I was alone with my guilt. It almost felt like survivors' guilt, I felt bad that I was okay while you were being torn apart.

There's so much more I could say about this but no one wants to hear it, maybe a lot of those days are just meant to die with me and then be forgotten like everything else. I feel that same guilt now more than anything because I *wish* it was you sitting here writing these stupid notes for a therapist. You went through so much more than me and it's not fair that you just—

But right now Jax has made dinner and for once, I think that I'll join him instead of drifting away on my lone raft of remorse.

II

Sunday, October 7th

I have nothing new to report about my current life—maybe I do, but I can't think of anything right now.

To be fair, I *am* halfway done with the bottle of whatever it is that I had hidden away so that Jax and Spencer couldn't find it. Someone took Maisy to the park so this seems like the perfect time to write about what happened next in our story because it's too hard to think about sober. I never even told you what really happened other than the night I broke apart on the phone, but we never talked about it again because you felt too bad and I couldn't think about it while continuing on but there is no reason to hold back anymore.

This is everything I couldn't tell you about that night.

The day after I talked to you on the phone was another one of the milestones I keep talking about; one of those split-second moments that had the power to change the outcome of our lives without realizing it. That morning I put on whatever I had ready and started the trek to the gym since it was in a nice part of town compared to our neighborhood. At that point, the gym was a world I had never entered without you and I was terrified of what would be behind the doors. My hands were shaking as I walked up to the door, I took a breath before stepping over the threshold. It was so new yet so familiar at the same time, I had lost track of how many times I had sat and watched you train, how many times I had fallen asleep in the same seats I was now walking past. The constant smell of sweat and blood was no longer threatening but somehow comforting; it smelt like you.

I walked through the gym and looked at the photos on the walls, all of them of some girl who I had never met—*no one* had really met but they said that she owned the building and ran the gym through proxy. Some people thought she was a drug dealer laundering money, others thought she was rich and had no use of money and some people question whether or not she was real in the first place, but either way, she was a striking image to see. I walked past a particularly nice photo of her outside the ring, she had kind eyes and she stood with a man who looked a little bit like you. I don't know what I thought about her, all I know is that not very long ago the gym burnt down and the police said she was found in the flames. Maybe you and she are the same.

I walked by the photos in order to see the training mats more clearly.

"Collin! Is that you?" I turned around to see Jax leaning against the wall looking at me as though the addition of new clothes somehow made me a different person.

"You guessed it." He walked over and gave me a hug; it had been too long since I had seen him and as I would later learn he was never one to shy away from affection. I was shocked to admit that I missed him.

"What on earth are you doing here man? Finally decided to take me up on my offer to hit some pads?" He moved away and looked at me with a raised eyebrow.

"No, no not that. I'm actually here to talk to Rob, Seb told me to come get some stuff?" I didn't know any more than that but it looked as though Jax knew something I didn't. He wouldn't meet my eyes as he played with the hem of his shirt.

"Yea id goes ask him, I'm not sure where he put everything." He pointed down the hall towards one of the offices. I thanked him before walking towards the door I didn't want to enter for fear of what I would learn once I did. When I stepped through the door, Rob was on the phone with someone who was obviously not telling him what he wanted to hear because he hung up before looking at me. He seemed j as confused as me as to why I was standing in his doorway

"Collin, what can I do for you today?"

"I don't really know; I've been told to come get Seb's stuff." Rob nodded with a sigh before looking around at the photos on the walls

"You take photos for his fights, don't you?" I didn't know what to say because he had my photos on his walls. I sat down in the adjacent seat with uncertainty.

"My photographer and me and are having, let's call it creative differences, but I have Jarred fighting tomorrow night so I'll pay you to come do the photos." I didn't know what to say, Rob wanted my help? It was Jarred, but I needed the money.

"I'm not totally sure."

"Please, you would be saving my ass." I looked down at my hands; It was a decision that changed my life, it's the reason I can afford to do things and live places that 23-year-old Collin could only imagine.

"Sure, I'll do it."

"Great! Be there by 4 pm tomorrow." He turned back to his phone as though he was done with me completely.

"I still need Seb's stuff?" I asked, more confused than ever before about my role in the gym.

"Oh yea, it's in the locker room, can't miss it." It was dismissive but I understood better than to push him.

I walked to the locker room silently, trying to keep to myself as much as possible. Of course, jarred was standing by his locker as I walked in and his eyes ran over me as though stalking his next victim, and in a way he was. I grabbed the garbage bag sitting on the floor quickly before turning away.

"Where's lover boy now?" He said in a cool voice. I put my head down and walked away.

I could go into detail about what it was like to go to the fight the next day alone but I don't want to, instead, I want to cut straight to the truth of this story. But for the background information, Rob hired me on to do all his fights after one day with Jarred because apparently, I was pretty good at it. This thing that had always been a hobby was something I was started making decent money from and all I had to do was take photos of people beating each other up. I felt a new normal set in as the weeks without you turned into months, and still every time I found myself having fun with Spencer or Jax I couldn't help but think of you alone in your house for more time than we thought. Every piece of my life was starting to fall into place, all except you, and you were always the biggest piece of all.

If that was what it felt like when my life was coming together, then this is what it feels like when my life falls apart. The main event of this evening, however, happened around three months after I saw you for the last time in the airport. Buckle your seat belt because—here is the story that I've only said once.

. . .

It was a Thursday and I was going through the photos from the weekend because I had quickly fallen behind schedule once Spencer got back from vacation, but it was a beautiful evening; I had a new bottle of wine opened and my favorite band playing on the record player Jax brought over and I was eating a bagel from breakfast. It was perfect. I wish I could skip this part, but I owe it to you to tell it, maybe I even owe it to myself. I was on the phone with you and for once the world stopped ending and it was like we were young again.

"You *cannot* say that to your mom," I said past the laughter that spilled like ink from my lips; Someone knocked on the door. I wiped my eyes before looking at you. "Hold on a second," You muted yourself as not to disturb whoever was trying to talk to me. My face was flush when I answered and I thought it was Sam or someone else who would laugh with me through the night.

"Hey—" But my thoughts disappeared when I saw the man standing at the door with a smile. Jarred towered above me, a beer in one hand and his keys in the other. He was obviously drunk as he leaned against the door frame messily. I moved away slightly. "What are you doing here?" How did he know where we lived? My hands started sweating when I realized that despite your voice, I was alone and no one was going to help me.

"Just stopping in to chat." His words were harsh and laced with something I couldn't recognize. Maybe he was jealous of us, of the two of us because he was too ashamed to ever let himself have something like that, or maybe he was just really drunk and made a bad choice.

"I don't see why." My words were careful and considerate.

"He's still gone yea?" He walked straight past me into our space; He was bigger than me and there was nothing I could do to stop it from happening. I watched as he poured the rest of his beer onto the floor.

"He will be back tomorrow." I lied, of course I lied to while I walked over to my phone and placed a hand over the top of it in order to block your face. I tapped the screen three times before Jarred turned to me, his eyes going to the phone as he turned his head.

"I think your lying," like a snake he moved closer and I couldn't move, all I could do was look at your face through the phone before Jarred took it from my hand.

"Goodbye lover boy," He stared at me the entire time.

"*You son of a bitch, Jarred I swear to god—*" He hung up before you could finish and I wanted to cry because—I was alone, and you were halfway across the country.

"What—what are you doing Jarrad." I tried to make my voice strong, I *swear* that I tried to do anything to help the situation but I couldn't speak when his smile resembled the devil. He ran a finger up my arm.

"He's not here to protect you anymore." I tried to push him away but he grabbed onto my shoulder tightly.

"You don't want to do anything stupid—he *will* come for you." I spit the words through my teeth and he seemed to weigh it over in his mind before coming up with a choice.

"Or, he won't." He brought a hand to the side of my face and ran his fingers down the side of my jaw because he wasn't afraid of you, not anymore.

"Please—" I whispered as his face inched closer to mine. I tried to move, to rip away from him but I *couldn't*, his hand was around my waist and I couldn't get out of it.

"No one is going to stop me."

I was paralyzed as he brought his mouth to mine, I couldn't move or breathe—or think, all I could do was stand there as he bit down on my lower lip until it bled. I felt his hand run down my chest and over my sides, felt them sprawl out on my lower torso before moving to the waistband of my pants. Like a switch in a split second before he could re-adjust his grip, I put *everything* I had into pushing him away; I moved my hand back in order to throw everything I could into the side of his face. He just stared at me, barely flinching as my fist hit his cheek.

I had forgotten that he was a fighter who had been trained and conditioned to take a shot. He wiped the blood from his lip with a smile.

"That all you got?" Before I could do anything else his fist was connecting to the side of my face, a hit that made me stumble against the cold table behind me. For a moment I couldn't see, the shot went straight to my head but I couldn't—I *couldn't* let him see me break like that. I stood up straight and looked at him.

"Is that all *you* got?" He turned his head with a smile.

"Not even close sweetheart." He threw again and the world started to fade and this is where my memory of events gets a little blurry. All I really remember are singular moments.

I remember the world spinning around me after the second punch and he was trained to see the moment I was injured and—and he did. Before my eyes could focus, he was pushing me against the table, the action so hard it knocked the air from my lungs. I remember feeling so afraid that I couldn't feel anything at all because I knew *exactly* what was about to happen and I *couldn't* stop it—my cries *wouldn't* make him change his mind and you weren't about to walk through the door to stop it. I remember opening my eyes in a last-ditch effort to save myself and I remember my phone still sitting on the counter from where he had placed it. I reached for it blindly while Jarrad played with his belt and in an action faster than time I threw my arm back and hit him in the throat with my phone. The one moment was all I needed. His grip in my hair startled into loosening and I took the chance to basically crawl to the other side of the table, my vision was blurring and black but I knew enough to run.

I ran faster than I had ever run before. I didn't know where to go—the ground felt like rolling waves and I couldn't understand my surroundings because it was all just too much, every breath was deafening and I couldn't do it—I could *feel* his lips on mine like a ghost; his hands running up my back but I needed—I *needed* to keep going. But I don't think I got very far as I'm quite certain that I collapsed in the middle of the street when my legs stopped working. I pulled out my phone and called Spencer.

"Hello my darling," I think he said, but I had to struggle to understand. "Collin? What's wrong?"

"I—I need you to come get me—I—" I brought my knees to my chest and maybe I said more or maybe Spencer said more but I don't remember, I'm sure that there are a lot of details I blocked out about that night because I had to in order to survive what happened next. I don't think I felt real in that moment, like my voice was loud but it wasn't *mine*, and I could taste the metal of my own blood in my mouth yet it was foreign. I don't know how long I sat on the ground.

"Collin," Spencer said and I looked around to see him running out of a car. I clung to him when he put a hand on my shoulder because I *needed* to feel something real. I'm sure he was terrified but I couldn't do anything to stop it. "What—" He didn't continue, something on my face must have told him that I wouldn't answer anything. He picked me off the ground, I'm sure he carried me to the car because the second I stood up the world was falling away and I could do nothing but succumb to the darkness surrounding me.

Thinking back on it, it feels as though I'm watching It all through the eyes of someone else, as though it happened to someone else because it all seems far too blurry to have actually happened to me. But it did, I have the scar on my chin to prove it.

. . .

When I finally woke up, for the second time in my life the first thing I saw was someone close to tears sitting beside me.

"Oh, thank god," Spencer said although I didn't realize that it was him at the time. I looked around the room, trying to find something grounding but my eyes landed on nothing but Spencer looking at me with big wet eyes with a bloody cloth in his hand.

"Hey," I said, still confused as to what was happening but then as though a bullet, I was hit with it and couldn't breathe.

"You're alright, C—it's okay." Spencer grabbed my hand carefully, I watched his eyes desperately search for something, maybe it was you that I was trying to find in that moment. I brought a shaking finger to my cheek and took a breath when the skin was sticky with blood.

"What happened?" I asked, suddenly having no idea how I had gotten from the street to his apartment.

"I don't know—you were in the street and you were bleeding and then you were unconscious and I was about five seconds away from calling an ambulance." He gripped my hand tighter and now I can realize how afraid he must have been. I wanted to hide in a dark room away from everyone else because I felt as though I had *let* something horrible happen.

"Thanks, can I—can I take a shower?" I said, trying to calm my breathing.

Spencer nodded as I slowly walked away to the bathroom trying to ignore my pounding head. I knew that he kept clothes under the sink. I don't know what I thought about while I stood under the boiling water, only that I clawed at my skin until it bled because I *needed* it to be gone, I needed *him* to be gone and when I stepped out of the water my skin stung with the reminders of what I had done. I remember looking in the mirror, at the black eye and cut lip, and the tears that I couldn't keep from falling. *Everything* was a reminder of It, of *him* and his words and his fist. I put the clean clothes on numbly before walking out of the steam-filled room. Maybe it would have affected me more if I grew up as Spencer did, maybe if I hadn't already almost been killed by my father then I would have reacted differently, but I had, and the only thing I wanted was to go home and lay in my own bed with you because there was nowhere in the world, I felt safer. It's the only time that I missed my mom. I couldn't go home; I wasn't sure that my home even existed anymore. I heard him talk to someone in a hushed voice when I walked towards the couch.

"I don't know, I don't know what happened," He was talking to a video call, someone was on the other side looking back but I was too far away to see it, and his headphones stopped me from hearing it. "He wouldn't say anything but It looks bad—he's in the shower, yes, yes I know it's important" I watched as Spencer's eyes widen with whatever you were saying to him. "Well, fu—," as though right on cue I made myself known and Spencer looked towards me with grateful eyes. "He's right here, yes just—" He took out the headphone before handing me the phone and then he was walking away. I heard a door shut down the hall.

"Collin, can you hear me?" You said and your voice was utter panic, it was the last piece before I finally broke, the last act of my defense came down as I let out a broken cry. I moved in front of the camera, letting you see my face and I'm sure you gasped but I couldn't stop myself from crying; whether I was scared or embarrassed or ashamed I don't know but I cried. "Collin," you said again and finally, I looked at you.

"Seb—" I spit out, unable to say anything more. I can't imagine what that would have been like for you, having to watch me fall apart while being completely unable to stop it.

"I'm going to kill him," you said and I think you meant it, your voice was so dark and real that I think you would have killed him if given the chance. "Please look at me." But I couldn't, I *couldn't* look at you because I *let* this happened—I should have tried harder or done something more. I took a deep breath, trying to compose myself but it didn't work.

In small words and broken sentences, I told you for the only time some version of what happened because it was you, and I didn't know how to keep anything to myself. I clenched at my chest, feeling as though my heart was going to beat right out of it.

"I'm sorry, I'm—I'm sorry I should have—" I said between breaths, finally looking at you only to see tears running down your face; your hand gripped the blanket beside you.

"Please don't—don't apologize for this." Your voice was strained and I knew it was killing you to just sit there and watch. I heard someone yelling on the other end of your screen and then I saw you set your jaw with regret. "Collin, I *promise* I'm going to call you back but I—I have to go I'm sorry. I love you, and I promise I'll call you." I held up three fingers instead of responding, no longer able to stop myself from letting everything out and suddenly I was on the floor too exhausted to miss you or wish you had stayed or to admit that I was spinning away from earth faster by the second. At some point Spencer moved towards me and his arms were around me and it wasn't you or my mom but it was something real. I let myself be held that night until I drifted into a pitiful sleep.

But this story didn't have a horrible ending like ours did my love, because you, you are unlike any human I've ever met and of course you weren't going to just sit there and watch me break.

I was opening my eyes what felt like seconds later. The sunlight was streaming in through the windows and it took me a minute to realize that I was on the couch for the second time. I let my head fall against the pillow, still in the same place I had fallen asleep but Spencer must have put a blanket over my shoulders while I slept. I slowly sat up only to see him sitting at the table drinking coffee.

"Morning," I said with a weak voice.

"Coffee?" He offered and there was an unknown gentleness that I hated. I didn't want his pity.

"I'm okay, thanks." My voice was sharper than I wanted it to be but he didn't notice, or maybe he did and just chose not to comment on it. I wanted to go home but I knew that I couldn't. I walked over to the counter, keeping the blanket wrapped around my shoulders tightly like a shield.

"How did you sleep?" He asked trying to keep the conversation light and easy. For a moment I wanted to tell him the truth; that all night I saw Jarrad's face and felt his hands and that my eyes weren't just black from being punched, but he had already been through enough with me, I didn't want to put anything else on him.

"Good, thanks for letting me stay." I poured myself a mug of hot water.

"Course, stay as long as you want." I moved to sit beside him on the counter, leaning my head against his shoulder.

"Thanks, I just need a couple of days." I felt him put a hand on my back.

"Course, I can go grab your stuff later." He suggested into the odd silence that had been created between then and the night before. I felt grateful in a way I never had before. I didn't have time to voice my thoughts however because someone was knocking at the door. Spencer just looked at me with guilt.

"it's Andi, but I'm going to tell him to leave and how about you and me just stay in today, order take out and rent movies or something?" He moved towards the door while I got up, he deserved some privacy.

"Sounds great." He gave me a thumbs-up before I disappeared behind the corner to the spare room. I sat on the bed and looked around at my temporary living space, the room was almost as big as our entire apartment.

"What do you want—you can't just come in—if you don't leave, I'm phoning the cops."

My blood went cold when I heard the front door slam shut, when I heard Spencer's panic and hurried words. Slowly footsteps approached me followed by Spencer yelling and I wanted to hide, to block the door or do *anything* that would help the situation but I couldn't—I had to face it, whatever it is, I had to face it. I held my breath as the doorknob seemed to turn in slow motion. Everything stopped when you stood there staring at me from across the room.

Neither of us moved or breathed because—because you were there and real and standing across from me with your long messy hair and hoodie and I could feel your eyes run over me as though trying to make sure that I was whole and alive—and I couldn't look away; not even when Spencer ran in from behind and started talking. It didn't matter because you were there and the war seemed to have stopped for a second.

"What the hell is going on—" His voice broke the spell that had tied me to the floor and before I could think twice, I was running across the room and then you were holding onto me as though we would never see each other again.

"Seb—" I whispered as I felt my feet leave the ground, I moved my arms tighter around your neck while pressing my face into your shoulder. You were there, you were holding onto me and your fingers were gripping into my shirt and there was nothing left between us. I wrapped my legs around your waist because I just needed you—

"Thank you," I heard you whisper into my shoulder again and again and again as though sending a prayer to something you no longer knew and your fingers bit into my skin and I swear I could feel your heart pounding against mine but none of it mattered.

"*You're here,*" I murmured, feeling your warm skin against my lips and then I heard the door close but I *couldn't* let you go. You walked us both over to the bed, sitting down so that your arms were wrapped tightly around my waist. Everything, the past three months without you and the fear and horror and shame and guilt, all of it came rushing and I was too tired to stop it. But despite it all, I took my first real breath in months. You moved away slightly and I followed; I needed to see you in order to know you were real.

"I'm here." You said with glassy eyes, you ran a hand over the plains of my face, wiping away a tear that had started to fall. I leaned my forehead against yours tightly.

"How are you—" I started, running my fingers up your jaw and into your hair, anywhere I could reach without having to let you go; a part of me was trying to rememorize your lines after such a long time apart and the other half was just trying to convince myself that you were real.

"I got on the first flight that I could." I just looked at you, unable to comprehend your words because you would have flown for most of the night yet you were standing with me now as though it didn't matter. "You're crazy if you thought I was gonna leave you here alone, especially now—" I moved my face into the palm of your hand, placing my own against it to make you stay.

"But your family, your brother—" I would have never been able to forgive myself if something happened while you were away.

"They can wait, your my family too." Your answer was fast and held no hesitation. There is still no way to explain the way I felt in that moment, but it consumed everything I was.

"Thank you," I said instead, nothing else could escape my mouth because of the selfish gratitude I felt. You looked at me like you were asking permission before closing the gap and kissing me slowly, as though you wanted to remember every single second of it because it might never happen again.

"Don't thank me." You whispered against my lips before pulling away. Both your hands went to the sides of my face so that you could really look at me for the first time in months. You ran a hand over the cut on my lip and the bruise on my face, you waited for me to nod before you moved your hand to the hem of my shirt; moving it only to reveal the massive bruise forming on my shoulder in the shape of a hand.

"It's alright—" I tried because I didn't want to see you upset, not when I just got you back.

"It's *not* alright." Your voice was stronger than I think you meant it to be because remorse painted your eyes the second the words were in the air. I played with the hem of your hoodie.

"I'm sorry," I said softly, unable to look you in the eye because I didn't know how to; I didn't know how to look at you while being able to talk about what had happened. Your muscles tensed under my hands. You brought a finger under my jaw to make me look at you.

"I need you to listen to me alright?" I didn't look away. "This *wasn't* your fault, none of this—" You took a deep breath, "None of this is your fault. Jarrad is—I swear that ill—" You stopped mid-sentence and for one of the first times in your life you didn't say what you wanted to. Instead, you took a sharp breath to stop your hands from shaking. I let my head fall onto your shoulder, suddenly I couldn't keep my eyes open, not with you sitting here and not when I felt warm and safe and alive and just—I was suddenly so tired that I just wanted to sleep forever.

"I'm so tired," I said honestly and you rubbed a circle onto my back, moving us both so that we were laying down with the blanket from the couch covering us. I curled up on your chest, letting myself listen to the certain and endless beat of your heart.

"Close your eyes, we can talk later." I could feel myself sink farther into sleep. "I'll still be here when you wake up."

. . .

That was the story of how you saved the day. Or maybe it's the story of how I started to save myself.

It's crazy how life works, like the fact that you and me were born in different years, to different families, and grew up without really knowing each other. The very *idea* that there was ever a time in my life when I didn't know you—when our lives weren't strung together like the fates in myth seems crazy because how do people unknowingly become *everything* to each other? How do two people, who have never met change everything just by saying hello in a hallway at school? And even more impossible, is how is one just supposed to carry on when their person—*my person* no longer exists? How—*how* do I do this now that I've been with you longer than I lived without you? Maybe the first step is writing this down, maybe the second step involves holding onto our daughter and eating dinner at the table instead of alone in my room. Maybe the only way to get through any of this is to hold onto the pages of this book as though they can possibly save me.

Or maybe—maybe the only way I stand a chance at survival is to throw *everything* away.

12

Sunday, October 14th

Everything is different now than it was before.

The last time I wrote I thought the most important thing in my life was nothing, and that things worth nothing were everything but then—Jax had been at your dad's house with Maisy and something happened. It was like the past was repeating itself because all I could think about was you—when the phone rang, I jumped, falling from my paralyzed state onto the floor as I scramble to the phone. Nothing mattered but getting to that phone and when I answered it, I couldn't breathe. Your dad called me with a ragged voice as though he was running—he was panicking and I could hear it and I could hear Jax talking in the background but I couldn't move, all I could say was her name and your name and then some combination of the two of them. Maisy was sick and she was just getting worse and no one knew what to do—it was just the three of us, all of us raw and ragged from you, all of us thought the worst. Your dad said that he was taking her to the hospital, and I was still half asleep but told him that I would meet him there and I did despite my blinding fear. But don't worry, I promise that she's okay. The doctor said she has croup—which is some lung thing and even though I know that she's alright, it doesn't feel alright. In one of these *stupid* entries, I said that nothing scares me anymore—but I was wrong; *she* scares me—the very *idea* of losing her—I wouldn't survive it. I thought that I could, that I wanted to be alone, and that she didn't mean anything but she does, she is *everything*.

Right now, we are sitting outside while Jax throws some food together, the cold air is apparently supposed to help so she's all bundled up against my chest as I write this with one hand clutching at her jacket and I just—*I promise you*, right here in writing, that I will *never* leave her. Maybe I don't know how to do this—*any* of this and maybe I don't know how to look at her without seeing you and the future I lost—but it doesn't matter; she, this helpless child whose heart I can feel beating steadily against mine—*she* is going to be the reason I try to breathe again.

Even if it still feels like glass.

. . .

Later that day I woke up to your fingers softly running through my hair, something that threw me so much I thought I was still asleep. But you were real, and you were there and when I opened my eyes you were already staring at me gently.

"I thought I was still asleep," I said in a happy daze, content to stay exactly where we were forever because you were so warm. I moved closer to your chest.

"Sadly, you're stuck with me till tomorrow." I didn't let you see how much my heart hurt when you said that, I just got you back and before I could even soak it in you were leaving again—one day would be enough, I wouldn't ruin it by missing you.

"What time is it?" I asked, watching as you checked your phone beside me.

"9." I relaxed into it, we still had time.

Soon your lips were on mine and things seemed like they were going to be okay, or more so that even if things weren't okay, I knew that they would be one day. I wish I could say that I was different after that night, but I think I pushed it so far away that I didn't let myself feel it, not when there were so many other things that needed to be talked about. "The guy out there told me, to tell you, that he wanted to talk when you got up. I'm assuming it's about the handsome stranger that burst into his home unannounced." I laughed as you pulled away, taking a deep breath before letting myself fully wake up for the day.

"Good assumption." I stood up slowly before offering you a hand. "Come on, let's introduce you two before he really does phone the cops." You placed a hand on the back of my spine as we walked through the door; you needed the contact just as much as me.

"It's about time," Spencer said the second we were in his view, I started to laugh slightly but stopped it, trying to pretend as though I was the least bit sorry when in reality I never was. I sat down on the same couch I had called you on the night before, this time with you at my side. "So, I'm going to assume that you must be Sebastian?" You nodded, suddenly shy now that you weren't trying to find me.

"Uh, yea. Sorry about before." Spencer looked between the two of us as though he was trying to hide his smile.

"I'm less concerned about that presently, and more concerned about the fact that you knew where I lived."

"I called Sam." It's an admission that made me smile, Spencer just seemed to bow his head in defeat because there was nothing he could do to change his friend's nature but when he looked back up, he was smiling.

"Of course, she told you, any idea how long you're staying?" I pushed my face into your shoulder.

"Just for the night, if that's alright with you, I have a flight back tomorrow afternoon." You put a hand on my knee. Spencer watched your movement with an unreadable expression, before looking at me.

"This man just flew here, in a plane, for *one night* because you needed him? Andi won't even get me a coffee from a place two minutes away." I laughed at that because I didn't know what else to do. You were a different kind of person and I couldn't articulate what it felt like to be able to love someone like that, what it felt like to love *you* like that.

"Course." You said smiling.

"*Course.* You say that as though it's a normal thing everyone does." He looked at me with his kind eyes and growing smile. "I'm glad you did though, I don't think I've ever seen him look so *young.*" It was my turn to feel embarrassed, but I smiled at him and I think that smile said all the words I could never say. "What are you two getting up to today?" He walked over to the kitchen to grab a container of muffins, as though he could sense my growing hunger.

"I have to talk to Rob," I said quietly as though if I whispered the words then they wouldn't become real. But my voice must have carried because soon it felt like everyone was looking at me.

"I think, you're mistaken," Spencer said as he sat down once again in front of us, his face changing from kindness to concern. Your hold on my leg tightened too.

"I have a job—I can't just not show up for his fight tomorrow."

"Yea, so there's no way in hell you are gonna do that." You said and your voice was serious, but it was more than that; you were afraid and I was the only one who could hear it but it was there. You were afraid of going back to that gym, afraid of what would happen once you got back on the plane and afraid of going back to a place you didn't know when you would leave again. You were afraid of what you would do if you saw Jarrad, I think you were afraid a lot back in those days but you never wanted me to know.

"I actually agree with blondie on this one, no way." The two of you teaming up was something I wasn't ready for because you were more similar than you wanted to admit.

"I can't run away—that's what he wants—" If I ran away, then he won. And I think you knew it.

"That doesn't mean you have to go explain yourself to them, you don't owe them anything."

"I'm not gonna be alone, and plus I do work for Rob, he does have a right to know." I watched as you decided what stance to take on the matter but you knew that I was right, this was something that I *had* to do. "I have to grab some stuff anyways; we can just run in on the way back."

I knew you hated the idea.

We left quickly after that. Both of us wanted to get the whole thing over with as quickly as possible so that we could enjoy whatever time we had left. To be honest, the last thing I wanted to do was go to that apartment, not yet, when I still saw it every time I closed my eyes but I knew if I had to go back, then I wanted to go back with you standing guard at the door. I didn't miss the protective arm around my shoulders as we walked down the street.

. . .

All too soon we were standing at our front door, the door of the place that we had built for ourselves; it was almost poetic, walking through that door symbolized the literal destruction that we were running full speed towards. It was at that point that I remembered I had left Jarrad alone in our place and that he could have stolen everything we had or worse, maybe he was still sitting at the counter waiting.

"You really don't have to do this, I can go." You said softly against my hair. I reached out to open the door.

"I'm fine."

That was our home, the place we had created and I wouldn't let someone else take it away from me again. The lights were out which was a good sign, but I still let you go in first. The lamp we kept in the corner was smashed on the ground, the contents that were supposed to be on the table were scattered around the floor and Jarrad's beer can was still on the chair. I didn't let myself look at the bloody fingerprints on the counter, or the way the chairs near the table were on their sides because he pushed me into them—I just looked away as you stared at it all as though you could make it disappear, I wanted to disappear—I walked away from you, stepping over the broken pieces of my life as I made my way to our bed that was still untouched. I grabbed the clothes still in their bags instead of trying to sort through my old ones as I forced myself to take deep breaths. My skin felt like it was on fire and all I wanted to do was run. It was the same feeling that comes over me when I'm walking alone at night and feel as though someone is watching my every move.

I couldn't focus on anything other than the fabric falling between my shaking fingers, your hand on my shoulder made me jump and I knew the action broke your heart.

"It's me, let me do it." You said and I let you, handing you the beg as I walked over to grab my camera and laptop from behind the couch.

I didn't look at anything else as I walked out the front door and I didn't know that we wouldn't live there again, not really. Never again would we be in that space the way we used to be and I didn't even know it. I felt exposed and seen as I waited for you outside, I couldn't stop looking at the elevator as though he was about to walk through it. Soon you walked out the door and locked it behind you. You didn't say anything, just walked over and placed a kiss on my forehead.

"Thank you." You said but it wasn't for me, later I learned the story behind it and it broke my heart. But at that moment, I didn't care who you were talking to because it didn't matter. You held my hand in a vice grip as we walked silently down the hall and down the stairs, neither of us said anything as we walked down the street towards the gym. Neither of us wanted to walk through those doors again, maybe you more so than me.

"I think I'm going to throw up." You said as a panicked admission and I forgot that you still wouldn't tell me what had happened between you and Rob; Your hand was shaking in mine.

"it's alright, I can just run in." I didn't want to put you into a situation that made you feel like that, not when this was supposed to be a break from it all

"Absolutely not."

I tapped the side of your hand the way I always did when you were anxious.

"Together?"

"Together."

The doorbell rang above our heads as we took the first few steps inside, the whole gym knew we were there. You didn't look at any of them as you walked ahead to Rob's office, Jax looked at me with surprise and I just gave him a look that screamed *later*. We walked into his office without knocking as though we owned the place and the second he saw me looking as though I had just gotten out of the ring, and you suddenly returned, standing above me, he hung up the phone.

"Collin, Sebastian—what are you doing here?" He said while folding his arms in front of his chest like a jealous ex.

"This isn't about me." You said and I took a breath.

"I'm not going to Jarrad's fight tomorrow—or ever again for that matter. I'll take photos of the other guys but not his—do what you want, I'm not doing it." I held my breath as though waiting for him to get mad but he didn't. I saw him look at your dark eyes and my bruised face and decide that he couldn't argue what I had said.

"That boy does some stupid things, but he has a good heart." I didn't know what to say because he—he *didn't*. But I didn't want to fight, not when I knew I would lose.

"I'm done."

"Understood. I'll see you next Saturday for Jax?" I nodded and realized that he was going to let me do this, maybe he was afraid of hearing what his prizefighter had really done behind closed doors. Or maybe he was afraid that I would go to the police. "Sebastian, can I talk to you for a moment?" You turned to him with ice

"I'm not back Rob. I'm leaving tomorrow but either way, I think you said everything you needed to over the phone." Before he could respond you were dragging me out of the room. When we got to the main room everyone was watching us, Jax was the first one to move.

"We miss you, man." He said while pulling you into a tight hug. I moved away to let you two have a moment. When you pulled away

Jax turned to me, he moved closer and ran a concerned finger across the bruise on my face. He just looked at me as you stood seemingly confused as to when we had become close enough friends that I didn't flinch at his proximity.

"I told you to stop getting into fights," he said before looking towards you as though that's where the answer would be.

"Like I would ever do as I'm told." I would tell him something real later, but now was not the time and he seemed to realize it as he just laughed.

"Next time you decide to fight, give me a call, I'll bring back up." He said it to me but I think that a part of him wanted you to know that he would make sure I was okay, even if you weren't here. And he is, I promise.

"Will do."

I moved to grab your hand but you weren't looking at me anymore, or at Jax or your friends. I didn't have to follow your eyes to know exactly who was standing across the mats. I didn't breathe as I turned around. Jarrad was staring at us with something unrecognizable, maybe it was fear. I searched his face and saw the place that my phone had connected with his neck, just below his jaw, a bruise was the only proof. He knew that he couldn't fight you.

"Seb—" I tried but you were gone faster than I could get the words out and before I could do anything else Jax was holding onto my waist.

"Collin, stop." He said against my ear as I tried to escape his grip, he just held on tighter as we both watched in slow motion as you stalked over to where Jarred stood with an impressive smile.

"Hey buddy—" he tried but your fist was connecting to the side of his face before he could finish and soon, he was on the ground with you kneeling above him, relentlessly throwing shot after shot as though you really were the soldier that I keep pretending we were.

"*How dare you.*" You said between gasps and no one moved because no one in there could beat you, everyone was too shocked even if they could. Jarrad threw a shot of his own but it didn't make you flinch, maybe it was adrenaline or maybe you had been through too much to care anymore.

"He came onto me man!" Jarrad spits with a blood-stained smile and it's like the room understood what had happened; Suddenly everyone's eyes were on me and the proof of it presented on my face. Jax held onto me tighter, his breath changing and I knew he was trying his hardest not to help you. No one stepped into the fray to save him, not now that it was apparent what he had done.

"Seb—*Stop*" I pleaded but you didn't hear me, your every sense was trained onto hurting the person in front of you and in that moment, you were no longer Atlas carrying the world, you were Achilles to suck in his own rage to realize what he was doing.

For a moment I thought that you were going to kill him. But when it became apparent that you weren't going to stop, the room broke free from the trance keeping them in place, and ran to get involved. It took three men to restrain you. Before we could do anything else Rob came running out with wide eyes.

"If you *ever* come near him again—I will *fucking* kill you." We all knew you meant it.

"What's going on?" Rob asked, stepping between you and Jarrad who was still bleeding on the ground. He stood waiting for someone to answer him but no one did. The only sound in the room was your heavy breathing.

"Ask him."

"Seb, come on, let's go," I said again and this time you looked at me as though only now realizing that I was still there. Jax seemed to think that it was okay to let me go because I was running and then I was in front of you; you still had your hands pushed behind your back but the longer you looked at me the less you tried to fight them and I could see the emotion building in your eyes.

The people let you go and I grabbed your hand, and we were leaving. Jax just gave me a worried smile as we walked past him. I didn't stop walking until the gym was out of sight and we were truly away from it, even then when I tried to slow down you just kept walking without saying a word until we were walking through the door of Spencer's apartment. I was thankful that he was at Andi's. I grabbed your arm to make you standstill.

"Look at me," I said, moving so that I was completely in front of you, I brought both hands to your face and it only then hit me that you were crying. I can count on one hand the number of times I've seen you cry but it was all too much; the past three months and Jarrad and all of it came to the forefront of your mind because you couldn't stop any of it. "It's alright." You shook your head.

"I'm sorry—I, he just, I couldn't stop and—" It was easy to forget that you were a trained weapon; you had fought and shaped yourself to hurt people.

"It's alright, it's over, it's all okay." I grabbed your hands that were balled into fists and made them uncurl until they were flush against mine.

"He deserves worse—"

"But not from you, it's not worth it." And it wasn't. The only reason that he wouldn't press charges was that we had the other side of the story.

"I should have been here, I should have—" Your eyes were wild and bright and horribly sad and I didn't know what to do. You were *so* scared. I wish I could find a better way to state it, a way to twist and turn the events to make them more poetic but I *can't* because you were sad; horribly, and tremendously sad.

"You're here now, nothing matters other than *this* moment, okay?"

Nothing else did, the past and the future, the uncertainty, and the fear, none of it mattered because you were here and I was okay and there was a cease-fire in the war and I wanted to live in it instead of always being lost in a future where the shooting resumed. There would be endless amounts of time to be sad, for once I just wanted to live in the feeling of you, instead of the thoughts of constant doom. I brought my hands around your neck, pulling you close.

"*Nothing* matters but this," I whispered as I brought my lips to yours.

Although it started out like sweet poetry it took less than a second for you to deepen it; for my lip to be in-between your teeth and your hand to be on the back of my neck. I couldn't stop the sound that ran past my tongue. Soon your hands were under my shirt exploring the smooth skin of my back as though trying to remember the words to an old favorite song and my hand was tangled in the gentle strands of your hair and I couldn't think; all my thoughts were gone other than ones of you. I pulled you closer and before I knew what was happening you lifted me off the ground and we were crashing into the closest wall with laughter consuming the space between us. I tried to catch my breath but you were everywhere, your lips were on my neck and my shoulder and it was *everything.*

"Spencer—would kill us if he walked in right now." I breathed against you, you didn't pull away only kissed me as though you were frantically running out of time and we were; we just didn't know it yet, the only thing I knew was *you.*

"Then let him." You whispered and I had no idea how I had existed this long without it, without your hair and your eyes and your mouth moving over every inch of my skin making me feel every kind of alive.

"I missed you."

I couldn't help it. You took my jacket off in one movement, my shirt was gone before I could breathe, and then your hands were running over my skin and you were so warm. I didn't hesitate to rid you of yours, letting my eyes fall on your collar bones and we were laughing and young and just—*nothing* else mattered but the way your breaths came fast and hot against the side of my cheek. I smiled as you moved away, pulling me towards you and together like a tornado we somehow found our way to the spare room, I'm sure we left chaos in our paths but it didn't matter because—because we were *laughing* and soon my back was against the bed and you were looking at me as though I was the only thing in the entire world worth looking at. The only sound was our breathing as you took a moment to catch yours.

"You—you mean *everything.*" You said in a hushed breath and your eyes were filled with so much emotion that I wanted to cry because how could I be the reason for that look, how could someone look at *me* the way you did? I didn't know how to articulate it so instead, I pulled you back down and kissed you until I knew you understood.

We were happy; for a moment in the middle of it all we had been granted a moment of joy, even if we didn't deserve it and that day as your hands ran down my sides and your mouth placed soft kisses down my ribs I knew—*I knew* that whatever the future held, we were going to make it because—because we were still laughing.

I'm unsure whether it's harder to remember the good moments or the bad ones; is it easier to long for what we had, or feel guilty about what we didn't? All I know is that my neighbors must think I'm crazy because I'm sitting on the balcony holding my child while tears fall onto her blanket because—*we laughed* and it was real, and right now *nothing* feels real other than this one moment when I can see my breath appear before me. Maybe it's easier to think of the past when darkness is the only thing left to judge me.

. . .

After things had settled and our breathing slowed, we laid there tangled together under the thin sheets in Spencer's spare room unable to tell where one of us started and the other one ended. Your head was on my chest and your fingers were running circles up and down my sides. You let out what sounded like a sigh.

"That was *awesome*." You said. it reminded me of something a teenager might say instead of an adult but you said it anyway and I couldn't help but smile; every nerve in my body was heavy with bliss as I placed a kiss in your hair.

"It was." For a moment we just laid there enjoying the silence. But then I remembered something you said earlier. "Why do you keep saying thank you when you think I'm not paying attention?" You looked up at me through your eyelashes and for the first time in years, you looked genuinely nervous.

"You can't laugh at me." I nodded and braced myself for whatever could be so bad that you thought you had to give me a warning before starting. I played with a piece of your hair.

"Before—when Jarrad hung up—I've never been that scared before." You took a breath and even though the words were heavy, they somehow didn't scare me anymore under the false safety we created. "Not when your dad left, or when I fought—It felt like I was dying because there was *nothing* I could do—absolutely nothing and I *knew* that he—" My hand rested near your eye and I felt you lean into it. "I felt helpless; suddenly I was just a powerless kid again—so I did the only thing I could think of; I prayed—and hoped with every fiber of my being that whoever I prayed to would remember me." I didn't say anything, your words hit me deeply because I didn't think that you believed in anything anymore. Not after what we had been through. "I quite literally *begged* anyone listening to help you—to make sure that I could get there in time and yea I—"

I knew how hard it was for you to admit what you were saying and maybe you wouldn't have if the air wasn't still soft. You moved closer to me, placing a kiss on my palm before pushing your face into my neck. You were hurting in ways that I couldn't imagine. While I was out there living and expanding and creating, you were simply still trying to survive and it made me remember that although sometimes I felt as though the war was over, you were *still* huddled in the foxhole trying to make it through the night. I dug my fingers into your back as though it would ground you to the moment instead of letting you float away again. You prayed to something that ruined your life, and it broke my heart. For the only time in your life, you were powerless to save me from what you knew would happen and I think deep down it changed you.

"—then at the apartment, I saw the mess and, and the blood and it just hit me—how bad it really was and I just, I said thank you because—you are *okay*." Your breath hit the side of my neck and I knew that there was *nothing* I could say, any response would betray your honestly so instead I simply held you tighter.

There are lots of things I could write about that day or the ones that followed, but I think for once this story needs a moment of humor before we all forget how to laugh, or maybe I need something to laugh about before I go back inside.

A while after your words had sunk in, I threw on a hoodie and ventured out to the kitchen to steal some food, I didn't think anyone was home. That is until I got to the living room and saw Spencer quickly throwing whatever was closest to him into a duffle bag. I blushed at the mess of clothes and items on the ground but I wasn't sorry.

"What—where are you going?" I asked with as much innocents as I could muster. He looked at me with wide eyes while pointing around the room.

"Anywhere. I am going *anywhere* other than here until he is gone because—" He pointed at the clothes still lying discarded and then at me, who I'm sure looked the same. "I have heard shit that I am *never* going to unhear, and I have far too much money to sit and witness all of this so, text me when *this* has finally ended." I didn't know what to say, all I could do was stare in pure embarrassment. He looked at me as though he was having war flashbacks.

"I uh—" I cleared my throat. "Okay?"

What else was I supposed to say? Instead of responding Spencer smiled at me and suddenly, I didn't feel bad anymore, although I still wanted to launch myself out the closest window. And then he left as though he hadn't said anything at all leaving me able to do nothing but stand there in his kitchen trying to figure out how I was ever going to face him again.

I think this is a good place to leave things for tonight. Even if it's not, I have to go because Jax is calling us and I think Maisy should go inside now.

Maybe tonight doesn't have to be horrible, maybe it's okay if I give myself a moment to breathe instead of constantly throwing myself back into the waves. My therapist said that it can be hard for people to let themselves live after death, and now more than ever, I think that she might actually be right.

13

Thursday, October 18th

It's been 75 days since I last heard you laugh or saw you smile.

75 days since the walls came crashing down and I lost all sense of reality. I remember sitting in the car the day after and not being able to possibly imagine getting through a single minute with the extinction-level pain radiating through every nerve and I didn't want to—I didn't want to even *think* about how my life would somehow just keep going now that you weren't in it because—it felt like a world-altering event; it was the kind of thing that should, by all means, make the stars fall from the sky and the world stop turning because how—*how* could we all just continue to simply exist now that Sebastian Morgan didn't? I still don't know how but I made it 75 days.

That's over two months of this relentless nightmare and it's farther than I ever thought I would get. Today was almost even a good day. Please don't hate me for saying that.

. . .

Honestly there's not much I want to say about the short 24 hours that you were there; not because it was boring or uneventful, but because I think it's something that I want to keep for myself. It was as though we were stealing time from the fates, time that didn't belong to us and I think there are still some sacred things that exist nowhere but between you and me, and that's where those 24 hours live. What I will say, is that we stayed up all night because we both knew you had to leave in the morning and we talked.

We talked about everything and anything; about the universe and philosophy, we talked about politics and the things that still scared us, under the gaze of the night we talked about everything we could because *no one* could make better conversation than us. We were one in the same back then, always seeming to be thinking the same things or wondering the same questions and now that it's gone—I think the thing I miss the most is just *talking* to you, and hearing the crazy things that your mind would come up with. But that night I couldn't stop time from ticking away, I couldn't stop the sun from rising and the world from waking and soon enough you were gathering the little things you brought and we were heading to the airport. It felt like the first time we had done it, but also as though we had already said goodbye a hundred times.

"Call me when you land," I said into your shoulder as you held onto me in the airport line. I let your sent wash over me for the last time as I tried to take it all in because who knew when you would be back. But I didn't feel scared like I did before. Not when you kissed me and turned away, not when I watched you walk out of frame because I knew there was life on the other side of this. I had friends and a job and somewhere to go to instead of just having to wait for you to come back. Although, I did miss you before your plane left the ground.

I could continue on with the details of what happened next but honestly, it wasn't very exciting.

Life just went on the way it had been for the past three or four months. I stayed living with Spencer, and Sam would joke that in our last life we must have been married because we fought like such and life was actually good. I had a stable job and was starting to make a name for myself doing photography, people other than your coach wanted to work with me and slowly but surely, I was making my name known. Something that did change however was Jax. After the day in the gym with Jarrad, he came around a lot more; he partied with us on the weekends and hung out at our place on the weekdays. He and Spencer became friends faster than I, but after a few weeks, he had somehow become a part of our circle. A few months went by before anything worth reporting happened but those mundane months were nice, they were peaceful and normal and it was almost easy to forget that for you things were falling apart. But Dr. Riley doesn't care about the everyday stuff I did, so ill skip ahead to when we fell apart for the first time.

Throughout everything we ever faced, all the hardships and wars and danger, we had *always* stayed a strong unit; both of us acted like a shield for the other and I think sometimes it's the only way we could get through it. But then my life started to move forwards and yours was stuck in the same constant state of fight or flight, suddenly *our* war became *your* war and I was just standing on the sidelines. But before I continue with that, we must talk about what led up to it first. It can't be more than a few months after you left because I had my 24th birthday and I think you were gone around six months in total, so we should start about two months after you flew back.

The first memory I have is walking down the street towards the gym. Since you left Jarrad had been "let go" from the team and then after that, things started to fall into place.

I was doing more and more events, not just for Rob but for other people who saw my photos online. Now when I walked into the gym, I didn't feel fear or uncertainty or like I was out of place, instead it was starting to feel like home. I had to drop off a disk to Rob, I smiled at a man named Ethan, he waved and your team had somehow become mine, your friends became closer to me than I think they ever were with you and a part of me almost felt bad, but I couldn't feel bad for the sense of belonging that came from being one of them. It was the first time I truly understood why you worked so hard in the gym, it was because it meant you got to belong to something bigger than yourself and for people like us—it was something we desperately searched for. I threw the disc on Rob's desk and turned to leave but before I could get to the door someone was wrapping their arms around my neck from behind, but it didn't scare me the way it used to, instead I laughed and leaned into it.

"Your very clingy, you know that?" I said while Jax laughed, moving so that he was standing in front of me. It's come to my attention that I haven't done right by him on these pages. I don't think I've ever really given him a character even though he has become such a large one in my life.

Jax was a fighter on your team, but he was also a friend, who always tried to do right by you, I think he may be one of the few people I've ever met who just wants to do the right thing. He never has bad intentions or wants something from me, he just wants to help and now—now he just sits in the house and watches Maisy; he makes me food and makes sure I eat and no matter how mean I am to him, he stays. Every day I wake up and he is still in the kitchen or living room doing this or that, he takes her to see your dad because I can't bring myself to face him, and I don't know why he's doing any of this but I think it's because he is one of the rare good people this world has left. That day, however, he laughed while standing in front of me, somehow without realizing it he had become one of my best friends.

"Me? Never." He leaned against the wall beside him, dramatically folding his arms as though in mock offense. I just looked at him.

"Sure. How did the date go last night?" He had gone on a blind date that I had *strictly* advised him not to go on, he looked at the ground.

"Well, she didn't kill me so that's good I guess, but the date was pretty much over when I said I didn't want to sleep with her." I just shook my head as he leaned his head on my shoulder. "Why are people so complicated?"

"I am the wrong person to ask about that," I said because really, I was. I had been with the same person since I was 16 and you and I were so far past the complication phase that I didn't remember what it was like to be there.

"Let's run away together, we can go live in the forest and avoid people forever."

"Sounds perfect, other than the fact neither of us have any survival skills whatsoever." He laughed.

"Yea that's true, plus, I think your boyfriend would kick my ass," I nodded with a smile. "Are you and Spencer still coming over tonight?" He walked over to the front desk to grab his bag.

"Of course we are, the movie is not going to watch itself." Thursday nights had somehow become movie night, a tradition that we had started after you left and I was alone for the second time. Spencer wanted to go see some new superhero movie and Jax said he would go if I did, so we went and now months later, we still tried to do it. But that week it happened to be my turn to pick the movie and I knew exactly what I wanted to see.

"Are you sure that out of *any* movie in the entire world, you want to watch that one?"

No, I actually thought it was going to be a horrendously traumatic experience, but I also knew that it would make us all laugh and there wasn't nearly enough of that in our lives.

"Positive. Think of it as comic relief so that you can stop thinking about the fight for a moment and instead think about A-list celebrities dressing up as human-sized cats." He had a fight coming up soon and he was nervous about it, out of everyone on the team, he fought the least.

"I can't wait." His voice was laced in sarcasm but I just smiled.

"In other news, are you ready to go mattress shopping?" I said with as much energy as I possibly could. Spencer had insisted that it was time to replace his mattress and for some reason, Jax and I were being dragged along as accomplices.

"Let me think; am I ready to go sleep on expensive mattresses, that I could never afford while Spencer shops? Yes, I very much am." He started towards the door and I followed with a smile.

That's how we found ourselves sitting at the third mattress store hours later after being forced to sit on every single bed available. The problem was that none of them seemed to be what Spencer wanted.

"I just—I don't know." He said in frustration before moving towards a sales associate who we should all feel sorry for because Spencer was in a mood that could have ended up with him being the star of a viral video.

"That's it, just kill me," Jax said while falling forward onto the bed I had chosen to lay on like a wounded soldier. He placed his head on my chest as though it were a pillow.

"This is pretty bad yea."

"Want to know what the worst part of all of this is?" His voice was soft and sweet, he looked as though he was close to falling asleep.

"What?" I said because I would play his game. I turned to look at him.

"This is the closest I've gotten to a break in weeks." My heart ached for him because I could understand, I had seen first-hand what it was like for you to train like that and I could only imagine that Jax was going through the same thing, maybe even worse because unlike you, he was the underdog.

"Well, I'm glad something came from this then, because I don't think Spencer is ever going to find a mattress." We both sat in silence for a moment as we watched him talk to different people and sit on the same beds again and again. Even the sales lady seemed at a loss for what to do. Before I could comment on it, my phone was going off and I knew it was you. I smiled at Jax but he was already close to sleep.

"Hello my love" I said dramatically, liking the way you smiled when you saw me. We almost strictly used video chat instead of the phone by that point, it made it easier to be away.

"Hey." You said and it hit me how much I had missed the sound of your voice. I didn't comment on how dark the skin under your eyes was; it was a reality check to the fact that you were very much still stuck in the crossfire.

"Hi from me too," Jax mumbled softly which made your face turn.

"Who was that?" I didn't answer, only turned the camera the other

way around and panned down so that you could see his face. "Hi Jax."
You said laughing. Jax smiled. "I've been gone for a few months and
you're already in bed with someone else, I should have seen it coming."
We all laughed at that, Jax pushed his face closer into my side.

"He's all mine now Morgans." I moved the camera back to face me
because I knew Jax was trying to sleep and you were smiling, it was
beautiful despite the pain lining your eyes.

"What can I say, I'm irresistible."

"Damn right," you looked down. "What are you guys up to?" You
asked but I knew you wanted to say something else, I could hear it in
the tone of your voice that there was a real reason that you had called. I
think sometimes you used to call me just because things were too heavy
at home, it was like a window into the outside world where things could
be okay.

"Spencer needed a new mattress, Jax needed a nap, and I had nothing
better to do so we are hanging out while he shops." I made sure to turn
the camera to the very aggressive conversation Spencer seemed to be
having with the saleswoman.

"Sounds as though it was very productive then." You said but there
was something else in your voice, something that made your walls stay
up instead of lowering as they should have.

"Yea, is everything okay?" I watched as you took a breath before
looking at the ground.

"Yeah, I just wanted to hear your voice."

"Is there anything I can do?"

"No—this is enough." Your voice was quiet as though you were trying
to make yourself invisible, and I hated it.

"Are you sure? Because I can ditch these guys and we can talk." I
looked down at Jax's sleeping figure on my chest trying to figure out the
best way to get him off that would preserve his unconscious state.

"I'm okay, I just wanted to check-in."

"Alright, I'll call you later though, okay?" I couldn't help but feel as
though I was blowing you off in order to live my life without you.

"Sounds good, love you." Before I could answer you had already hung up.

I wish you would have told me then what was happening, that your brother was on the verge of death and everything was falling apart faster than you could fix it. I wish that you would have told me because there's nothing, I wouldn't have done in order to get there faster than I did. I wish I could have been there for you because you had to go through it alone, surrounded by people who didn't love you. I couldn't have done it—the only reason I've made it this far is because of the people around me, but you—you were alone.

But at that moment I didn't know any of that, instead, I looked over to Spencer who seemed to have found a mattress, and smiled because in my world, things were okay, *we* were okay. That is until the sales associate seemed to realize me and Jax had no intention of buying a mattress and promptly made us get up.

. . .

As planned, that night we all made our way to Jax's small apartment near the gym. Thinking back on it we weren't living in the real world anymore, in the same way that you were living in an alternate reality before I told you about Christian. My peace didn't have any right to exist in your world anymore and I didn't even know it. I also didn't know that I was living in the last few moments of normality before the calamity. I didn't have the heart to tell Spencer that the movie we were going to watch had been reviewed as one of the worst films ever made, not when he seemed so excited to watch it.

"I'm sure it's going to be great," I said instead as Jax looked at me as though I was crazy. We all settled down on his big couch with drinks and pizza for me and Spencer, and water and a piece of celery for Jax who was still in the last few weeks of a substantial weight cut.

"But why eat celery?" Spencer said in disgust as Jax took an unimpressed bite of his snack.

"Because, If I just close my eyes tight enough, I can almost pretend it's real food."

"That's rough babe," Spencer said before taking a bite of pizza while looking Jax straight in the eye."During my second year of law school—someone I knew was doing something like that and we all joined in for solidarity," he took another bite. "And it was hands down the worst thing I've ever done." Jax threw himself over the two of us as though he had been shot, his head landing near me with his feet on Spencer and we laughed while trying not to spill our drinks. But then he stopped and looked up at him across from the couch with pure confusion.

"Wait—did you just say that you went to law school?" Spencer looked at him with a raised eyebrow.

"Yes Jaxton, my family owns one of the biggest law firms in the country did you really think all I did in school was graphic design?" Jax looked at him as though unable to comprehend what he was hearing. I couldn't help but laugh.

"Yea—and you graduated? Like seriously, you're an actual lawyer?"

"Technically speaking as far as my parents are concerned. It was the only way for them to fund my lifestyle." He said these things as though they were nothing, as though he went to law school because it was expected of him and graduated without breaking a sweat but he was smart, Spencer is still one of the smartest people I've ever met. Who cares whether or not he ever actually practiced law and did graphic design instead? He passed the bar on his first attempt and when you have money, who cares how you spend it.

"No shit, I'm actually impressed." Jax laid his head back down but there was something new in his eyes. I pushed play on the movie in order to stop the shock from spinning out even further.

Somehow, the movie was worse than I thought it would be. I'm still not sure why I thought it was going to have some redeeming factor, but it didn't. It really was a horrible creation that had no right to exist. When the credits started playing none of us moved or spoke, we all just sat there looking at a blank screen trying to forget what we had just witnessed.

"C, I'm sorry, but you have officially lost your movie choosing rights forever," Jax said strongly and I nodded my head without hesitation.

"That's absolutely fair."

"I feel like I need to pour a bottle of bleach on my eyes," Spencer said without looking at anyone, and then suddenly we were all laughing, the movie mixing with the alcohol making everything seem warm and blissful.

"I second that." Jax agreed and it was the kind of laugh that reached everyone's eyes, all of the stress and anxiety from the real world melted away between the three of us that night because we were safe and happy, and nothing seemed as though it could touch us. When I checked my phone, it was almost 2am.

"Do you mind if we crash here?" I asked because there was no way I was going to walk home; I think it was raining. Or maybe I was just tired of being alone.

"I guess so, but Spencer has to sleep on the floor."

Spencer agreed due to the fact that he was on his fourth drink. Jax' eyes were alive and a smile split his face in half. For a moment I starkly remember thinking that everything would work out.

Not even five hours later, I was asleep on his couch. To be honest I don't remember anything else before that, but at some point, we had all fallen asleep and then the phone was ringing. Anytime I've received a phone call after 2 am my world has changed, and it did that night too. I picked up the phone confused and disoriented and *very* hungover.

"Hello?" I said and instead of words the only thing I heard was you gasp for air. All of the emotion you had been trying to hide came rushing out and you were crying, you never cried. I was standing up and out the front door before my body could understand what I was doing, the world spun but I knew this wasn't a conversation the rest of them needed to hear. It felt like someone was pushing a hole in my chest because you were strangled for breath and making *horrible* sounds filled with so much pain and I couldn't do anything to get you. I didn't need you to tell me what had happened. I didn't say anything because I knew that you needed a moment to be human while constantly around people who pushed any form of vulnerability away. I brought the phone tighter to my ear as though it would somehow bring me closer to you. After a few minutes I could hear your breathing even out slightly.

"—he was 16 years old—" Your voice broke and I had to close my eyes in order to stop it from consuming me. It hit me in that moment that Christian would never grow up; he would never have that first drink with his dad when he turned 21, he would never know what it felt like to drive too fast down the highway at 2am with music blaring, he was never going to fall into the kind of love that made him do stupid things—he was *never* going to move away and start his own life. He was forever going to remain a barely 16-year-old kid who was too sick to live the short life he had, and I wanted to throw up because just like that, it was over. An entire human life was *gone* and at that point it was the first time I had ever witnessed it.

"Want to know what the worst part is?" You started again and I could hear your sharp intakes of breath, could hear how hard you were trying to catch it but you just *couldn't*. I sat down against the side of the door. "She thinks it's *my* fault—she thinks that it's some punishment for her and I just—" I heard you take a horribly desperate gasp. "I didn't even get to be there—"

"Seb, I need you to take a breath." I'd never felt that helpless in my entire life, the only other thing that felt like that was when Maisy was sick and nothing I did could make it better.

"I *have* to get out—I, I have to leave I just, I need —" I couldn't help you, not over the phone. The only thing I could think of was to turn the audio into video and soon I was looking at the broken image you presented me with and it took my breath away. Manic is the only way I can describe it; your eyes were wild and sad, and your hands shook hard enough that I could see it from across the camera, you looked around *desperately,* as though searching for something to bring you back to life and I couldn't think because you *never* got like that.

"Look at me." I said and your chest was heaving too fast and I couldn't fix it. "Sebastian, I need you to look at me." And you did, maybe it was because I used your full name but either way you looked at me, and your eyes were bloodshot and dark and I had to steal myself from falling apart in proxy. "Good, now take a breath, okay," I took a deep breath and watched as you followed, we did that for a few seconds until you stopped breathing as though you had lost a marathon. I couldn't imagine what you felt at that moment, not only were you grieving something irreplaceable, but you were doing it while being attacked by people trying to blame you for the ineffable.

I wonder if it's different to mourn the loss of someone when you've known your whole life that they were going to die. "Good, you're doing so good." I saw you nod.

"I have to get away from here—" I wished that there was something I could say, but we didn't have the money to get a hotel and you couldn't leave yet. "My mom won't look at me and my dad left but hasn't come back and I just—"

You were the picture of pure destruction; the people who still believe that abuse is something beautiful or poetic—or something to romanticize for aesthetic have *never* had to taste the metallic fear of it in their throats or watch helplessly as the person they love blindly goes through it because trust me—there is *nothing* beautiful or poetic about *this*. Don't let my choice to write about it take away from the reality of what it really was; it was dirty and raw, it was broken sobs and bloody faces and the *constant* feeling of being at war with the people who created you, yet still constantly blaming yourself for their actions. It's not TV or fiction created only for entertainment; it was real, it *is* real and don't let my soft words diminish the bluntness of what they describe. I talk as though it was a war because that's exactly what it felt like and, in that moment, as you cried about your endless situation it was as though you were bleeding out on the ground while your allies stood by and watched.

"You know you can't leave yet—Seb you have to say goodbye." And we both knew I was right. If you came back before the funeral, if you

gave up your last chance to say goodbye to him—you would never forgive yourself. But you were afraid and alone, and just wanted the pain
to stop. I heard voices around you and it was at that moment I realized
you were still sitting in the hospital hallway.

"I can't—I—" You shut your eyes tightly as your own realization sunk
in. "I know." You whispered and I wanted to do something, or say something but I couldn't because you were all the way over there and I was
still outside Jax's apartment. I saw you look over your shoulder to the
right and at that moment another realization hit me; it had *just* happened. "I—I have to go but I'll call you back." I nodded before you hung
up and then you were gone as though the call had never happened, yet
I knew nothing would be the same again. I didn't move from the hallway, my own built-up emotion falling because I just wanted things to
be okay, and finally, for the first time in my life they were starting to
be, and then this had to go and happen, and I was *so* tired. I was so tired
of the constant struggle and blood and war and I just wanted it to end.
I know that it's selfish, but I just—I just wanted things to be okay for
longer than a second.

At some point, the door opened and Jax was running to sit beside
me, his face full of concern but I was almost numb to it, so tired and
spent that I didn't have anything left to give. He moved a hand up my
arm.

"What happened? Are you alright, why are you just sitting out
here—"

"Seb's brother died like ten minutes ago," I said point-blank, he just
sat in front of me with a sigh.

"Shit."

There was a collective feeling of uncertainty felt between us. No one
knew what to do, or what would happen when you eventually came
back.

"I think Rob kicked him from the club," I said in the same monotone
voice. Jax just sat there because those were his people.

"What? Why would you think that?" There was a hint of protective-
ness to his voice because the gym was his family before anything else.

"Because not only did I have to clean out his locker, but when they saw each other—it was like estrange exs finally running into each other after years apart." I looked at my hands. "And because no matter how much I try, he won't talk about it."

Maybe it was easy for you to ignore your life in New York while you were there, but when you came back everything was going to be different and the only one who didn't know it was you.

"Shit," Jax said again. He put a hand on my shoulder. "You're going, right?"

I didn't know what to say. Was every nerve in my body telling me to get on the next flight out? Of course it was, but would it just make everything worse for you in the end if I was there?

"It's just going to make things worse if I'm there," I said and I knew it was true, no matter how badly I wanted it to be false. Jax just stared at me until I turned to look at him.

"Collin, you have to go. He's alone, and in pain and his entire world is falling apart right now and you can't just—you can't just let him deal with It alone. You'll regret it if you stay." There was something fierce in his voice, something real that left no room for argument.

"What if I just make it worse?"

"I don't think things get worse than this." He was right. You were alone and needed your family, and I was thousands of miles away. I knew I had to go.

"Your right."

The decision was made. Maybe a part of me was trying to find reasons to stay because I was so afraid to go back there, maybe I was scared of facing the demons I never learned how to fight or maybe I was afraid that when I saw you again everything would be different. But I couldn't hide from it, I had no choice but to face the reality we had created and learn how to live within it. If we could create peace once, then surely, we would be able to find it again.

There isn't a lot more to say about what happened right after that; I booked the first flight that I could while Jax woke up Spencer, Spencer demanded to pay for the flight out if not more because he was the only one in the room other than me who knew what going home meant. And then before I could really think about it, I was sitting on a plane. I don't remember any of the details from that day because my brain was in a fog, like it was putting up battlements and walls to prepare for the on-coming siege. But I think I might finish that story another day.

Jax has Maisy and they are both sitting in the living room by the TV, and I think for once ill join them. Maybe there's some traditions that don't need to be forgotten

14

Sunday, October 28th

Last week Jax decided that we needed to get away for a few days.

I, of course, was perfectly happy staying held up in my apartment because *your still here*.

You're in the blankets and the dishes that we picked out when we finally made enough money; you're in the curtains that you found on-line and the couch that we slept on when we didn't have a bed, you are in every corner and every floorboard of this place, and as long as I'm here then—then I'm *always* going to be stuck constantly replaying the moment's we shared and the words you said because they are written on *every* single wall with still drying ink and—I can't breathe while sitting in the midst of it, but I also can't breathe without the safe feeling of suffocation it provides.

There's a bloodstain on the rug in the living room from when I broke a wine glass and you stepped on the individual pieces—I *can't* stop looking at that one single spot because it's this constant reminder that you were real—that we really were more than just words strung together in this book; that you breathed and bleed and laughed and—and I guess some days it's easy to think of you as nothing but a character I wrote up in order to fill the emptiness sitting at the base of my spine. I guess that's why Jax wanted to leave for a few days; to breathe without you wrapping around us. Maybe it's impossible to move on when every night me and your ghost dance through the halls of this place we built together. Either way, last week Jax packed some bags and we drove out of the city in order to get away from the ghosts that follow us here. We only have a few days left before returning and there is a part of me that never wants to leave these quiet rooms where the only sound is ourselves instead of the never-ending traffic, but that same part of me longs to hold onto the calamity that is slowly becoming safer to me than not.

. . .

I won't bore my therapist with the details of me sitting in the airport waiting for my flight because anyone who has ever flown out of New York knows that its horrendous and not worth writing about so instead ill skip to the moment I remember the most, mostly because up until that moment my head was stuck in a blur of fear and exhaustion but by the end of the day I was standing on the front steps of your house. Before I left Spencer had transferred me some money and told me to get a hotel room so that we weren't forced due to circumstances to stay with them and I was thankful. I hated taking money from him because it always felt dirty and cheated but just this once I was grateful for it. I wanted to run away. I was standing in front of the door that I hadn't seen since we were kids and I was trying to breathe because this *wasn't* like last time. The last time that I'd seen that door we were running away from it, but you needed me and I couldn't run away again. I didn't breathe as my knuckles came in contact with the door.

It felt like those few seconds between knocking and answering were hours because the only thing I could think about was seeing you, but I also knew that it wasn't just you who I would have to see. Spencer said something in passing one day that has always made me smile because of the truth that's held in the words; he said that you and I are basically two inseparable people who are constantly, due to necessity, being separated, and I think that those words, more than anything, sum up how we lived. At that moment I was just trying to get back to you. Your dad answered and for a moment we both stood there and looked at each other. He looked exactly how I thought he would look; his face was that of a parent who had to helplessly watch their child suffer and die. I couldn't begin to imagine the extent of it back then, but now that depth of emotion feels personal, and I wouldn't handle it as well as your dad did. I also realized that he had no idea who I was. Of course, it makes sense that he didn't, he had seen me exactly one time and it had only been for a few moments while we ran, and I had changed a lot since then, I wasn't the skinny little kid I had once been. I stood up straighter as he looked at me with a question. I remembered him as kind and I relaxed a little bit under his eyes.

"Hello—is Sebastian home?" I asked, trying to keep the longing out of my voice because really, I just wanted to push him to the side and run to where ever you were hiding in the house but I didn't, instead I played with my necklace so as not to lose my nerve. I watched as he looked me up and down, his face pale compared to his robe.

"Who are you?" He asked and maybe there was something familiar about me that he couldn't place. I wasn't like you, and I couldn't tell him the truth.

"I'm just an old friend," I said and I promise that I felt bad about every word. I wish that I could have just told him but I needed to see you first. He nodded his head.

"Just wait here." He shut the door and the second he did I let out a huge breath. I bounced up and down on my heels as the seconds turned into minutes, I couldn't react when I heard the sound of someone opening up the door and suddenly you were standing in front of me with hooded eyes and a worn sweater, your grief plastered into every line of your face for the world to see; once again you looked like a fighter. I watched recognition come over you as you ran your eyes over me and then before I could move, we were both stumbling backwards due to the raw force of you wrapping your arms around my neck. The moment was beautifully painful, emotions of both ruin and salvation interwinding until I wasn't sure what was what anymore but it didn't matter because you were there and I could feel your entire body shaking against mine. Your fingers dug into my back as you held on as though it would somehow save you, and I held on just as tight.

"You're here." You said in pure disbelief and I could feel your breath hit the side of my neck.

"I'm here"

Should we have seen the warning signs back in those days that we were already walking down a broken road? That even though we tried—and *God* did we try—we were never meant to last a lifetime. Maybe we were only ever supposed to be as permanent as the rain.

But I didn't care then and I don't regret it now. Not that, and not you. It was only us, no one else in the entire world existed because I was prepared to jump into the foxhole with you even though I had found peace on the surface.

You pulled away but kept your arms around my neck tightly, leaving only inches between the two of us. There were a thousand things we said in that space despite the fact neither of us could speak. You leaned your forehead against mine as though you wanted to be close and then you were kissing me, and every word that you couldn't get yourself to say was being pressed to my lips and I understood. It made me dizzy to think that we were kissing outside your childhood house where anyone could see and I wasn't afraid. What a crazy upside-down world we had fallen into.

"Who's at the door—" Your dad, Ben, came into view again as he walked down the stairs and he really did look as though he had aged ten years in the last five, his face so different yet so familiar then it had been all those years ago. He lacked the venom of your mom, as well as the conviction and condemnation and I'm glad every day that you got to know him before you—that our *child* gets to know him because he is as close to you as she can ever get. I won't just write you out of the book as though your arc is over because it's not. You knew that if your mom had been different and if Christian wouldn't have been sick, he never would have let you leave. He took a deep breath in realization as our eyes met. He smiled.

"Andrew, right? I'm sorry I didn't recognize you— been a while since we saw each other." He said and I was shocked when he leaned in to give me an awkward half-hug but I hugged him back.

"It's Collin actually, but it's nice to see you again." I didn't know what to say, what could I say at that age to a parent who had just watched their baby die? "I'm sorry for your loss."

"Thank you." He motioned us into the door, "please come in Collin."

We did, shuffling into the tight entryway as your dad made his way to the living room wordlessly.

It's stupid, but there was still a part of me that wanted them to accept us, for a parental figure to turn to me with kind eyes and accept me for being with you. We all settled down on various couches, I didn't know where to sit; did I sit with you or did I create some distance as to not make the situation more awkward than it already was? In the end I didn't have to choose because you pulled me down beside you before I could make up my mind. There we were; you and me, and your dad who didn't know either of us anymore, it was uncomfortable and tense, but my therapist said that sometimes healing can be the most uncomfortable thing of all.

"It was very considerate of you to come all this way for him." Your dad was trying to make conversation, the key part being that he was *trying*. He was trying to understand us and it makes me smile just thinking about It, because it was the first time anyone in our home lives had ever tried before.

"Of course, it's what we do," I said because we did, and you smiled because you knew.

"Still, it's nice for a parent to know that their kid has someone like that." His words shocked me, but not in a bad way, but in a *I never thought anyone related to us would ever say something like that* way. A part of me wanted to come back with something spiteful because it was weird to hear you referred to as their kid, they should have lost the rights to that when they made you leave and then blamed you for your brother's death. But there he was, trying to act as though you had some sort of family unit still standing behind you. But it was also the closest thing to acceptance that we had ever received.

"What have you been up to these days career-wise?" He asked and I was so tired. Tired from the flight and the last few days and just from life, and all I wanted to do was go to bed and deal with this tomorrow but it would have been rude to leave.

"Collin does photography, he's one of the best fight photographers around." You said and there was a tone of pride that made something in my heart feel less sharp.

"I'm alright at it, it pays the bills though so that's good." There was a piece of me that desperately wanted to ask about my family; if they had ever come back to town, or if the house still sat there abandoned, maybe someone new was there; would they ever know the story that started within those four walls? When they ripped out the bloody carpet, did they ever wonder whose blood they were replacing? But I didn't ask, not then, I knew that there would be time for it later.

"That's great, I'm happy you've found something." He said with a smile and maybe he just needed to hear that we were alright; that we were living a good life with good jobs and maybe Ben thought that it would somehow make the guilt from the past ease, and maybe it did.

I felt suspended in the hot air around us, as though I couldn't breathe while it was pressing down on our shoulders. I knew you felt it too when you leaned against me as though needing the support to stay awake. Your dad leaned closer.

"Listen—" we both took a breath at the same time, both of us not wanting to have whatever conversation that your dad wanted to have with us. But we couldn't avoid it. Instead, we just hung onto each other a little bit tighter. "I know that there's been a lot of things in the past—but your mom—she is just traditional, you understand that right?" He was trying to keep the peace because we all could feel the only thing standing between total destruction was one wrong word. I nodded, I didn't need her approval because it wasn't about her anymore, but you just stared at him.

"And you understand that I'm not going to change, right?" Ben nodded his head.

"Of course, and—I might not understand It, but I want you to be happy—"

"Sure, that's why you never tried to find me right?"

It was hard for you to forgive your dad, and at this point it was still new, it was fresh and the pain was still there and you couldn't understand it.

"You know it wasn't that simple. Just—be careful around your mom when she gets back okay, she's hurting right now."

There was more he wanted to say but he also knew that it was not the time for you to listen. But the words he did say were the wrong ones. But your dad was exhausted and I can't imagine what he was going through; not only was he grieving a child, but he was trying desperately to regain some kind of hold of the estranged one he still had and I can't imagine it was painless. You looked at the ground, all the fight you once carried gone.

"I'm hurting too."

The words were so quiet, so fragile and broken that it didn't even sound like you anymore. I grabbed your hand from where it rested on your knee because I had to do something, I was ready to go to war if it meant your voice never had to sound like that again. Your dads face changed to something akin to regret, as though no matter what he did, he could never say the right thing to you.

"I know you are; I know and I'm sorry, I'm—it's not your fault—" I couldn't believe it.

Maybe it was better that my parents just left, at least I got to be mad and stay mad without them trying to behave as though the past didn't happen, of course it wasn't your fault. The fact that he even had to say it meant that someone told you it was and I wanted to take you and just go home, we didn't belong there anymore and I was more than okay with that because for the first time I realized that I didn't want to.

We all sat in silence for a moment before I realized it was my turn to save you.

"Where is Hannah anyways?" I said, taking the pressure off of you and throwing it back onto him as it was too soon to just get up and leave, but it was also too soon for that conversation. Your dad ran a hand over his face slowly

"she's picking up her aunt a few hours away," I remembered that we were all still here because of the funeral. I didn't want to ask, but I couldn't stop myself from saying it.

"I'm sorry if this is blunt but—when is the funeral?" I said and it was silent for a moment but I had to know, I had to book flights and figure out my job, I couldn't just leave for an unknowable amount of time as you had and no one was going to ask about it other than me.

"A few days, on Saturday." It was Wednesday. I nodded my head, we could stay for a few more days. I looked at you and the only thing I could think about was the fact that it was almost over.

"Okay. I think it might be time for us to leave." I said while standing up, keeping your hand in mine so that you had no choice but to follow. You looked at me with your head tilted to the side. I leaned closer to your ear. "Spencer sent me some money, and I'm exhausted."

"Where are you going? We have lots of room here." Your dad said, following us up from our seats and a part of my heart broke for the desperation that covered his face. It was an ode to the past; both of us headed for the door but this time your dad wouldn't just sit and silently watch it happen. You turned to him and I knew a part of you wanted to stay, maybe you wanted to be mad, you wanted to be mad just so that he could prove that he wouldn't walk away from you again.

"You don't want us here." Your voice was cold and unattached but there was something hidden underneath of it, something I couldn't place but knew was a pure want for things to be different. He looked at the floor, and then at us.

"Sebastian please—I know I've messed up, trust me I *know* but just *please*—stay tonight, don't leave me here alone." Any resolve you might have had about the situation fell apart and all I wanted to do was hug him, because he was just as alone as you. You looked at me and I nodded. Even though staying was the last thing I wanted to do.

You sighed before looking at your dad.

"Yea, okay fine." You shut the door and took off your shoes, your dad relaxed. I really did want to go to sleep. "But I do think we are going to go to bed, he's been flying all day and I just want to sleep." You said, slowly walking past your dad in the direction of the stairs.

"Yes of course, let me know if you need anything—have a good night." He was just trying so hard to make things even slightly okay. I smiled as I passed him.

"Thank you." I said and he smiled.

We didn't talk as we walked up the stairs, everything weirdly the exact same as it had been all those years ago like it was a time capsule that had remained untouched. Your room was exactly the same as it had always been, the same pictures on the walls and books on the shelves, it was almost shocking to stand back in that room when it felt like everything other than us was the same. If I tried hard enough, I could almost pretend that we were the same too. The second the door shut your arms were around my neck as you pressed your face into the side of my head, and you hung on to me so tightly. I laughed slightly as I wrapped my own around your middle, I felt you release the breath I knew you had been holding since you arrived. Finally, for the first time in months, we were completely alone, save for the new ghosts that seemed to sit in corners and remind us of the past.

"I missed you." You said quietly, as though you didn't trust your own voice to speak. I focused on the way your breath hit the top of my ears. I just nodded, there had been a lot of I miss you and goodbyes spoken in the last few months and for once I didn't want to live in them because we were together, who cared about anything else. I moved us over to the bed, and when we sat down you just pulled me closer until we were inches away.

"Hi," I said stupidly and your face was so different then it had been downstairs. The pain was still there but it was almost softer now, less jagged and defensive and more honest, as though you weren't hiding anything anymore. I moved a hand to the side of your face, letting my fingers gently play over your features until you became you again.

"Hi," You said back and for a moment we both just lived in the silence, in the feeling of having each other this close after so long apart but it couldn't last forever. I couldn't ignore the feeling hanging in the air.

"I'm so sorry."

The words felt wrong and stale because how could that make anything better?

Why do we always think that saying sorry is going to help a grieving person heal, or make them stop feeling as though the world has ended? It doesn't, it doesn't make anything better because sorry is just a five-letter word and nothing more. But I didn't know what else I could possibly say. You nodded your head but didn't say anything else, instead you buried your face into my chest and finally, *finally* let yourself fall apart over what you had endured. When it came to you and me, it was always me falling apart and you trying to keep it together while pretending as though the bullets never made you bleed, but they did, and for once you couldn't act as though you had come out of this whole thing unscratched. The whole six months of this had taken you to the edge and now you were finally letting yourself fall off of it because it was almost over. I couldn't do anything; it was too soon to pretend as though things would be alright. Instead, I just move the blanket so that it was surrounding us like a shield and hung on until your storm had passed

. . .

That's how we ended up back in that town. It turned out to be one of the most important trips of our lives because it was the first steps that led us to Masiy, as well as the first time I would see any member of my family since they left. But we didn't know that then, all we knew was that your mom was gone leaving the house quiet and safe. But I think I'll wait till I get home to say the rest of it, tonight the sky is pink and it's still warm enough to go outside. I can see Jax and Maisy playing in the yard, and I think it's too nice to get lost in the past, even if it's the only moments that I get with you.

15

Thursday, November 1st

Jax is gone.

I don't know where he went, and I don't want to talk about it because I don't care. I don't give a shit whether he stays or goes.

Or maybe I do—I don't know anymore.

I got mad, and then he got mad, and then suddenly I was yelling and he was yelling and then he left and how doesn't he see what this is like? He just walks in and acts as though he is a part of our lives now but he's not—he *can't* be—because what about you? How am I supposed to just keep going without you for the rest of my life? How do I just act as though it never happened and raise our daughter and go through every single day of my life as though you were never here at all? Jax acts as though life is just going to continue on but it can't, it *can't* because I don't *want* it to go on without you. He wants me to move away from this place and I just don't know how to do it, so I got mad like I always do and now he's gone and your gone, and everyone is just gone and I don't know how to make any of you stay.

I don't want to write this today, screw my therapist.

The rest of my life can wait a day.

16

Thursday, November 8th

The last few days have been rough.

I apologize for my last entry; I was half a bottle down and panicking, but it's been a week since then and things are less inconceivable. Jax came back after a few days and I have never been so happy to see him. Masiy missed him too, she's been basically attached to him ever since he walked through the door. I know that I'm not easy to live with at the best of times—especially right now, and I don't know why he keeps coming back but he does, every single time. I hate how much I want him to stay. We haven't really talked about what happened though, maybe he is just trying to make peace or maybe he doesn't want to make it worse but eventually we are going to have to talk about it like adults but—

He came back.

. . .

The morning after I got to your parents' house the world seemed less violent than it was the night before.

We woke up in the same position we had fallen asleep in and I think despite everything going on, it was the best sleep id had in ages. I ran a hand through your hair while looking around the room for the first time. It was strange to see it now; everything was so different yet still so similar. A part of me thought that the second we left your mom would have packed everything up and turned your room into a yoga studio or an office or something, anything to dig in the point that you didn't exist any longer, but she didn't. Or maybe your dad didn't let her.

"Remember what happened the last time we were here?" You whispered against my chest, your voice was ragged and harsh from crying. I took a soft breath.

"How could I ever forget it?"

"We have come a long way since then." It was true, we were different people than we had been and I was so proud of who those people were.

"Bet no one thought we would make it past the first highway exit." You looked at me with a smile.

"But we did."

We had made it, and we had done what everyone thought we wouldn't; we were bruised and broken and had more problems than I could count, but we were still standing and we should have been prouder of that fact.

"We did." I echoed your words back to you and honestly for some reason, in that small childhood bed I saw the past, but I also saw our future. When you said those words with conviction—I had this startling realization that you really were the rest of my life. I wanted it *so* badly—for you to be *it*—I never thought I'd have to go on another first date, or have another first kiss or be nervous about meeting someone's else parents but now—I just wish it was *you*.

"How long are you staying?" You asked and maybe you thought I had just come for a few days; we both knew I had a thousand things on the go at the moment and that it was a lot for me to walk away from it but I would do It for you. I remembered saying the same words to you months before and I was done. No more goodbyes, no more leaving, no more quick hellos.

"I don't plan on getting on the plane alone, so however long that takes," I said and I meant it. I wasn't willing to go home alone, not again.

"Do you ever think things will get better for us?"

I wanted to laugh because I *felt* it.

Of course, what I didn't say was that things *had* gotten better, they had started to even out and become stable and I didn't say that a part of me was terrified about what would happen when you were faced with the reality that the life you had known in New York was gone. But instead of saying any of that I just nodded and placed a kiss in your hair.

"Of course they will. Think of this as character development."

You didn't respond, instead, you brought your lips to mine and kissed me as though you were willing to wait forever. I felt your hand on my jaw slowly, as though making sure I couldn't get away and there was something just heartbreakingly sweet about that moment. I had missed you, a lot, and it wasn't until that moment that I realized the extent of it but God—I missed you. I tangled my hands in your hair, letting myself surrender to every moment of it. You smiled as my lips parted under yours and it felt so out of place but I didn't care, too caught up in the way your fingers spread across the skin of my stomach to care who was sitting down the hall. I only cared about you. You pulled away slowly only to take off your sweatshirt in one smooth motion and then I was laughing as you pushed us both back against the pillows. You seemed more like you than you had in months, your eyes started to seem like mine again instead of lost to senseless violence and I wanted to remember every single second of it because we made it. You kissed my jaw and the place below my ear and It felt new, as though you had never done anything like it before and we were kids again. I loved every second of it and I can never find the right words to describe what that felt like, but it was something completely *you*, I don't think I'll ever tell anyone the details because no one—not even my therapist, has that right to our life. Not when it was real and true and—I watched with rapid breaths as you ran your eyes over me like you were still convincing yourself that I was really, truly there with you instead of thousands of miles away and maybe we were allowed to have that one moment of surrender in the midst of the battle, even if we weren't, we were never people who listened. But then someone was knocking on the door and I remembered where we were, you laughed as you let your head fall onto my chest.

"We should have gotten a hotel." You said and I found your lips again with a smile.

"It's not too late to change plans."

"Deal." The knock came again and you moved away, but this time I wasn't being thrown off the bed or pushed into the corner, instead, you sat up beside me and faced the door. I don't even think you put on a shirt.

"Sebastian—I'm coming in, okay?" We heard your dad through the door and it was the last thing on earth that he wanted to do. I pulled the blanket a little tighter around my shoulders as though somehow that would hide the fact that my clothes were thrown halfway across the room. You staired with no intention of hiding anything. He opened the door slowly, as though not sure whether or not it was a good idea and I wanted to jump out of the window when I saw his embarrassment as he looked at me. I can only imagine what I looked like; all flushed-faced and bruised lips, I'm sure I looked exactly as I should have, only made worse by the fact your dad was trying not to intrude.

"what's going on?" You said as casually as possible, I think a part of you loved his discomfort. Maybe he had almost forgotten that I was here.

"I—uh I am going into the city to pick some stuff up and won't be back till tonight." I watched as he took a breath as though to collect his thoughts. "But id, I'd love to have dinner tonight if you wanted—with both of you of course." I nodded my head without asking you because I wouldn't let you throw this away, not when you had a chance to have what I never could.

"Sure." You said but only after you saw that I had already agreed. you laid down dismissively

"Great, great okay I'll see you then," he went to walk away but stopped. "Morning Collin." I waved as he shut the door and the second, he did you laughed harder than I think you had in a long time.

"That was horrifying," I said while pulling the blanket above my head only for you to pull it back down. I kissed your cheek before sitting up. "What should we do today?"

I played with the hand you put on my knee. We really did leave everything behind that day, even the photos and random knickknacks still sat on the countertops completely untouched. I knew the next few days were going to be hard for you and I just wanted to make the day as nice as possible.

"That breakfast place on main still exists, could be nostalgic to go there again. Especially with you." That place was old even when we were young.

"Are you saying that you finally want to go public with our scandal? This will be the talk of the town Sebastian" I said as dramatically as possible. You kissed me as though to prove your point.

"I mean, unless you're worried about mommy and daddy finding out your big secret."

"I think it's a little late for that." I said while going through the small bag you took when you were last in the city. I don't think my bag had made it up the stairs yet.

"I miss home." There was something closer to longing in your voice and I think it wasn't the city you missed, but your life in it. You missed going out on Fridays with our friends and walking around in the endless sound in the middle of the night, you missed a life that had moved on without you. I thought you would be more upset than you were, but maybe it was different to mourn the death of someone you had been grieving your whole life.

"Good, because I don't think we can ever afford to travel again." It wasn't as true as it once had been, especially when our friends were always trying to find something new to drop money on. But I wanted you to laugh. And you did.

"I'm okay with that."

You put out a hand and I grabbed it.

. . .

We walked to that little breakfast place the same way we had done a thousand times; except this time *everything* was different. You held my hand as we walked down the quiet streets, no longer afraid of what anyone would say or who saw because it didn't matter, it wasn't our home and we didn't owe them anything else. I wasn't afraid anymore, not of what they could say anyways. I heard the bell ring as we walked through the door and nothing had changed. I'm positive that the same bugs sat in the corners of the window. The walls had the same photos covering them, the same tile in the middle of the entry was cracked in the corner and it smelt like coffee and cinnamon in exactly the same way it always had. Everything was the same except for us. Instead of sitting we walked down the stairs into the little book store in the basement. When I was growing up, I spent a lot of time there, it was somewhere I could hide from the rest of the world and it was a place where no one expected anything from me. I walked over to the seat in the corner where I would sit with a coffee and I could basically see my younger self in the reflection of the shiny table.

"I basically lived here before I met you," I said in the direction you were walking. Of course, you found a section of interest and got drawn in faster than I could grab you and I knew we were going to be there for a while. But it was your day, and if you wanted to buy books that we already owned then so be it. I left you alone to browse, knowing that you wouldn't say much anyways and instead I looked at funny comics and socks, at random toys and keepsakes that tourists would love, and then something happened that changed my life.

It was one of those moments that although seems small, changes everything. If we wouldn't have gone to breakfast that day, and if you wouldn't have gotten distracted by books, then we never would have got Maisy, everything we are would be different if not for that one moment. Just as I was about to comment on some stupid bar of soap, my world changed.

"Andrew? Andrew Collins?" Someone said from behind me and the voice cut straight to my chest making me turn around in search of the person I left behind. You weren't the only one who walked away from their siblings, and you weren't the only one who would have to face it. Walking towards me was a man—he had to be almost 18 but he had my eyes, the twelve-year-old girl standing beside him had my nose. The last time I'd seen them—he had been 14 and she had barely been seven and now—now I could barely understand who they were, every feature was so strange yet there was no denying it.

"Jaccob?" I said slowly and he nodded, a piece of hair fell into his eyes than before I could figure out my next move, he was walking towards me and we were hanging on to each other as though I had never left. I still don't know how to describe what it felt like to hug my brother that day—someone who had the same blood running through their veins because I had forgotten what that felt like—to have biological family holding onto you as though they couldn't let go and we didn't. We just stood in the middle of a book store holding onto each other with no thought of the past. We grew up close, as close as we could be considering the age difference but at one point, he had been my best friend due to the fact we both lived in the same war.

"Holy shit." I heard him say and I was laughing, really and truly laughing with my brother and I never wanted to let go because letting go meant confronting the past. I knew it wasn't his fault, it wasn't any of their faults. He moved away and then my sister was staring up at me with uncertainty. I looked at her with a smile.

"Hey—" I didn't know what to say to her, she was so young when we left—she was young and I didn't know what they had told her but then she was holding onto me just as tight as Jaccob had.

"You're here." She said quietly and I couldn't find any words for what was happening. They didn't hate me. I had spent years thinking about what would happen if I saw them again, of what I would say and if they would understand but I never thought it would have an ending like that. Once Annie pulled away and moved to stand beside Jaccob, we all just looked at each other.

"You're so old—I can't believe it—" Jaccob said and I nodded with a smile. I ran my eyes over him as though I was still trying to convince myself that he was there.

"You were like, four feet shorter the last time I saw you," I didn't know what to say, what does one say when they are met with their estranged family who they haven't seen since a horribly traumatic event occurred? It hit me then that Jaccob was the same age I had been.

"luckily, I grew in high school, and thankfully high school is over. Five—six years, that means your like what—"

"Twenty-four." I smiled, thankful that he got to finished high school even if I didn't. His eyes went wide and there was something hidden behind them. He looked at Annie.

"Hey, why don't you go find some books?" He said and she nodded before heading in the direction of the boyfriend I had momentarily forgotten was standing six feet away. Once she was gone Jaccob looked at me, but he couldn't meet my eyes.

"Drew, I—I don't know where to start—You know, I've thought about this every day since, you know—"

"Since dad tried to kill me, and then left me to die," I said and I wasn't joking or trying to make it better because we had to live through it; I wasn't going to hide my pain when I had to deal with it every single day, I didn't care if it was hard for him to hear because at least he didn't have to live in it.

"Yea, since that. He's not around anymore you know, he and mom split a while ago—I don't know where he is now but mom—she talks about you all the time." Did she talk about me? The kid she walked away from and never tried to find? I could have been dead and she never would have known. "Noah, well you know how he can be—he just kinda became dad."

He looked at the ground as though trying to find the right words. Noah was the oldest after me, he would have been twenty-two or three by that point and I could only imagine what he turned into. Jaccob looked at me and I wanted to hide. "But I've always thought about you—they never really told us what happened that night, only that you had forsaken God and wouldn't be there when we came back from grandma's house—." I nodded while trying to keep my composure because, it wasn't his fault.

"Why—why did you never try to find me?"

"I didn't know where you went, or if you were okay or wanted to hear from me—" I could see the guilt forming on his face, and for once I had to push down my own feelings about the matter.

"Of course I wanted to hear from you—I had nothing Jaccob, no friends or family or money, and I—we slept on the side of the road for weeks—" I took a deep breath because there was no point in getting mad at him; not when all it would do was destroy any hope we had for the future. "New York, we live in New York"

"You always wanted to go there." I nodded

"It's not quite as glamorous as I thought it would be. But it's home."

There were so many things I wanted to say to him but all the possible things that I wanted to say were gone. I didn't want to believe for even a second that he would still be smiling when he knew who I really was.

"You got out—why on earth are you back here?" I looked towards you with a smile. I pointed, and you must have noticed because soon, as though finally realizing what was happening you made your way over to me with haste. And then you were standing beside me with an arm on my back.

"Jaccob, I'd like to formally introduce you to my boyfriend, Sebastian," He just looked at you, and then at me. I turned to you. "And Seb—this is my brother." Your eyes went wide as though you didn't know what to say to him. I didn't either. You stuck out a hand for him to shake.

"It's great to meet you." You said, trying to be nice when I knew that you didn't like any of them. Jaccob shook your hand.

"You too—I used to watch you play soccer." He said and it's like all the things he had been wondering about came crashing down as he looked at the two of us. "I *knew* it." I laughed because I didn't know what else to do.

"Yea, dad didn't love it," I said to keep it light, this wasn't the setting to rehash a past that didn't matter anymore. "It's why we left," I said and Jaccob nodded his head with sad resignation.

"I'm sorry—truly I'm sorry but I—please know that we, me and Annie, we don't care—at all and I would really love the chance to know you—both of you, if, of course, that's what you want." I could have cried because there it was. The thing I had always wanted on some level was happening and it was real and I just—I couldn't believe it.

To this day I'm grateful for them both, Jaccob has been by a few times in the past month but maybe I should try harder to keep him around. Because in that moment—he was *trying*. I nodded my head, unable to put anything else into words because I just—it was something else.

"I'd like that," I looked to where Annie was collecting books and she reminded me so much of you and I wonder if Maisy will take after her too. I needed time to be able to talk to them, and I couldn't do it in a public book store with the rest of the world listening to our sins. "Listen we—we have to go but," I took a deep breath. "This is my number," it was weird to give him a piece of my life, He quickly put my number into his phone and sent me a text to make sure it worked. He smiled.

"Thank you—I'll call you, I promise." And he meant it because he did call me. He called me and texted and we began to form a real relationship as adults. He stayed with us for a while when we were trying to figure out what to do with Annie and I hope that he will be in our daughter's life forever.

"If your ever near the city, stop in." I said and then he was hugging me and this time I let myself experience it, I let myself hold onto him just as tightly. Before we left Annie was walking back to our group and all I did was smile at her. "I'll talk to you soon alright?" I said and she smiled and nodded and then looked at you with a turned head. I would let Jaccob explain.

Together we walked away from the past without looking back, except this time there was hope that they would be in our future. Maybe once me and Jax figure things out we can go visit him, I'm sure he would love to see Maisy, and maybe it will help to get away from people constantly wanting to know if I'm okay. We slowly walked down the winding roads and I don't think we said very much, both of us too stuck in our own heads to be able to vocalize our fears and we didn't have to. There were people watching us, it's not as though they didn't know who we were and I can't imagine what our families told people after we left; maybe the people around us thought they were seeing a ghost when you grabbed my hand tighter. I knew where we were going, where else would we go other than the one place we always went back to? Although I have to say that the little playground seemed a lot bigger when we were younger. By then it was close to being condemned but it didn't matter, it was still ours; I could basically see us sitting under the platform in the rain, or on the roof when it was clear, we fell in love on that condemned ground. You walked over to the swing set, I sat down beside you.

"That was a lot," I said into the silence. We were sitting in a photo, everything around us was exactly the same. If I was standing there now, I'm sure I would feel your ghost against the metal chains. You laughed a little.

"Yea, not bad though, right?" You let me decide who I wanted them to be; whether I wanted them to be the heroes or villains.

"No, not bad, I just—I don't know how to believe them." It was honest and raw and true, I didn't know how to trust them, how to believe that they would call or that they weren't running home to mom in order to tell her what they knew. I didn't yet know how to believe that they were on our side. "I want to—I just, I don't know." I kicked at the sand with my feet, watching the way it moved and fell to my whim.

"I don't think you have to know, even if he never calls you again, at least you were honest with him."

I was so far away, I don't think I cared about my brother or sister, seeing them was like re-opening a door that I had bolted shut and now my mom's face was filling mine and I wanted to yell. It shouldn't have been this crazy thing to see my siblings, it should have been just another day and I should have been here visiting them, I should have been able to go home and hug my mom while spilling the horror that we had seen and I should have been able to get a drink with my dad because I think you two would have liked each other. *Everything* should have been so different and yet there we were alone, sitting in the same place as though we had never left.

"I don't understand them—sometimes I still feel like a kid whose playing pretend because I just—I just don't understand how they did that, how they just left me like that." I felt stupid for being upset, especially when we were there for you, it was *you* who should be upset; *you* who had just lost your brother but I just couldn't stop. You reached across the empty space and took my hand.

"Our parents are just kids too," When you looked at me your eyes held the same pain, both of us connected by this one piece of truth that we lived with. Time was funny like that, sometimes it felt as though the past was far enough away that I could barely remember it, but then sometimes it felt as though it happened seconds ago and I was still trying to stitch myself back together.

"How could they just leave like that," I whisper again because I *didn't* understand, I still don't but I was young, and I was in more pain than I realized. You held my hand tighter.

"But can you imagine what our lives would be like if we stayed?" Yes, I wanted to say; yes, I could imagine what would have happened, I would have finished school and gone to university, we still would have gone to New York except we wouldn't have been homeless and alone. But then I thought about our family back in the city, about Jax and Spencer and Sam and—and if we would have stayed then I probably never would have met any of them. It didn't take away the longing for normalcy, but it did lessen the weight of it.

"Things would be so different," I answered, not voicing what I really thought because it wasn't your fault.

"We may not have everything, but I wouldn't give any of it up."

You really did make me smile.

It was you and me against the world. You always tried to be optimistic, always one to say the right things even if you didn't believe them and that's all you were trying to do at that moment, you were trying to save the world from burning and I think that you did. You stood up with a smile and started walking and I couldn't believe what we were doing but soon we were once again sitting underneath the bug-infested platform, something which was considerably harder as adults than it had been as kids but there we were; face to face as though we were sixteen again. You rubbed a small circle on the inside of my thumb as I looked up at the place our initials sat unmarked.

"Tell me about the rain," you said, and I had to stop myself from laughing.

"Who in their right mind would have an opinion about something like rain?" I said what I had wanted to say all those years ago but lacked the nerve to. You smiled and it was real, despite your dark eyes and sunken face, your smile that day was real and I wanted to cling to it. I took a breath, "But if I had to, I would say that I think the rain brings second chances." We were a thousand miles away from those words yet it seemed the same, the same energy sat in my chest as having you so close, I had the same inability to look away when you met my eyes; all the things that mattered the most were the same as they had always been. You laughed slightly.

"I can't believe I actually asked you about the rain, I don't know what I was thinking." I could see the embarrassment forming but I smiled.

"I'm glad you did."

You were new and exciting and unlike anyone I had ever met, and when you asked me about the rain that day all I wanted to do was understand the way your mind worked, I wanted to hear you talk about it forever.

"Want to know a secret?" I nodded "I didn't need bio help, you actually needed more help than me as everything you told me was wrong, but I just wanted a reason to hang out with you." I shook my head in disbelief.

"Asshole, you could have just asked! Do you know how long I spent studying before we met? The entire night, I spent the entire night teaching myself the concepts because I was so afraid of messing up in front of you!" You kissed me against the side of the broken playground a thousand years away from the moment in question. "I'm not letting you off the hook that easy." I said between breaths, but my smile betrayed me.

That's how we spent the first day, we sat and talked on the ground about everything and anything, you told horrible jokes I thought were funny and I think we both felt invincible hidden on the ground like that, as though we could forget about our real lives and go back to a simpler time when we didn't have anything to fear. By the time we started walking home, my fingers were numb from the cold and the sun was disappearing from the sky, it must have been close to November or October because I remember being frozen to the bone as we started walking back, not that it mattered because I felt lighter than I had in years. You wrapped an arm around my shoulders as we walked, reminding ourselves that we were so much more than we had been back then. I remember that we took the long way home, we walked down the winding streets that painted our childhood, I used to ride my bike up and down that road, the same trees created the border of my young life.

"See that tree right there?" I pointed behind us to a tall spiky tree. "That tree, to the end of that corner, that's as big as my world used to be," I said and it was only then I realized we were standing on the street to my house, that my childhood home was within eyesight. I could see my mom's old car in the driveway and was hit with the realization that she had come back to that house; I hope they all saw the blankets and mattress in the middle of the living room and known it was us. We stopped walking before the house, both of us taking a second to look at it without any of them being able to see us, not that they could have anyways as it was dark.

"The number of times I jumped out of that window is impressive." I said, looking at the spot my old room would have been, they would have had to replace the carpet. I leaned into you as you laughed, I think it took you by surprise when I kissed you right there in the middle of the street, but soon your hand was in my hair and you were holding me even closer and despite everything else I almost felt invincible too; our very existence was a big fuck you to the people living a few feet away. I could feel you smile against my lips as I pulled away.

"Sorry, I should have asked." I said the words back like a ghost and you laughed against the side of my face as you pushed me up against the street post. Of course, the sound made the people inside become aware of us, and soon the lights were on. You looked at me with a smile and grabbed my hand and together we ran down the street, as though we were still teenagers drunk on the invincibility of youth.

The entire night was honestly one that should never have existed in that space, it felt odd to feel something good in the middle of all the pain, we were there for a funeral and yet that night we would laugh harder than we had in ages. When we stumbled through the door, your dad was in the kitchen with a glass of wine. True to his word he was making dinner. You looked at me and we had a choice; we could leave or go upstairs and act as though we didn't know he was there, or we could join him, and you could try to understand each other for no other reason than that you were both going through the same thing. You pulled me to the kitchen and poured yourself a drink.

I once read that the more we try to explain something, the harder it is to feel what the experience was like; the same goes for this. The harder I try to find the perfect words to explain everything we felt that night, the further away from the truth it gets and that defeats the purpose of writing any of this and instead dishonors the purity of our joy. So, instead of overcomplicating that night, I'll leave it at this; In the middle of endless war, we laughed.

Jax is waiting outside the door and I can hear his foot tapping against the floor with secret anxiety. I should go talk to him. Sometimes I just sit here in my chair holding this notebook in between my fingers for hours as though I could somehow make you stay, as long as I grip the pages tighter. I don't *want* to do this whole life thing without you, I don't know how to—but, no matter how hard I grip these wordless pages, or how many 11:11 wishes I promise to you—*you're gone.*

You, Sebastian Morgan, died at 31 years old, leaving behind me; a man unable to stand on my own and a daughter who deserves you instead. I *can't* bring you back my love. But right now—right now Jax is standing at my door asking me to *stay*; to stay with him, and Maisy and our friends and family instead of getting lost forever in these words with you and I, I—I think that I have to go talk to him because—I'm tired of always fighting.

17

Saturday, November 17th

I have to tell you something and you're not allowed to hate me for it.

Please—*don't* hate me for what I have to do in order to survive you.

The night after we drank more then we fundamentally should have, we woke up on the couch.

My head was pounding and I was regretting every choice that led me to that moment, but still, I smiled because my chest was light from the laughter that still covered the walls around us. I didn't remember falling asleep but at some point, I must have because I also didn't remember the night ending, but there I was sleeping on the couch with your arm around my waist, that's when I realized that you were lying on the couch beside me. You laid there with your feet on the coffee table and your arm holding onto my waist, your face was pressed into the pillow.

I looked around the room, trying to ground myself to where I was but all I could think about was the blanket wrapped around our shoulders and the Tylenol sitting on the counter away from anywhere your feet could reach. When I looked further around the room, I saw half of your dad sitting in the kitchen reading something, the other half of him was hidden by the wall but it was unbelievable none the less. A part of me, even in my hung-over sleep deprived state, was suddenly so mad at our situation because I realized how unnecessary it was. Your dad made sure we were warm and taken care of and sat reading a book no more than ten feet away as though the two of us sleeping on the couch together was normal, and all I could think of was that—you didn't have to leave, if your mom would have been anyone else and if your brother hadn't been dying, everything would have been different and it was the most frustrating feeling—you went through so much pain for nothing. We both did. Slowly I sat up, placing your arm on the warm spot I used to lay as not to wake you as I disentangled myself. I took the drugs without asking, knowing that it was going to be a rough day and a pounding headache was not going to make it any better. The funeral was the day after and it was going to be hard. I also knew that your family was showing up which meant that your mom was going to come back and we were both going to have to deal with what that meant. The only thing keeping me from freaking out was the knowledge that we had the means to leave, we could go anywhere else and we would be okay.

That morning I made my way off the couch despite my head spinning and I walked to where your dad was sitting with his coffee. I didn't know what side to take; on one side he never tried to find you, never checked in to make sure you were okay and alive and healthy, he left you just as much as your mom did but on the other hand, I knew what it felt like to live with a weapon like your mom, and I knew the things you were willing to do to keep something close to a cease fire when all you known was war. Not only did he live with your mom, he also had to keep it together for the dying child who needed his parents to seem as united as they could be. Do I think that he did the right thing in letting you go? Of course not, but there was a small part of me that understood what abuse looked like, and how it made you do things you wouldn't normally do in the name of simply surviving. Maybe that's why I always found him so easy to talk to; abuse recognized abuse.

He smiled as I awkwardly stood in front of him, unsure what to say now that it was the two of us alone.

"Morning, I hope your feeling alright—please, sit down." He stammered and I did, feeling lucky that wine was something I could hold down relatively well.

I always thought your dad was like mine; that all dads where like mine, all harsh words and violent eyes. But really, your dad was just afraid. Afraid of you leaving, of saying the wrong thing and making it worse, he was afraid that there was nothing he could do to fix what had been broken between the two of you. I sat down in front of him.

"Thanks. I'm good, not my first time drinking more then I should." I looked at you from across the room. "He on the other hand, may feel less then okay when he wakes up." In the past, wine had never been your friend and I didn't think it was going to start now. Your dad laughed softly while filling an empty mug with coffee from the pot sitting in front of him. I thanked him before taking a sip.

"I remember this one time—come to think of it, I imagine he was out with you—he came home and let's just say I'm not sure he knew his own name." We both laughed as I took a sip of the warm drink. "He just stood in the living room smiling and talking about absolutely nothing comprehendible, but he was happy." I looked back at you because it's easy to forget that for a moment we were, before things went sideways and we had to pick sides, we were happy in this world. "Me and his mom just figured he was out with his friends, or better yet some girl who somehow made him look like that," he looked at me with something soft. "Obviously, it was you. The next morning, he woke up and all hell broke loose, he's horrible in the morning without drinking, I can't imagine how you put up with it." I let myself imagine that this was our world.

"With struggle. I've seen him drop a coffee cup because he missed the handle when I tried handing it to him, and then he blamed me for making the mess."

"That sounds like him." He said but then stopped, I watched as his face changed slightly and suddenly the weight was sitting on my shoulders again. "Although, I guess I don't really know him."

He looked at the ground, or maybe at his coffee cup. I didn't know what to do; did I try to comfort him, or did I agree and make things worse?

Maybe it was his grief that softened me.

"He drinks his coffee with two sugars and no milk," I started, trying to find things to say that wouldn't give you away, because it wasn't my place to forgive him. But I had to give him something. "But he doesn't like to drink it first thing in the morning, instead he waits until he's gone for a run and eaten, or on Sunday mornings he waits until noon." I didn't even know if I was right anymore, that thought alone made me stop but I didn't faulter. "Every Monday morning, he eats a bagel with cream cheese for breakfast even if he has a fight coming up, because he likes the routine. Well, maybe not anymore but—" your dad looked at me, as though silently taking in every piece of information I was willing to give up and I didn't have the heart to tell him that I could be wrong. "He has flat feet and hates to run, so he will complain about it for hours until it's over but then he's always happy he went."

All those little details of you; your flat feet and crooked nose, the way you sang off key while driving out of state, the way you played with your hair when you were anxious, all of those things are imbedded in my brain as though they are as much my habits as yours, and now that your gone—what am I supposed to do with my unlimited knowledge of you?

In the moment I only smiled while trying to ignore the growing uncertainty that maybe you weren't the same person you had been six months ago.

"Thank you."

It seemed crazy that such small facts could mean so much.

Now, now I don't want to say those words to anyone else. I want to hoard every single fact of you to myself so that I may preserve them, but then again if no one knows your name, then they will never get to know who you were. Do I tell my daughter who you were? Do I show her the photos that we took on Christmas or the hundreds that sit in boxes and phone cameras? Do I tell her your name and describe your voice, do I show her your gloves as though they still contain an unsaid piece of you? Or do I let her grow up in a home without a ghost in the walls? I don't know yet, maybe I'll never know, maybe it's better to spare her the pain of loving someone that death has already claimed.

I put my hand over his because I wanted him to hear me, I wanted him to hear my words and understand how much I meant them. I was never going to be able to sit and have a coffee with my father, or my mother no matter how badly I wanted to, it was something I was never going to be allowed but you were, and because you were, it was almost a second chance for me.

"Thanks for trying." I said, I didn't forgive him for what he did, but I understood. "My dad tried to kill me, and I mean he quiet literally beat the shit out of me, the only reason he stopped was because Seb showed up." I gritted my teeth together tightly in order to share my story, I didn't know what I was saying or what point I wanted to make, maybe I just needed to be accepted by someone who acted like a dad, since from birth I had always been rejected by mine. Or maybe we were all trying to focus on something else in order to avoid Christians body lying in some cold room waiting to be buried. "It's going to be hard; I don't think he's going to come around easily, but *please*—don't stop trying with him." I said and I meant it.

This was a chance for us to have a family, a real family who knew us. It was a chance to go home at Christmas or thanksgiving, someone to call when we were in trouble or unsure what to do, it was a chance and I wanted him to hold onto it as hard as he could. Your dad nodded his head with firm resolution.

"I want, I want to make it better." I knew it was true. I could see it in everything he had done since we arrived, he was trying so hard to hang onto the only son he had left even though you had already been lost for years. "Do you have any other stories?"

"I think our entire life has been one."

"Then please, tell me more." And I did.

That morning while you slept on the couch to ignore the hang over waiting for you, I told your dad all of the crazy things I could think of. Nothing too personal, mostly I talked about the good things, the stories we told people when we wanted them to be impressed with who we were but I think I also told him about some of the bad times. Of course, I said them with a smile, as though to pretend that they were not nearly as bad as they sounded because I didn't want to share our secret pain; for some reason there was something sacred in being the only two who knew exactly what we had to survive. But it was a nice morning, a soft moment with your dad where I got to finally be accepted. He laughed as I spoke, his face full of joy but also hiding his own secret war just under the skin and I think we both needed it. But all to soon you were waking up and walking over with a heavy sigh as you sat down next to me. You didn't hesitate to lean your head against the counter, we both laughed around you.

"I told you." I said to your dad while I placed a hand on your back in some sort of moral support. You just grunted roughly in response.

"Shhhhh." You said against the table and things were light, and easy and exactly the way they should have been. I think that day, despite its issues, was one of the last normal days we would have for a while because once we got home, and after the initial relief of having you back wore off, everything we had made fell apart.

That day we were still blissfully unaware of what would happen next and I want to live in the yellow wallpaper and floor tiles because as the sun rose through the window, they held nothing but family. That was until the front door opened. The sound made you sit up quickly, heartbreakingly I saw you automatically look at your dad in a moment I'm sure you would have denied.

It was like the second she entered the house, the air went stale, instead of warm and inviting it was thick and disgusting, the very energy seemingly turned against us leaving us both barely breathing. I gripped my fingers into the fabric of your shirt as though somehow that would keep time from moving forward. We all watched as your mom came through the front door with another lady in tow. Your dad smiled at me sadly before standing up.

"Hannah, Rebecca, in here." He said and I could see how much he hated what was about to happen. I watched your jaw tense when you heard their names.

"Who is the lady with blond hair?" I asked quietly.

"My Aunt Becca." You said without looking away from the door. "I haven't seen her since I was 8" I understood. No one other than your mom knew what she had told her, or what she knew. I moved my hand away from your back, you looked at me with betrayal.

"Whose all here—" the words were taken from her mouth as she saw the room, more so me. She didn't take her eyes off me as an older lady with blond hair walked in with a smile.

"Sebastian? Honey, oh my goodness it's been ages." You got up despite your pounding head to give her an awkward hug, I stayed seated, still engaged in a staring contest with your mom. Her eyes were fire when they turned to you

"This—he needs to leave, we, we are *mourning* Sebastian—"

"And so am I."

I looked at your aunt "I'm Collin." I said with a smile, she just nodded while trying to read the room. I never thought of the fact that your mom wouldn't have told anyone what happened, but once I did it made sense. It was embarrassing, we were an embarrassment to their family that she wanted to erase.

"I'm Sebastian's aunt, Rebeca—"

"Don't. He's not staying long enough for it to matter." It was in that moment I realized who she hated; it wasn't you or your dad or God, it was me. I was the man who took away her child and broke her family, not you. Suddenly I was a kid again and had nothing clever to say. I watched as your dad stepped in, moving to create some space between me and her.

"Hannah—"

"No, you listen to me. Ben he, he *can't* be here." She said and you grabbed my hand quickly, I knew it was too late to turn back.

"What is the big problem? I think it's great that this young man is standing by his friend in hard times—"

"Oh, he's not my friend."

Before I could do any of the things that could have defused the situation, you kissed me right there in front of your family and I hated it. I *hated* the fact that you were using *us* as a weapon to hurt them—as though we were just ammunition. I quickly moved away, looking at your dad with an apology because it was the wrong move; you were mad and frustrated and wanted to show them exactly who you were and I understood, but still, I couldn't help the urge to punch you. You turned to your aunt with a smile. "We are getting married."

All I could do was look at your family with an apologetic smile because I had no idea what you were doing. When your aunt staired at you without speaking, you looked at your mom. "Bet you never thought you'd have to explain why I never came back, did you?"

"Seb come on—" your dad started but stopped himself, as though not sure who was right anymore. You didn't look at him, only at the women like you wanted them to start screaming.

"Alright, once again I'm sorry for your loss," I stood up and grabbed your arm, pushing us both away from the people and towards the door. "Ben, thank you so much for the hospitality but I know when I'm not wanted." He nodded his head and I understood. You just looked at the ground and I knew you already regretted what you'd done; we could have made a temporary peace, but instead you blew everything up and used our relationship as a *thing*; a thing to hurt them with.

You sighed but ran upstairs to grab the bags we had already packed. Your mom didn't take her eyes off me, not when you came running back down the steps or put on your shoes, but this time I didn't turn away, instead I met her because she held no power anymore. I did however, feel bad for your aunt.

"I'll come get the rest tomorrow." You said before following me out the door. We had a flight booked the next night, both of us just wanted to get home as soon as possible but I wish we would have stayed an extra night.

We didn't speak as we walked down the road, I knew there was a hotel if we just kept going straight and Spencer had graciously transferred me money before I stepped on the plane, but I didn't want to talk to you. I was frustrated that you couldn't think past the next five seconds, that every move you made was so short term instead of thinking of the long-term effects. I wanted to be mad that you kissed me in order to prove a point but I also understood why you did it. I walked fast, it was cold and my head was still spinning, you didn't say anything only walked faster to catch up.

"I'm sorry—"

"*One* day, all we have to do is get through *one* more day and then we get to go home, who cares if they thought I was your friend. This isn't about us Seb" And it wasn't, although it seemed hard to remember sometimes. It was about Christian, maybe that's why you were short with them, maybe you were tired of everyone making the two of us into something worth talking about when it should have been about him.

"I know, but she can't just speak to you like that—"

"I can stand up for myself. I get it, I get that everything is fucked up right now, and that your mom is out for my blood and I get that it hurts knowing she didn't care enough to tell them the truth," I stopped walking and turned to look at you, knowing that I had just taken all the words you were going to say. "I know that your brain is moving a hundred miles an hour right now but just please—tomorrow, remember why you're here." You nodded without meeting my eyes, I hated it. I grabbed your hand because I wanted you to realize I wasn't hiding anything.

. . .

The hotel up the road was small; I think all together they had maybe fifty rooms and I'm pretty sure half of them were available to rent by the hour. But it didn't matter because we were alone for the first time in months; no annoying yet lovable friends, no anxious parents, nothing, just you and me and it made the dingy hotel worth the price. We checked in and I knew the girl working the front desk. Although I really hoped, she didn't remember me. The brown-haired girl from church who wore red shoes; the girl my family thought I would marry one day; I think she thought that too. Did I look different enough to get away from the counter without her realizing who I was? Sadly, I wasn't.

"Collin? Is that you?" There had been so many introductions that I had to stop myself from rolling my eyes at the new one. I didn't want to deal with it, not right now when all I wanted to do was exist without anyone else around. I looked up at her over the other side of the counter with a small smile. I think you were outside talking to your dad on the phone because you felt bad about what had happened.

"Hey yea, Sally, right?" I watched her face light up as she walked around the counter in order to hug me. I responded awkwardly, not sure how to handle the situation. "We had history and English with Ms. Moray I think yea?" I said into her hair, she moved back with a bright smile, and really, she didn't look very different.; she still had the same brown hair and dark eyes, she still smiled the same and looked at me as though she wanted to know everything I was about to say. I could see how we would have worked out in a different world.

"Yea! We also went to the same church; our parents are friends." I just nodded at her, not sure what to say because she didn't want to hear about my life, not really. "What happened to you back in school? One day you were there and then the next you just weren't and no one ever heard from you again, I don't think you came to grad either?" I just sighed. I wasn't trying to hide you, I promise that I never wanted you to be a secret but I knew when to pick my battles and I was tired, I didn't want to fight this one so instead I lied.

"Yea, some stuff happened and I just had to get out of town. I went to New York actually; I've been there ever since." Her face was kind and understanding, I hated it.

"That's so great, I never believed all those nasty rumors about you, I knew there had to be a good reason." I just nodded, not adding in that all the nasty rumors were more likely than not true.

"What about you? What are you doing working here?" I asked, a part of me realizing that it could have been us. If we never left, or if things were different, I would have been working there too.

"I took a semester off to work, my husband has a good job here, so here we are, I plan on going back to school one day though." I smiled at her, not telling her that she was living my nightmare. It didn't matter because she looked happy.

"I'm happy for you, you deserve it," I said and I meant it. She was always nice to me. She grabbed my hand tightly.

"What about you, what are you doing now? Are you married?"

"I am actually a photographer. I do mainly sports stuff right now, like fights and such but I'd love to get into editorial stuff one day," her eyes were wide as though I was living in a dream, as though my life was exciting and new and something she couldn't have imagined.

"Wow, I'm impressed. Fighting is such a crazy sport," she frowned a little in disapproval. "I've only seen it once—my friend wanted to go watch because we knew someone fighting, one of our classmates actually, what was his name—"

"Sebastian?" I smiled.

"Yes! Him, he did all that fight stuff and she wanted to go see it in person, I couldn't bare to watch." I just laughed.

"Yea, it takes some getting used to for sure." I watched as you hung up the phone outside, it was only a matter of time before you would be standing beside me. "Actually, funny story about that—" but before I could tell her, I watched as her eyes found you and it was over. I just hung my head in defeat, wishing that I had gotten the key to our room before the little conversation.

"Is that—"

"Sebastian Morgan, yes," I said, you looked at her, then at me, I couldn't help but laugh. "Seb, this is Sally." You put out a hand to shake.

"Hey, I think we had English together one year?" You asked and she slowly shook your hand, but I didn't miss how she moved back around to the other side of the desk.

"Yea, I think so. We were just talking about you." She said, and you just looked at me.

"Only good things I assume" I nodded.

"Always." You placed a hand on the small of my back and together we turned to Sally who just stared.

"It's safe to assume that the nasty rumors from high school were true," I said because her rejection couldn't hurt me if I beat her to the punch line. "It's been great talking to you, but we actually have to run." She handed me the key to our room but when I went to take it, she grabbed my arm.

"I'll keep you in our prayers." She said softly and her tone made me pull back.

"Save it for someone who needs it."

With that we walked away, you grabbed my hand as though to prove what she was already thinking. Her words didn't affect me, I knew who the people in this town wanted me to be and I knew that it wasn't who I was, I didn't need or want their approval. Instead of thinking about her for longer than a second, I thought about the funeral, about your aunt and dad, and about you. And about the fact that we were truly alone. I was almost nervous, it had been a long time since it was just the two of us with no distractions, when it came down to it, did we still know how to talk to each other? Were you a different person than you had been when you left? The nerves sat at the base of my spine and I couldn't make them go away. Not when you kissed my cheek while I opened the door, and not when I watched you dramatically fall onto the bed. I didn't realize until then that this was the first time in months that you weren't at your parents' house.

"It's so quiet," I said because it was. There wasn't the traffic of the city, or the sound of other people moving around, the air was calm and silent and it was odd.

"It's beautiful." I laughed while laying down beside you. It was nice. I wanted to let the silence sink into my skin because it was so unusual, so unlike our normal lives. I think we both could have slept right there on top of the bed with our shoes on. But instead, you turned on your side, making me do the same so that we were laying there face to face.

"Hi." You said, a small smile growing on your face

"Hey," I whispered, and just like that my nerves were gone because it was still you. I ran a finger down the side of your face slowly, giving my skin time to relearn yours, and God I just—I loved you a lot in that split second of silence.

You leaned closer; your eyes stuck on mine as though asking. Maybe you thought I was still mad about before. When I smiled you kissed me as though the act itself was a challenge, and I kissed you back because I knew we had won. I could say more about the rest of that day; I could spin a love story of the way your hands ran up the lines of my back, or compose a sonnet on nothing more than the sound that escaped through your teeth when I pulled on your bottom lip, I could spend hours writing about a single second of that day, but I don't think I will. Because writing about it means giving a little more of you away and I think I'd rather keep it safe.

. . .

I can't ignore what I have to tell you, I wish more than anything that we were still sitting in that silent hotel room but—but we aren't. We aren't there, I am in my home and Jax is sitting a few feet away. Maisy is sitting on the floor with some colorful toys while she watches some shows on the TV. Your gone, no matter how much I would give up for you to be sitting here instead, I can't make you come back, *I can't*.

After the last time we talked, I went and made up with Jax. He said that he was sorry for intruding my space, but he wasn't sorry for what he said, and he's right. It's not just me, I have to do what's best for Maisy and I *have* to be there for her because I'm all she has.

I hugged him and confessed how glad I am that he came back because I don't think I could do this without him. I have to do what's right for her, for him, and for me so I—I think we have to leave.

This apartment, these walls and floors, and rooms, all of them are yours—*ours*. This is the place that we created between the two of us, the place we had family dinners and watched stupid reality TV, this was the first real adult apartment that we had and every time I walk into our room the only thing I can think of is how excited you were to have a room at all. How can I be the person they need me to be when I still can't sleep on the right side of the bed? When I still can't look in our bathroom because your hair elastics are still stuck under the counter? I think I have to find somewhere new. Of course, we are going to stay in the city as our lives are here, but I just—I just need to look at the walls without seeing you in them.

Please don't be mad about what I have to do now that your gone.

18

Wednesday, November 21st

I started packing today.

We found a place near Tribeca and it's beautiful.

It has three bedrooms and an office with large windows, there are great amenities plus it's close to Spencer and Andi. It's a place where Maisy can grow up; one day she and her friends are going to have sleepovers in the spare room and they can watch movies in the living room. Jax will teach her how to cook and I can show her how to slow dance in the kitchen.

You would hate it; you would say that the white walls were cold, and the dark floors were harsh, you would have thought it was something meant for other people, never for us, but I can see myself in this place, maybe the fact that I can't see you is what makes it right. Either way, I put an offer in, and I guess we will see how it goes. I thought it would be easy to pack, as I've done it a thousand times but this time it's different, this time I know a lot of these boxes are never going to open again, and that's—that's hard. I haven't even gotten to your stuff yet, your clothes are still in the closet and your photos are still in the box that Jax threw everything into when he first showed up, I can't touch it, not yet. I don't know how to yet.

. . .

We spent the whole day in that hotel room; wrapped in scratchy sheets and each other.

When you put your hands on me or kissed the spot under my ear, you did so like you wanted to forget everything else; as though each moment was the last and you wanted to remember every second before our time ran out. It was beautiful and tragic.

Before we could catch it, time was gone and the sun was setting. We ate takeout and drank shitty coffee, the TV didn't work so instead we just talked. There was no rush to our words, no necessity for them to be anything different than what we wanted them to be, you talked all night so that you didn't have to think about the fact that you had to bury your baby brother in the morning. But no matter how loudly you spoke, or how many words you tried to cram into the small finite space, we couldn't stop the sun from rising. Before we could grasp what we were doing I was eating a granola bar I had in my bag from the flight and you were staring out the window as though moving would make everything too real; like the second we opened the door and let reality see us, the fake world you had created would fall apart. I didn't know what to do, I knew nothing I would do could make it hurt less, I was just as powerless as we always seemed to be and I hated it.

"Ignore your family, it's not about them," I said as we walked out the door, did I grab your arm? Or did I let you be? When you—I didn't want anyone to touch me; it felt as though I would implode indefinitely if anyone's skin touched mine and I just wanted to be alone. You were different though; I think you just wanted someone to hold onto you and make everything else go away. I waited to see what you wanted to do, and when you grabbed my hand, I made sure to hold it tightly. You nodded your head but didn't speak.

There were a lot of things at play that day, not only was it Christian's funeral, but it was the first time you were going to see your extended family and friends in years and neither of us knew what they had been told, and on top of that, the event itself was going down at the church we had both walked away from. It wasn't my family, but I wanted to throw up at the thought. We walked to the church in silence, ignoring the people who passed us wearing black suits or holding flowers because it wasn't time yet. When we did get to the church doors there were people everywhere, all of them having the same awkward expression on their face; no one there knew how to live with a dead child hanging around them. I tried to let go of your hand before we entered the fray because this wasn't about us and if we went in there together then it's the only thing people were going to talk about. But when I tried to move away you just held on tighter, who was I to fight you?

To be completely honest, there was a small part of me that thought we may burst into flames after walking through the threshold of the holy, or that lightning would make the place go up in flames or that there would be some ultimate act of God to cleanse his halls of the sinners as they taught us in Sunday school, but nothing happened, nothing other than the sound we heard as the large doors closed behind us.

Once again, I felt like a soldier standing in enemy territory as I ran my eyes around the room of strangers, maybe I thought I could find the gun before it fired, or if I could catalog everything about everyone, then they could no longer hurt you, I tried to take in everything I could. I saw your parents standing at the front near the coffin, your mom's hand was on the polished wood and your dad seemed to be talking to someone older than the building. I wondered if there was any possible way, we could get through this without them seeing us. Other than them, people were scattered around in various places, most of them waiting to say their goodbyes to someone they didn't know.

I bet everyone's waiting for me to tie this funeral to yours, to compare the two events—but I can't write it down more than once. *I can't.*

We walked deeper into the room and I knew everyone was looking at us, we were an unbelievable sight to those people, I'm still certain a lot of them had been told you died years before and thought they were seeing a ghost. But either way, I went where ever you wanted to go, and I knew that you didn't want to stay longer than necessary. I held my breath as we walked towards your parents. Thankfully, your dad saw us first. It was then you let me go, and for the first time in six years, you hugged your dad tightly. I smiled despite everything else.

"I'm glad you came." He said quietly but I could hear it, he looked at me over his shoulder. "You too." I gave him a secret nod before looking around at the people staring.

Your family, they were the ones to see, the ones to pay respects to, the ones to hug and be there for, and everyone in that room was watching your every move. Your mom seemed too busy dealing with one thing or another, her conversations so in-depth that for a few moments I don't think she knew we were there. Your dad pulled away from you only to move to me for a quick embrace. I saw you smile from behind us. I moved away and stepped off to the side, this wasn't my moment and I didn't want to intrude on something this personal when I didn't know what to say. All I did was watch as you put a shaking hand on top of the coffin, your dad put a hand on your back in support. Maybe you said something in that moment, maybe you apologized or begged for forgiveness for leaving him for so long, I'm not sure what you said in that first moment because it wasn't for me, it especially isn't for this book. But no matter what you said, you didn't move, just stared down at the dark wood as though it could change if you looked away. I understood why you stayed silent; everyone was looking for a weapon and you refused to give them any.

"You shouldn't be here." I turned at the sound of your mom's voice and it took everything in me not to lose my temper. We were at a child's funeral, *her* child's funeral and she thought that right now was the time to pick a fight? I don't know why she cared so much but she did, maybe more than ever.

"This is an open event, is it not?" I wasn't playing her game anymore,

I was tired and mentally ready to get away from that stupid town and this was the last thing we had to do, we were *so* close to going home and I was done. Especially when I knew what it was doing to you to stay.

I looked her dead in the eyes as she came closer, I could have gotten out of the way but if she needed something to hit then so be it. I was done being afraid of her.

Before I could say more, she slapped me across the face but I didn't let myself flinch. It didn't matter that her ring cut my cheek; she wouldn't know that my hands were shaking at my sides. I think I almost felt bad because it was so obviously not about me being there, it was about the past and what I did to them, I watched as tears ran down her face and everyone around us went silent.

"Not for you." She was so close, closer than I think she had ever been but her words were so loud, loud enough that everyone else in the church could hear them.

"Not the first time I've been hit by a parent," I said under my breath, I refused to look away.

"*Get out*, just—just get away from us—now just get away—" There was *so* much hate laced in every breath she took, every time she spoke it was another repeated verse of condemnation.

"Did you just—is that blood?"

Before I could defuse the situation or make it known that I was controlling it, you and your dad were there in the middle and it became so clear how similar you both are; both of you ran in to save the day without question or thought. Your thumb was running over the small cut. It really wasn't a big deal and I could have handled it myself, but you were there. And when you saw the blood, I knew it was the last straw. I grabbed your arm tightly.

"It's fine—really," but then you ripped my hand away and were looking at your pouting mother as though your will alone would make her disappear. Something changed in your dad's face.

"Hannah—"

"They need to leave—our little boy is dead Ben, he's *dead* and these two they are just—they need to leave—"

"Stop acting as though this has anything to do with Christian," Everyone seemed shocked by your dads' words because normally he stood by and let her do whatever she wanted, but that day he looked at my face, and your eyes, and I knew what he saw; he saw two kids desperately pleading with him to choose *them*. He looked back at her and made a choice.

"If this was about him then—then you would be embracing these boys because he is our *son* Hannah. We lost Chris—but *he* is standing in front of us and you want us to act as though he's already gone—" He looked at us and nodded, your mom didn't know what to do.

"Ben—"

"No, you *don't* get to decide this, not when he is *all* we have left and you're driving him away based on nothing more than your own stupid prejudice. He has every right to be here, so does Collin because, because they're *my* family. I don't care about what you want anymore." Your dad moved closer to us before looking at me.

"Are you okay?" I nodded, then he looked at you, "I'm sorry. For everything." You nodded and I can't imagine what was going through your head because he chose *you*. He stood in front of us as though making sure everyone knew what side of the undisclosed war he was on. "So, let's just be civil with each other and get through this. And Hannah, please don't ever hit *either* of them again." With that he grabbed your arm and pulled you to sit down, I followed and we acted as though nothing strange had happened at all.

It's funny, that funeral was closure for a lot of things; it let you say goodbye to your brother, it let your dad finally stand up for you instead of being a bystander, and it was also the final chapter of your parents' marriage. In the end, she never could forgive us for what we had done, and it turns out that she couldn't forgive your dad for not choosing her when it came time to pick sides. That day softly closed a lot of doors that we had been trying to desperately keep at bay. Out of respect for you and your family, I don't think I'm going to talk about his funeral, it feels wrong to sit here and discuss it when the person reading this has no right to the intimate knowledge that was shared, somethings don't need to be written about in order for them to be true.

. . .

Once it was all over, we were standing outside and unlike what they show on TV, it wasn't raining or dark out; it was sunny. It was a rare sunny Friday near the end of November and to anyone else, it was just another day, but you, me, and your dad stood on the edge of the cemetery because we knew otherwise.

"I'm glad you're here." Your dad said quietly and I think it meant more than that day. "I know it hasn't been easy, being home with Chris and us over the past few months," he looked at the ground. "But, it made a difference for him, you—he thought the world of you and I know, I *know* It made things better." You slowly put a hand on his back as he tried to keep himself together, and it was the first step to forgiveness. "Thank you." The words were so soft and drenched with pain that it hurt to hear them, but I owed it to you both to listen.

"I thought I would feel more." You said out of the blue. For most of the service, you had remained silent, never speaking up or saying something in front of the group. I thought that maybe you would have, like in a movie you would have given a big speech that said all the right words to reunite the broken ones before you, but sometimes things just stay broken; sometimes there are no words left to say. But when you spoke now, I knew why you had waited. "I thought that I would cry more, or feel *something* more than what I'm feeling right now, but I just—I don't." We both nodded, everyone deals with the finality of death in a different way. "He was in so much pain, all the time for his entire life and now, how—how can I be upset when it's finally over for him?" I held your hand tighter. "I wish—god I *wish* things would have been different, that I would have been there, that I would have used the time we had—but I didn't, and I wasn't, and I'm sorry. I'm *so* sorry Chris." No one said anything, because your words weren't meant for us,

I'm sure they were just a repeat of what you told him when it came close to the end.

All we could do was hold on to you while you let everything out. I couldn't help the guilt that started to make its way up my back. I know it wasn't my fault, but sometimes, especially at that moment, it was easy to act like it was. I watched as you recomposed yourself and took a deep breath.

"Pacem invenies" I whispered, you looked at me but didn't say anything. It was the only thing I could think to say, something I had seen someone do in a book and it felt right.

We all stood there for a while, neither of us able to piece together something encouraging, it was the end of one chapter but the start of a new one. Eventually, whether we liked it or not, we had a flight to catch, a flight that would take us back to our lives and away from this weird reality we had been living in. It would bring you home. I watched as you looked at your dad as though afraid to leave.

"We have to go." Your dad smiled and I think both of you were afraid that once we got on that plane, things would go back to the way they used to be. But instead of letting you go he pulled a loose piece of paper from his pocket and wrote down his number.

"I know that there's nothing I can ever do to fix what happened," he looked towards me. "But if you'll let me, more than anything I'd love to be a part of your life, both of yours," you nodded. "so, call me when, and if, your ever ready, okay?" You moved closer and hugged him one last time and I knew without speaking that you would call him soon. All you ever wanted was for them to call you, and now here he was with his heart on his sleeve asking you to forgive him. His fingers dug into your back, he was afraid that he may never get another chance to hold you.

"I will." You said and he understood that there were a thousand words left unspoken. He turned to me and soon he was holding onto me just as tightly.

"Thank you, for everything." He said softly against the shell of my ear. "Keep him safe." I smiled.

"Always do. Thank you for trying." I pulled away and for a moment we all just stood there smiling at each other, none of us wanting to be the first ones to leave and break the momentary peace we had made. But we had a flight to catch.

There's not a lot more to say about that trip other than that fundamentally it changed us.

It changed the course of everything that would follow. But we will come back to that later. That day we went back to the silent hotel and grabbed our bags, you decided that anything you left at the house was better off staying instead of having to go back and face them. We got to the airport early and you let your head rest against my shoulder with a sigh, as though you were afraid but still couldn't stop time from moving and it was odd. On one hand, I was scared to go back to our life because I knew that you were going to have to find your place in it, you were going to figure out where you fit in your own world because I had created something without you.

I thought of the day in Florida when we were walking back to the hotel and you told me that everyone else had to find a way to fit into our world instead of the other way around, but at that moment, I felt for the first time ever, that you and I were living different lives. On the other hand, however, I was so excited to show you what I had created; to show you my friends and photos, I was excited to go back to our apartment and sleep in our bed instead of the one in Spencer's back room. We boarded the plane without a word to each other and when we sat down, I held your arm tightly, because it was the last moment we got to pretend that everything was going to be okay the second we touched ground in the city. It was alright to pretend I think, it was okay to live in our own world for a little while longer.

I think that I'm done writing this for tonight, I'm tired and I have to pack. I don't know how to make my hands stop shaking when I touch your sweaters. Honestly, it's not even the big things that hurt the most, it's the small things that I can't stand to put away; it's your toothbrush on the counter, and your jewelry sitting on the dresser untouched, it's the small, everyday things that I don't know how to handle because I know—I *know* that once they go into a box, they are never going to come out again. Your stuff is just *never* going to exist in the same place as me again, the little things that made you who you are, are just going to be gone as though they were never there to begin with. In this house, in this space or our room, no matter how hard Jax tries, he can't get rid of you completely.

He can't get rid of the hair elastics still caught in the baseboards, or the hole in the drywall from when you tripped on a shirt, he can't erase you from the foundation of this home, whereas a new place will be completely void of you, its surfaces untouched by our limited history. The worst thing is that I know I have to leave you here.

I'm begging—*please*, just forgive me for learning how to get through this without you.

19

Tuesday, December 4th

I was talking to Jax about this book today.

He is the only other person besides myself who knows that I'm writing it, or mainly the fact that I'm *still* writing it even though my therapist doesn't ask to see it anymore.

But it helps to write it down, as though even if we both no longer exist, our story always will; you *will* live on as long as I continue to write about it. This morning we were having coffee in a silent house since your dad has Maisy for a few days, and he asked how the writing was going. Of course, I didn't really know what to say because I'm not even sure why I'm writing it, but I tried to find a response either way. I told him that it's going well, although I'm not sure whether or not to keep writing it. Our story is getting closer and closer to the end, and I think that thought scares me more than anything.

What am I going to do when I finally run out of words to write? When history finally fades into the present and I am no longer able to make stories of it? If I don't keep writing, then I never have to write an ending, and maybe that's why it's taken me a week to pick up the pencil again.

Or maybe I just don't want to admit that I'm smiling more these days, or that last week I swear I went an afternoon without thinking about the fact that you weren't there next to me. If I don't keep writing, then I don't have to admit to you that I'm alive; that I went out for dinner a few nights ago with spencer and Andi, or that I and Jax took Maisy to the park and I laughed as she chased a butterfly because the sun was warm on my face and I forgot what It felt like to feel. It's getting close to Christmas, which means it's getting close to your birthday, and that is something I am not ready to deal with yet.

. . .

This whole time I've been leaving out a lot of bad things that happened to us; other than a few moments, I've left out the fights and disagreements, all the times when you would sleep at your friend's house because we fought so loud the windows shook, or the times I was so mad I couldn't speak to you and I'm not sure why I've decided to disregard them. By no means were we a perfect couple, we had issues and problems and fights, but maybe I don't want to remember you like that.

I don't want to remember all the horrible moment's because it doesn't matter anymore. The stupid things we fought about and the horrible things we said to each other, none of it means anything in the grand scheme of things and maybe that's why I've decided to omit those moments from my narrative. I could skip over the first two months after you got back, I could ignore that we actually came close to breaking up and that you moved in with your dad for a while because we could no longer live together, but I don't think i will. I think you deserve for me to tell the whole truth, no matter how ugly it got.

I'm not sure what I was expecting when we got back to New York.

Did I think we would jump back into our lives together as though you never left? Did I think everything would be seamless when we hadn't lived together in months, or that I would have no issues going back to our apartment? I'm not sure what I was expecting, to be honest, I think a part of me really did just think that things would go back to normal, that you would figure out a way to fit back into our lives but somewhere along the line I forgot that we were supposed to be fighting the same war. I think we both forgot that we weren't supposed to be fighting each other. Maybe the problem was in reality, we didn't need to be fighting anyone at all.

When we first got home it was a weird situation, I didn't know where to go, did we go back to our place? Did we go somewhere neither of us had ever gone before? Because I didn't know what else to do, we went to Spencer's, if not for any other reason then I needed to get my stuff.

I've decided that I'm not going to go into details on things such as what Spencer said or what it was like to see them again because it doesn't matter in this story. And I honestly don't remember a lot of it. I know that he hugged me and it felt like coming home, like I was returning to a life I had missed even though I hadn't been gone from it long. I think you were surprised to see just how close me and Jax had gotten, I watched your face change when he held me tight to his chest. You were never jealous, unless you were around him and I'm not sure why he got to you like he did, but he made you into something nastier than you usually were. They both said hello to you, Jax pulled you in for a long time because he had missed you.

He still misses you—he doesn't talk about it, he never mentions you in stories or lets on any indication that he knew you, that he spoke at your funeral and raises your daughter, and I'm not sure whether or not he is trying to save me, or whether he is saving himself.

I think you just wanted to go home because you didn't say much, all you did was go into the spare room and collect all of my stuff while I talked to the boys, I couldn't help the knot forming in my stomach. A part of me liked the life I had been living alone, not that I didn't miss you, but I had a routine and a job and friends, I went to clubs and did my own thing, and I think I was worried about how you would fit into that narrative. Essentially, what I wanted was for you to fit into my world instead of making a new one for ourselves. Something I do remember from that first day back was going to our apartment

I hadn't been back since you and I went there, there was no reason for it and I didn't want to bring up a past that I had been working so hard to ignore, so I left it. Spencer helped pay rent because he said I should wait for you to get back, but I didn't really want to be back in that space. For me it was no longer home, or somewhere safe; it was violent trauma and anxiety and one of the worst nights of my life. I didn't want to be there but you did. All you had thought about since you left was being able to go home, to sleep in our bed, and look out the same window, it's what kept you going and I knew you needed to be there. So, I didn't say anything. Instead, I put a smile on my face and held your hand a little tighter as I walked in the door.

It was weird, it was the exact same as the last time I was there and I hated it; my blood was still on the counter. I'm not sure how you didn't notice my expression, you were normally so intuitive about that stuff, always so sure to check in with me but for some reason, you didn't notice the way my hands shook when we stood in the doorway. Instead, you didn't say anything and walked straight to the bed and laid down. Pure relief came from you as you curled up under the blankets, forgetting about the luggage as you kicked off your shoes. It's weird to think back on it now, that in that one moment our emotions were at war with each other; your exciting relief compared to my resigned horror at seeing this once holy place decimated. But I didn't say anything. Not when you looked back at me with your stupid smile and reached out a hand. You had just endured months of pain; I could put up with a little bit of anxiety. I walked over to you and took your hand, you pulled me towards you and soon we were both sitting under the covers of the small bed we had acquired instead of purchased.

"I missed this place." You said against the side of my neck.

You wrapped an arm around my middle and I knew you would be sleeping soon. It's like the world wanted us to go back to the way we were; same apartment, same windows and blankets, same pillows that we stole from Sam's place, you held me exactly the same way, except I *couldn't* be the same person that I had been. I almost couldn't enjoy the feeling of having you back because that place just wasn't my home anymore and it killed me. I didn't say anything, because I didn't miss that place but I had missed you. I placed a kiss on your forehead and I felt you smile against my skin. I honestly thought that I was going to live there, that I would make it work because I loved you, and you wanted to be there. I really thought I was going to make it.

But I didn't.

It didn't matter how many times I woke up there, or how hard I scrubbed the counters and the floors, or how many times I rearranged the furniture, I still saw Jarrad in the doorway, I still saw the bloodstain on the counter and I couldn't bare it. I started going out a lot more; before you left, we used to stay in and just exist within the walls of that room, and it didn't matter because we had each other and that's all we wanted but I started to make sure we were always out of the house, always with friends or at work, at a shoot or out of town, I had forgotten how to sit still and it didn't change just because you were at home waiting for me to come back.

I remember the first time I had to go to work after we came back and it was odd. I woke up first and by the time you were opening your eyes I was already about to leave. You just looked at me, and I couldn't place what that look meant but it was strange. You were always the one to be out in the world before; you fought and competed, you were outgoing and assertive while I tagged along but suddenly the power had shifted, suddenly I was the one with the job and the gym, with the friends and the experience and you didn't know how to deal with it. It was fine at first, you kissed me when I came home and asked me about my day, and I sat with you on that old bed and told you everything about it. I told you about the gym and your old friends, I told you about how they were doing and who was winning, and in return, you told me stories about walking down to get a coffee, or about how long you ran for, and for a while it truly worked. I think both of us were so excited to be together again that we let all the stupid stuff slide, but it didn't last very long.

Soon all those cute stories turned into nightmares, you stopped kissing me when I came home and instead sat there acting as though the world hadn't been fair to you. I still can't be mad at you for what happened, I know it was hard, and that your world was spinning out faster than you could catch it. But you became something meaner than you ever had been before, you stopped going out of the house and instead just sat on the bed waiting for the day to end. I kept coming home expecting you to have gotten a job, or to have talked to Rob about getting your team back but each day passed without you making a single move to exist again.

I think that was when you realized that everything you had loved about the city had changed, that all these small things were no longer yours, including me; I had a life outside of you and I wasn't willing to give it up any longer, not when I was living the dream I had thought about my entire life. I never got anything, I never got to graduate, or go to university, I never got the friends or the fame, I got nothing more than to be by your side, and *finally*, it was my turn to have something belong to me and all I wanted was for you to try. For you to make even the *slightest* effort to get your life together again but you didn't. For a while I let it go, I thought that you were just stressed, but then as time went on, things didn't get better, instead, they started to get progressively worse.

Before either of us knew what went wrong, we were sleeping on opposite sides of the bed facing the walls; we started fighting more than we ever had, and I don't mean big powerful fights that were worth the energy, I mean just stupid things that we never should have thought twice about. I think a part of you started to blame me for your situation; it was my fault you left home, to begin with, it was my fault that things went downhill in your personal life, I was the one who stole the gym away from you, everything you couldn't control became something I had done to you and it wasn't fair. I tried to understand, to be there and not let it get to me but it *wasn't* fair. I had done nothing to you but our foxhole had turned into a conflict zone and I didn't know what to do.

I realized for the first time we had nothing to talk about. Through everything we had ever gone through from the time I was 16, I *always* had you and I always felt as though I could bare my soul and you would hold it with gentle hands, it's the only thing that got me through the bad days—no matter what, we always had each other but then I woke up one day and realized that somehow, we had lost it.

I couldn't talk to you about my job because it would make you sad, I couldn't talk about the gym or my friends because you would get upset and feel as though you had been cheated out of your storyline. And I understood; everything you had known was gone but I cried on my way to work because I was losing you and I couldn't fix it, I didn't know how because you were unwilling to try. It's bittersweet, we needed to be apart in order to come back together again, but now I would give anything to fight with you like that; I don't care if all we did was scream and argue, if I cried and you walked out only to come back a few minutes later, I would take it all because you would be mine again. I think what I'll talk about today is the last argument, the one that made us both realize we were a bomb about to go off, it was the last time I saw or heard from you for close to a month.

The last straw was after I came home from Spencer's because I needed to change before heading to a fight, when I walked into the room you were sitting on the bed looking out the window.

"How was your day?" I asked while gathering my stuff from various places. You didn't say anything for a while, I didn't push.

"It was fine." I nodded; it was hard to breathe in our place sometimes. "Where are you going?" You turned to look at me and the skin under your eyes was dark with restlessness. I sighed.

"Damon is fighting tonight, it's a pretty big one too." I didn't want to tell you, because I knew what you would say. "You can come with me if you want, I'm sure they would love to see you again." It wasn't the first time I tried to get you out of the house, I knew that some stuff went down with Rob, but hiding wasn't going to fix anything.

"They want nothing to do with me."

"I think you're wrong, they talk about you all the time—"

"Do you not find it weird that your friends with the same people who made fun of you all those years?" I rolled my eyes because you were looking for a fight and I was over it. I was done because I didn't have time anymore.

"They didn't make fun of me—"

"Yes, they did. And I should know, they were my friends first." You turned away from me to look at the window again and I wanted to scream. I put down my bag with a sigh.

"Whatever, I'm sure you and your friends made fun of me in high school too. their good guys, you shouldn't just turn your back on them." I meant it, they missed you and no matter how hard I tried I couldn't get you out of the house to see them. They may have been the only people outside of our apartment you had left. "Everyone misses you, even Spencer and Sam miss seeing you."

"You act as though you know those guys, as though didn't get the job because of me, or because my career went to shit, you don't know them, like they just stood there and watched Jarrad talk to you, they let Rob kick me out without a word." I looked at you and had to stop myself from turning away; I didn't recognize you anymore. "You only have a job because I don't, how can you still be there after everything that happened?"

"How can I still be there after everything? Seb, you *left*. I know that you had to, you had to be with your family and no one is blaming you for it, but you can't just expect the rest of the world to stay on hold until you get back. They kicked you off the team because you lost a huge fight and then broke all your contracts by leaving and no one knew when you were coming back." I shook my head and my expression was mirrored in your eyes. The problem was that we weren't seeing each other anymore; you could only see the past and I was already in the future.

"*Those guys* gave me a job, the job which pays for this stupid apartment by the way, since you refuse to get a fucking job. We've been back for over a month, it's time to be an adult and contribute." There was a piece of desperation in my voice, I wanted you to come back to me; for your eyes to shine in the same way they had and for you to look at me without seeing your own mistakes, I just wanted you back.

"What am I going to do? I have no education, no skills, the only thing I can do is fight and they won't let me in the gym." You were standing up now, both of us were equals standing across a battlefield.

"No, you refuse to go back because your ego won't let you."

"Rob has never once reached out to me, no one has, why would I go back to a place that doesn't want me?" Your voice was calm and calculated but it was manic, your words lacked the substance you usually led with and instead were those of a child who didn't get their way.

"It takes two people to argue. I don't care what you do, get a job walking dogs for all I care, but I need you to help pay rent, you're the one who wants to live here so act like it."

"What do you mean?" I ran a hand through my hair in frustration.

"You know *exactly* what I mean; I hate this place—I hate it and I want to crawl out of my skin every single time I walk in the doors yet we are still here because you *refuse* to leave. If I can stay in a place that I hate then you can swallow your pride and apologize, or don't, I don't care, just do *something*."

We both froze.

"If you hate this place so much then—then why don't you just leave? Obviously, you don't care about us anymore; you are never home, your always with your new friends and out at parties or events, you hate everything we used to do together, like if I'm such a burden to your new little life then why don't you just leave?" I was mad and you were mad and I wasn't even sure what we were fighting over but once the words hit the air, we couldn't take any of them back, each one was permanent and real and we couldn't go back to the way we had been before we spoke them.

"I think maybe we just need some space—"

"I was just gone for six months, I guess I thought you actually wanted me to come back, but you've made it clear that you didn't," I hated the way you looked at me because I could see your heart breaking. "If we take any more space—you'll just completely forget about me." There was so much emotion in your voice, so raw and true and it was at that moment we both understood what we were fighting about.

"Seb I—" I knew that I was writing you out of the story without meaning to, I was leaving you behind and I knew it. "*I love you*, more than anything else but I—I *can't* keep doing things like this, not in this place, not with you refusing to take responsibility for your actions, I can't do it." It burned my throat to say, but I knew the second it was in the air that it was true. I knew how to be on my own, I knew the freedom of having nowhere else to be and I knew that I could do it again. Maybe I wasn't as ready as I thought for you to come back.

You didn't look at me, instead, you looked at the wall, at the counter or floor, anywhere you could so that you wouldn't have to meet my eyes and show me how broken you felt.

"Then don't." Neither of us said anything. We just stood there in silence that had the power to change everything. "Go stay in some beautiful apartment with someone you actually want to be with."

"Fine, *I'm done*. Call me if you ever grow up." I grabbed my bag off the counter and walked away without another thought. I wasn't going to fight to stay somewhere I wasn't wanted, I wasn't going to fight to make you want me, I was done trying to prove my worth to other people. I slammed the door behind me and the elevator ride to the lobby was filled with the most deafening silence I'd ever heard.

. . .

It was weird, I didn't know what to do or where to go, it was different than it had been when you were away, this time you were standing in the same city minutes away, yet you were more untouchable than ever. I don't think I was sad about it, not at first anyway. For a while, I just walked around the city with my head held high because I honestly thought that I had won, but of course, we both lost. I went to Damon's fight and I think everyone knew something must have happened because I was different. I spoke differently and walked differently; I wasn't sure what to do because for the first time I was unsure about what would happen to us. It wasn't until I was back at Spencer's and we were sitting around the table drinking that I really started to think about it. Because you hadn't called me. It had been at least 8 hours and you never called me or texted. Usually, you sent something after you had calmed down but this time it was radio silence.

"Did I—did I just blow up my relationship?" I asked while taking the last sip of my drink; my thoughts came pouring in. "Oh my god, like did I just destroy something—"

"No, and yes," Spencer said, I looked at him as though I didn't understand, mostly because I didn't. "Yes, you are not faultless in the situation, and no, because it wasn't just your fault. People need space sometimes; you've been together since you were what—16? That's almost eight years so just relax, space is good. He will call." I nodded, taking his words in stride because he was right, space was good, everyone needed space sometimes.

But then a few days went by and still, you didn't call me. Now, I easily could, and should have just swallowed my own pride and called you first, even just to see where we stood but I didn't, you needed to grow up and I was unwilling to put myself back in that situation until you did. Life went on as normal; I went to work, saw my friends, moved back into Spencer's spare room, it went on the same way that it had when you were thousands of miles away, but there was a certain level of despair to it now. For the first time since high school, I didn't get to text you about stupid mundane things I did, I didn't get to send pictures of random birds I saw on the way to work; I didn't get to hear about what you did on your way to get coffee. The conversations that had become such an important part of my life were just gone, and I couldn't stand the emptiness I felt whenever I looked at my phone.

Time moved really slow for a while, and it took too long for me to realize that I was just as wrong as you. I had left you out of my life.

When you came home, I didn't make any effort to include you in the world I had created, instead, I defended it because for some reason I was afraid that you would take it away. I didn't know who I was with you anymore because I had spent so much time alone, and maybe I liked the person I had become because I worked so hard to get it, but it took me two weeks to realize that none of it mattered. There was a time in my life when I couldn't imagine breathing without you when you left the first time, I couldn't even imagine how on earth I would exist on my own, but then I did, and by the time you came back, I no longer felt as though I needed you to survive. The difference I realized was that I could easily live on my own, I just didn't *want* to; my life was just better with you in it, every part of it and I wasn't willing to give it up.

So, by the end of the second week, I still hadn't heard from you and I was losing my mind. Any anger or frustration I had been holding above you was gone because I was afraid. I was afraid that I had gone too far or said too much, that I had pushed you so far away that you would find space in someone else's world. I was afraid that you hadn't called yet because you didn't care enough anymore to fight for us.

It's getting late, and I am still sitting in a kingdom of empty cardboard boxes. Jax said he would help if I needed someone else to pack you away, but I think I have to do it, I have to be the one to put all of your things in a box and seal them up—

It should be *you* putting my stuff into boxes, it's not fair—I shouldn't have been the one who survived

20

Monday, December 31st

Today is going to be short because I am running late, but I have news; I ended up getting the place I told you about; the one that you would have hated. It makes everything real; it's easy to think something, but it's totally different to live it.

Jax is excited, but I think he's just excited not to share a room with the baby anymore. He *does* have his own place, but he's rarely there, if ever and I think he talked about putting it up for sale. But maybe he was just testing the waters to see if I would ask him to stay. I'm not sure when he became a permanent part of our lives, but as we pack the boxes and look at new furniture, he is right beside me pointing out the things he thinks would look good. I think that this new place is going to be just as much his as it is mine. I'm not sure why he sticks around, only that every day I'm lucky that he is.

Me, Andrew Collins, feeling lucky, it must be the magic of the holidays.

He sat beside me on Christmas morning and watched as our friends laughed at the outrageous gifts, as Masiy tore into paper and draped it around herself; having him there made the pain sitting in my stomach seem almost survivable. Tonight, we are going out to dinner with our friends at an overpriced restaurant because yesterday I went to my first shoot since the accident. And it felt *so* good.

. . .

By the end of the third week without you, I was going crazy. But still, I wouldn't break first. It was stupid, truly I should have just called you because you were probably sitting at your dad's new apartment thinking the exact same things, but still, I refused.

I wouldn't break.

When I left, I had told you to call me when you were ready and I was determined to stay true to my words no matter how badly I wanted to give in. As much as I missed you, I knew things needed to change if we stood a chance and you needed to be in a place where you were ready to make those changes. It was near the end of the third week something finally changed. Jax and I were sitting at the gym waiting for Rob to finish some meetings.

"How did Spencer's sushi experiment go last night?" He asked as he walked around trying to clean up the mats as much as possible before we did some training photos. I smiled.

"So bad. For some reason, I just assumed that someone with that much money would have been taught by some crazy world-renowned chef, but I was wrong. I was so wrong." Spencer had decided to try his hand at making sushi, and we are all lucky that we didn't die. It was one of the biggest cooking fails I had witnessed.

"Come on, it couldn't have been that bad." Jax mopped the floor and for a split second I remember looking at him, *really* looking at him because for some reason in that horrible gym lighting, he looked beautiful, and the thought scared me so much that I refused to meet his eyes.

"It was, if you don't believe me, I'll tell him that's what you want for your birthday." Before that moment the thought of Jax being attractive—or beautiful, had never crossed my mind, but that day it did and I had no idea what to make of the new development. So, instead of thinking about it too much, I thought about the rice-covered counters and uncooked fish sitting at home. Jax turned to look at me with fear.

I lied. I thought Jax was beautiful the first time I met him.

"You wouldn't."

"Oh, but I would." We laughed and he threw the broom to the floor, seemingly done with the endeavor for a while. I watched as he looked over my shoulder with widening eyes.

"Don't look, but you are never going to believe who just walked out of Rob's office." For a moment I thought that it was Jarrad, that he had come back and I was going to have to face him, but then I realized that Jax was smiling and I instantly felt my heart get stuck in my throat. I watched him wave, and I stupidly stayed hidden behind the bench where I couldn't be seen.

"What is he doing, is he coming over here?" He didn't say anything for a moment and I watched as his eyes followed you and I knew that you were going to see me behind the bench like a child. Did I make myself known? Did I sit on my phone and act as though I didn't notice you? Were we going to be adults or were we going to be petty about it? Should I have been mad that you never called me? I didn't know what to do and I didn't have time to think about it, Jax smiled at me and I knew what he was going to do.

"Seb! What are you doing here man?" I was doomed. I'm not sure if you knew I was there, but I could hear you breathe and I suddenly didn't care about what I was *supposed* to do, because I just wanted you.

"Hey, yea I was just talking to Rob, I think it's about time I kicked your ass again." I watched Jax's face because I wasn't facing yours and my heart swelled, you had talked to Rob. I was *so* proud of you because I knew it was probably one of the harder conversations you had to have.

"We'll see about that," he laughed "but really, I'm glad your back, we missed you around here." I'm sure you nodded and smiled, I don't think you believed him yet, but you wanted to. I knew you were walking closer and I felt too stupid to do anything but sit there because I should have made myself known the second I saw you, but now it was too late and I couldn't do anything but sit there and play dumb.

"it's gonna be good." You said and then you were standing above me and I had no choice but to look at you, and I just wanted to be done fighting. It was too weird, it was weird to think that I wasn't going home with you, or that it was the first time I had heard from you in weeks, I just wanted the whole thing to go away because I wasn't mad anymore. I watched you for a moment, taking you in piece by piece and I think you looked better than you had the last time I'd seen you, the bags under your eyes were less pronounced and I didn't know how to take it; had things really been better without me? Your eyes were locked on mine, you smiled. "Hey C"

"Hey."

You nodded and then had the audacity to walk away. I just sat there, after three weeks all you had to say was hey? I heard the door close behind you and Jax stood there waiting for me to do anything.

"Get up and find him." He said, looking at me with expectation. I looked at him, still trying to process what happened.

"He just walked away!"

"Collin, I swear to god I'm going to tell Spencer that his sushi was the best thing you've ever had if you don't get your ass up and follow him. Please, I'm not sure we can take any more of whatever game you guys think you're playing. Go get him so that you stop complaining about him not calling." He smiled and I nodded, I knew he was right.

"You're an asshole, you know that?" I got up and walked towards the door.

"Yep, now go." I didn't respond, instead, I quickly walked through the door and tried to think of where you would have gone. I looked in the direction of our place and tried to find you amongst the hundreds of faces but I couldn't, I took out my phone and finally called you because I was done with the game if we played any longer then I knew we were both going to lose everything.

I dialed your number and waited for it to ring, but when it did, I could hear the ringtone from behind me. I turned around quickly and there you were leaning against the side of the building looking back at me. I wasn't mad anymore, there were a thousand things that we had to talk about but none of them seemed important because I just missed you. You were standing five feet away looking more like yourself than you had in months.

"I knew there was no way you'd let me leave like that." You said but there was no jaggedness to your voice, just a fond smile playing on your lips and I didn't respond. Instead, I wordlessly wrapped my arms tightly around your neck because the rest could wait. Your fingers dug into my back as you pushed your face into my hair and it's like I couldn't get close enough, no matter how tightly I held on it still felt like there was some invisible force between us and I just wanted it to be gone.

"I shouldn't have said all that stuff." You mumbled the words quietly as your breath ran across my skin, I just shook my head.

"It's alright, I was being an ass." I closed my eyes tightly for a moment before pulling back, we needed to talk about what had happened because it mattered. "Seb—"

"No, let me start." I nodded while you took a breath, your hands stayed curled in the fabric of my shirt. "I'm sorry, I shouldn't have blamed you because—because of course it wasn't your fault. I just didn't know what to do, and I guess watching you go out all the time and live this amazing life without me, it just made me feel as though there wasn't a place for me anymore." You looked at the ground. "But I get it, I was gone for a while and things change, I wasn't helping things either by just sitting around being mad and if you don't think there's room for us in your life now then I get it too—"

"Stop," you did, instantly and I couldn't hear you say what I knew you were going to say next because there was no version of myself that didn't want to be with you, "Seb, I, I thought that I had to choose between my new life and the one I had with you, for some reason in my head they couldn't be the same thing and I didn't know what to do. I should have tried harder to make you feel as though I wanted you there because I do, I'm sorry that I ever made you feel as though I didn't," I closed my eyes while trying to find the right words to say. "I like my life now; I like going out with my friends and I love my job, I like the fact that I don't need anyone else to survive anymore," I brought my hand to your neck and your heart was racing under my palm. "But the thing is, I like my life *so* much more when you're a part of it. I promise that I will try harder to keep you in it"

"I shouldn't have blamed you for my problems, I swear I'm trying to fix things—I talked to Rob and he's letting me come back, it wasn't fair to put everything on you when all you've *ever* tried to do is support me," you pulled me closer. "And I promise, I will never make you stay in that apartment again, I don't know what I was thinking, of course, you hate it there, I should have thought about it, and I'm sorry." I kissed you before you could say anything else because I knew we were going to be okay.

We both messed up and made mistakes, but there we were choosing each other despite them. I kissed you against the side of the building as though I was trying to make up for the lost time and you held onto me *so* tight.

It was the first moment in months where I felt as though I had you back—that you were something close to the man I knew.

"Are you really okay with moving?" I asked against your lips, I didn't want you to do anything that you didn't believe in, and I knew how much that place meant to you. You kissed me again as though it was answer enough.

"It's just a place." You whispered and yeah, we were going to be okay.

And we were, that day was the start of a new era for us, one that made me feel as though I was meant for this life because we got to live it; truly and deeply live and I wanted each and every second to last a lifetime. I don't have time right now to talk about it, but I promise that I will. What I will say for now however is that together we went into the gym hand and hand and talked to Jax, who hugged us both with a heavy sigh.

"Thank god, I'm not sure how much longer I could deal with him."

We all laughed, I took photos of you and him training together, both of you had smiles on your face while you messed around and had fun.

Jax doesn't know that I know, but he has one of those photos framed beside his bed.

Damon and the guys showed up later on and they were so excited to see you, I made sure we would all remember the day, and still, those are some of the best photos I've ever taken because we all felt content with our lives. I don't mean that we weren't before, but for a few hours that day, nothing else existed other than the people around us and the hope sitting in my chest that we just might, despite our circumstances, make ourselves a beautiful life. Even after when we were walking back to Spencer's we talked about life with something new, for the first time in months we lacked the baggage of history and instead focused on the present. We talked about where we wanted to move to, and that this time we should find someplace with a bedroom. You refused to go back to the apartment and instead I watched as you begged Spencer to let you stay with me until we found a place. He agreed but made you eat the left-over sushi as payment.

It was a day of new starts for us, one I still remember deeply and maybe that is the feeling I need right now. If I can just hold onto that, onto the feeling I felt that day, then maybe I can get through the next few hours without looking to my left hoping to see you sitting there.

Maybe I can ignore the fact that this is the first year you're not going to see.

21

Wednesday, February 2nd

It's been a while.

Things got busy since the last time we spoke; I had to pack, and I couldn't keep avoiding it, I had to put you into boxes and say goodbye to the ghost that will forever be in those walls.

Before we left for the last time I stood in the doorway and looked around at what we had made. I said goodbye to the elastic bands under the baseboards, to the bloodstain on the carpet and your initials scratched on the back of the balcony. I had to say goodbye and I couldn't then sit in the car and write about it. I needed to do it on my own, and trust me, it felt as though I was leaving a piece of myself there.

I was, in a lot of ways I wasn't just saying goodbye to you, I was saying goodbye to the person I had been *with* you, to the part of myself that would forever be roaming those halls beside you and it scared me to give it up. But my family needs me to leave us where we belong because there is no room for our history in my present. But I had to write today—I had to talk to you because the familiar feeling of drowning is sitting under my skin again. I didn't need to tell Jax, he knew and took Maisy away and left me in this unfamiliar territory alone.

It's February second.

You always loved your birthday, no matter how old you got you still woke up in the morning with a smile on your face because it was your birthday, and you had made it another year around the sun and thought that was a reason to celebrate. And we did, even when we had nothing, I still made sure that we did something to celebrate the fact that we had survived another year of the war, although I think the war found a temporary peace by the time you turned 26. Spencer used to do huge things for your birthday, the one year we all went out on a yacht; there was alcohol and a DJ, people were dancing under the stars and fireworks went off and you kissed me in the middle of all of it, it was one of the best moments of my life because we had made it. This year, we were supposed to go away. Spencer and Andi were itching to go back to Europe and asked if we wanted to come along, of course, we said yes. We figured that we would go in February because then we could double It as a birthday celebration while in Greece.

Instead, for the first time in fifteen years, I have nothing to celebrate today.

That's half of my life spent with you and your crazy birthday antics, Spencer keeps calling but I turned off my phone, I don't want to talk to anyone but you, not today. We used to talk about our favorite parts of the year when we got home from whatever party we had been at. We would sit and celebrate between the two of us and talk about our secret history while drinking wine straight from the bottle. There's not much from the past year that I want to remember but in the same spirit, I think I'll write about my favorite memories from years before.

. . .

It didn't take long for us to find a new apartment, and I remember how happy I was when we went to see it.

It was big for our standers, half the size of where I live now but back then, I couldn't believe that we got to have an actual bedroom, a *real* bedroom that wasn't just a sheet hung across the kitchen to give the illusion of one. That place had a bedroom and an office, a bathroom, and a beautiful balcony. The second we saw it we knew that it was the place we were meant to be. I was making real money at my job which was growing every day, and Spencer was more than ready to help us afford whatever we couldn't so together, we rented a place that was our first adult home—the *only* adult home you would ever have. I remember the first day we got the keys and we had nothing, most of the stuff in our other place had never belonged to us to begin with and so like broke students, we sat on our living room floor with a bottle of cheap wine and talked about the future that was waiting for us to take it.

You ran outside to the balcony, and with a sharpy wrote your initials on the back of the railing—you swore no one would ever find out—but you did it because you wanted everyone to know that we, high school dropouts and runaways, were living in that beautiful place and no one could take it away. You pushed me against the wall and kissed me as though we were untouchable, there was a new sense of hope sitting between us; we were going to make it, I was going to make sure of it.

That night was only the start for us. After *everything* we had been through, we finally got to be young and in love and do all the things we never had the chance to. By the time I turned 26, I was doing photography not only for high-level sports, but I had also started to make my way into editorial shoots. I took the money I was making and invested it back into myself and took classes at the local school in order to make myself better and it was paying off. For the first time in our lives, we weren't afraid of not having rent money or food, we could buy things we wanted or even take a trip if we found the time. We were free to make our own choices instead of always having to worry about keeping ourselves afloat. Not only was my career taking off but yours was too. Rob kept his word and gave you another chance and before long you were right back where you belonged. This time you came back with something to prove, you didn't complain as much while training or cutting weight because you *wanted* to do it, and you felt lucky that people were willing to take a chance on you again. We even convinced a few sponsors to take you on after we explained what had happened before. You were fighting, and not only that but you were winning, and soon you were standing in the ring for your first official professional fight.

It was a game-changer for us because it meant that you got paid real money to fight. You started traveling more and this time I didn't come with you, not all the time anyways. If I could, and if it was an important fight, I always tried my hardest to be there and watch, but I had my own life and unlike when we were kids, I didn't need you to hold my hand through every step of it. I remember feeling so proud of who we were and what our relationship had become, it was mature and independent; we were together because we *wanted* to be, not because we didn't know how to survive on our own. We each lived our own lives but always called each night we were away from each other. I keep saying our life was like a war, and if that's true, then for those few happy years with you, the war was over.

The thing I have noticed most about pain is that once it's gone, you almost forget how bad it felt; once it's passed and things get better, it's like your mind works overtime to help you forget about the horrible things you had to go through in order to survive it. We appreciated the good times more because of the bad, but I think we both almost forgot how hard we had to crawl through the mud to get to the surface.

There are so many things that I could talk about from those few years but few that I actually will because it's for us; they are my memories and I'm not ready to give them all away yet. But what I do want to talk about is when we went to Greece, because it was also Spencer's wedding. I know that I've talked about Andi before, but I don't know if I ever actually explained who he is; he and spencer started dating right before I met him, and they always seemed like such a mismatched pair. The story goes that they had met during law school and had become friends, which eventually led to something more. Andi is *exactly* the type of person you expect when you think of law school. He always looks professional, he sits with his back straight and has dark hair, and he always has something incredible to say. Not that Spencer doesn't, but when Andi speaks, no matter what he's saying, we have no choice but to stop and listen. He's calm and steady whereas Spencer is pure energy, always moving and changing, they never should have worked but somehow, they did. Andi keeps him from floating away from earth and Spencer shows him that sometimes it's okay to fly. They are one of my favorite couples because they really do love each other in an organic way; it's not for social media, they don't do crazy things because they want people to know about them, they do it because they *want* to, they do it for each other. I don't think Spencer ever thought he would settle down with someone but when Andi proposed, he knew that he was looking at the rest of his life. We were all there; we all laughed and drank and sang karaoke afterward because one of us was getting married, and I was so proud of the person I had watched him become.

We talked about marriage that night.

We were laying on the floor looking up at the ceiling with a bottle of wine between us.

"We've been together for ten years." You said randomly, I could hear the smile on your face. Ten years, that was longer than most people our age could fathom. "Like, Spencer and Andi are going to be 34 before they can say that."

"Yet, here we are." I grabbed your hand and played with your fingers "It's pretty cool actually."

"It's *so* cool, like actually, that is so cool." I laughed because you sounded like a child, you turned over on your stomach so that you were looking at me. "Tell me it's not cool."

"It is pretty cool." And it was, we had a real history in each other, the two of us had gone through more than most people ever would, and the fact that we did it together was unbelievable.

I was thinking about this the other day actually, I had this overwhelming realization that fifteen years isn't that long. Someday, not so far from now, I am going to have that much history with someone else. I can't even imagine it.

That night I could, I saw both the past and the future as we laid there.

"Do you think we should get married?" Your voice was light with an odd nervousness that never existed between us.

"Is it important to you?" Marriage was something I never needed, not when I had grown up in a house with two people who hated each other. To me, marriage was a word that held no meaning. You ran a finger across my cheek.

"No, not really. Although, I could get used to calling you my husband." You kissed me slowly, I played with a piece of hair that fell down the side of your neck.

"The whole concept is just so traditional; getting married in a white church with God as the witness in front of people who we barely know," when I was growing up, I would have given anything for the chance to get married like that, I just didn't believe in it anymore. "If it means something to you, then I'll marry you tomorrow," I leaned over you and my words made your face break into a smile. "But wedding or not, you're stuck with me." I leaned down to meet your lips slowly, as though to prove that we were more than some piece of paper from the city. We didn't need someone to tell us that we were one in order for it to be true. I wasn't going anywhere, and I knew you weren't either.

"This is enough." You said and I laughed as you pulled me down beside you.

We were always enough.

. . .

It was no shock that Spencer and Andi wanted to get married somewhere abroad, we found out that Andi's parents were from France and he wanted to get married there so that his extended family could come, who were we to say no? Spencer said he would pay for all of us to fly so that we could be there, and it was that moment that we realized we had never taken a real vacation before. *Ever*. And going to your brother's funeral did not count.

So, we decided to take two weeks and go to the wedding in France, and then fly to Greece because it's the one place in the entire world I had always wanted to go. We earned it. To make things even better I booked a shoot while we were there so that I could say it was a work trip. We packed all our bags and you told Rob that you needed a few weeks off. It was a period of our life where I kept waiting for something to go wrong but then nothing ever did. I kept waiting for the bomb to drop and things to fall apart again but they didn't, things were steady and getting better by the day.

I was in love with the world; without the constant pressure, I was able to finally look at the city without a constant haze around me. I looked at the sky and spent more time outside, I watched the birds and the traffic, all of the little things that I always hated about my life suddenly seemed beautiful because I was alive and genuinely happy. I am holding onto the feeling now.

We all flew to France in the summer and they had a beautiful wedding. Whenever I thought of Spencer's wedding, I would have thought Vegas and lights, I would have told you that there would be animals and fire spitters, I would have said that he road down the aisle on a sequined elephant, but his actual wedding was nothing like that. Maybe it was because Andi kept him in check, but it was a small, intimate setting that took place in the countryside between two mountains and it was breathtaking; truly, and utterly breathtaking.

I won't lie, I cried when they said their vows. It was one of the only times I wanted us to get married, if nothing else because it was beautiful and pure and I could see how much they loved each other. We cheered as they kissed and the officiant announced them as one. You held my hand and I knew that you felt it too.

Although the wedding was small, the reception was something straight out of a movie, a true representation of what money would buy if you were willing to spend it. We ended up on a mega yacht on the French coast and I honestly don't remember all of it. It was loud and huge, people anywhere they could fit and drinks everywhere. It made sense; Andi got the wedding and Spencer got the reception. The band was loud and we danced under the stars, you beside me and our friends surrounding us with the moon as our witness, it was a party and I let myself enjoy it, to truly enjoy every second of it because I never thought that I would be standing there—that I would get the chance to stand there with our friends on their wedding day and kiss you in the middle of chaos as though to prove that I could. I could and we laughed. That's the last thing I remember from that night.

The next morning however, the newlyweds jetted off to Tokyo for their honeymoon and we slowly, and hungover beyond belief, got on a smaller, cheaper flight to Athens and I could hardly contain how excited I was.

Despite the fact that I wanted to throw up, I couldn't help but run my mind over everything I wanted to do, the things I wanted to see, I wanted to see *all* of it; every rock and stone, everything I could from a not so ancient past. I planned it all out to every detail, I especially wanted to go to the modern equivalent of Thebes and see the ruins of a forgotten civilization, I wanted to see the temples of Apollo and Delphi, I wanted to see absolutely everything I could see because I didn't know when I would be back. I'll never forget the moment the plane landed, the second it touched down I wanted to cry because we really were standing on the *same* ground people did a thousand years ago. I wasn't hungover or exhausted anymore, I was in complete awe at what the world could offer and it was *right* in front of me. For once, I was in the position to grab hold of *everything* I ever wanted. We got off the plane and went to our hotel, it was beautiful, cheap, but beautiful none the less and I just wanted to start our adventure, but I couldn't ignore the fact that neither of us had slept in over twenty-four hours and my head was pounding, so instead I kissed you with everything I had before we both passed out on the bed.

Greece was the best two weeks of my entire life. Every second of it was something I want to remember forever, but more than that, I just remember feeling *so* much; I was high on my surroundings, nothing could hurt me because for the first time in my life I felt young and invincible and wanted to take advantage of every second of it. Starting in Athens, we did *everything* on my list; we saw all the temples, the famous ones and the lesser-known ones, one moment I remember particularly well is that we were at the base of the Pantheon, at the old theater of Dionysius.

I could barely breathe while looking at the marble seats still intact. We were standing at the birthplace of Greek tragedy, something I had spent my entire life reading about but to stand there—to read the inscriptions still on the marble from thousands of years ago, to actually see the places those people sat—I was *speechless.*

I would have stayed there forever to stand in the footprints of conquerors.

You smiled at me and it said more than words ever could. That whole trip was mine; you enjoyed it, but we went where ever I wanted without complaint.

There is one other moment I remember, we were standing at a temple to Apollo looking out over the sea and off the top of my head I thought that someone should have remembered them; I wished for a real way of knowing who those people were and the lives they lived because I felt *so* close to them, as though if I just touched the marble I could fall into their world. But then I realized in absolute astonishment, that I was standing in their recorded history. Someone *had* recorded it, and we were standing in the middle of it. Each word was shown in every crack and fracture of marble. It was the most surreal thing I've ever experienced.

Better than any of the sights or my constant bewilderment was what happened next. We traveled around the Greek world, and finally, we stood in the modern-day version of ancient Thebes, a place that personally, I loved more than Athens. We walked around the streets void of tourists, taking turns and pointing out things that we liked. I showed you the walls from the Spartan wars and told you about their endless history.

"Thebes was one of the most important places in ancient Greece, and it was forgotten," I said as we walked past ruins. You looked at me as though inviting me to share more. "They stood head-to-head with a Spartan army and won, that had *never* happened before. They had the first union that used the same currency, and they had one of the most untouchable armies in the country." We walked to the gravesite of the army I was referring to, and all I could do was stare at the ruins surrounding us.

"*This* is the field the battle was fought on, right here where we are standing. The Sacred band died before the fight was over and thousands of years later, their bodies were found here. They were still holding hands." It was unbelievable. "We are standing in a country that has *such* a rich history, the Sacred band was a 300-man army, but the catch is that it was supposedly made up of 150 pairs of male lovers. They thought the men would fight harder if they knew their loved one was on the field next to them." I looked at you, and I saw you look around at the enormity of what we were standing in front of.

"I would definitely fight harder if I knew you were beside me." You said, and I laughed but nodded.

"Exactly, this army was undefeated; they never really lost anything until this one battle when they were completely defeated, it's said that when the enemy leader realized who he had killed, he took a moment and cried due to the tragic nature of it." I looked around the surrounding area with the knowledge that at one point, thousands of years ago, something world-defining had happened in the place I stood with you. "What I'm trying to say is, it's pretty ironic that Thebes was once saved by men and their partners, or that there was a tomb men would go to and be married because, in our age, Greece is still one of the few countries in the EU not to accept gay marriage. It's weird how time changes things." It was odd, somehow, we had gone backwards instead of forwards.

"What do you mean they got married at a tomb?"

I showed you.

By the time we got there, the sun was setting and the people were going back to their homes, the streets were quiet except for us. I took you to the place the tomb once was, I stood you right in front of the place a statue would have stood, and together we stared at the emptiness.

"In myth, Lolaus was Hercules best friend, as well as a Theban hero, and when he died the Thebans buried him in a tomb right where we are standing. During the classical age of Greece, men would come from around the Greek world to make vows to each other right here, Thebes was one of the only places to recognize it as a binding marriage." I watched your face as you took in the words, the words that made up an entire generation of people but one that history always tried to forget.

"What did they say?"

"Anything, they gave their thanks to the fallen hero and then their loyalty and love to each other, it was an oath during a time when they still meant something. They didn't need anything else." You took my hand and I held it tightly. "In history from other parts of the world, all two people had to do was say the words between the two of them to be married, it's not a Greek idea," I looked at you. "But I think it's beautiful." You nodded with a smirk before looking down at the ground.

"Do you believe in it?" Your words were an echo from the past and I had to look away due to the overwhelming feeling forming in my stomach. I grabbed your hand tighter and rubbed circles with my thumb, I couldn't have smiled more. It was a picture-perfect scene with the last rays of light hitting the side of your face, your hair was gold and you looked a little like the Greek heroes I talked so much about.

"I believe in it." You nodded, and I did. Especially at that moment, I believed in it more than anything else.

"Okay, I can work with that."

You looked at the sky, then back at me, it was something straight out of a movie. I almost didn't write about it because it's something I hold *so* close to my heart, but I need whoever's reading this to know that we were more than our worst days. "Then right here, in the place of a forgotten tomb I don't understand, on land that I've never been, I promise to *love* you. No matter how simple or complicated things get, I promise you; I will, for the rest of my life."

I didn't know what to say, my words which always came so easily suddenly stuck in my throat because, because you were standing there saying things I *never* imagined someone would say to me, in a place I had dreamed about my entire life.

I knew that you were it for me, but to hear you say it out loud was something altogether different. You placed a kiss on the inside of my palm and I wanted to cry. I tried to steady myself because I had to say *something*, there was no way I was going to leave you hanging like that.

"I—okay," I laughed a little bit to catch my breath. "Then on this foreign land—in front of an ancient tomb as my witness, I promise to *always* stand beside you. No matter what happens I swear that I'll stay."

I couldn't believe what we were doing, but there I was saying the words anyways. We never needed anyone else to understand us; if we were the only two people who ever knew about what happened that day, it didn't matter, because *we* knew, and it wasn't for anyone else. "Oh, and I love you too."

I couldn't look away from you, everything seemed hazy and dream-like, as though I was living someone else's life, but it was *ours*. You kissed me right there on the forgotten shrine to a long-dead hero and I wondered how many people had done the same in the place we stood. Never before had I felt so connected to the past, as though we were all standing in the same place at the same time, it was the single best moment of my life.

"Then I marry you." You mumbled against my lips and the sun was gone but the light remained, the cold air wrapped around us but it didn't matter. I had to pull away due to the smile that split my face in half as I pulled myself closer.

"I marry you too." You bit your lip to keep yourself composed, I grabbed your hand and started leading us to our temporary home.

It was no more than ten minutes away but I'm surprised we made it back. There was a certain danger there, something I had forgotten about since being in New York but we were the enemy; the people around us didn't believe in us and every move we made was our own secret act of rebellion against their modern views. I felt like a teenager again, back to the times we had to sneak around and meet in darkened corners, every time you tugged on my sleeve or kissed me against the wall of a dark alley, there was a hovering knife waiting to kill, but that only made it better.

By the time we got back to the hotel room we barely made it through the right door, the second we crossed the threshold your hands were *everywhere*, your lips were on my neck and I wanted to stay in those seconds forever because it felt as though *nothing* was ever going to be the same, like we had somehow escaped the fire and were free to do whatever we wanted. I laced my hands in your hair as you pushed me against the bed, I felt the moment we both surrendered, finding the same peace within each other that we had when we were younger. We were no longer hiding in the fox hole, instead, we were on the surface and proud of the fact we survived the bullets.

"It's *always* going to be you," I whispered, suddenly feeling emotional over nothing because of *course* it was; it was always, *always* going to be you. If we lived a hundred lifetimes, I would have chosen you in every one of them and it's such a stupid thing to say, something that has no right to be said but—it's *true*, even if it's a cliché—it's still true. I'm never going to love someone like that again, for better or for worse, you were it for me. That night we whispered confessions into the space between our breaths; every time you kissed me it felt like a game, I smiled against your lips because I knew we had won.

. . .

The next day we walked around the streets with something new in our eyes, although we had been together for a decade, for those two years we felt like love-struck teenagers. Maybe it's because we were never allowed to have that when we were younger and now that we were secure, we wanted to make up for all we had lost; we were teenagers addicted to the feeling of each other. We walked around a market and pointed at the fresh fruit and small items for sale. In one of the most memorable moments of the trip I remember you walked over to me with a small smile as though you were nervous, I looked at you with a question. Instead of answering you just held out your palm and sitting in the middle of it was a ring. It was nothing special, something from a vendor that cost less than our lunch had but it meant *everything* to me. Wordlessly, I gave you my hand and watched as you slipped the medal around my finger. I still haven't found the strength to take it off.

They gave me yours—the hospital staff or whoever it was, they gave me your stuff in a plastic bag with detached eyes and sitting at the bottom of it was your silver ring, it caught the light and Spencer had to grab my waist to keep me from hitting the floor.

At that point, however, the ring was a symbol of the future I thought I understood. Of course, we were in the middle of a crowd so that simple moment was over before I could understand it, but I couldn't stop playing with it and feeling its weight. We never talked about it, not when we got home and Spencer and Jax commented on it, neither of us told them what had happened and they didn't push. It was ours, and now it belongs to this history alone.

Greece really was magical, but that magic didn't fade when we got on the plane and watched as we got further away. Instead, the things we saw and the places we stood stayed with me no matter how far away we got. I think one day I'll take Maisy and Jax there; let them stand in their footsteps, to feel the ancient power of that place through their veins like we did. I think those few years between you coming back and my sister showing up were the best of our lives.

Of course, the time you got with our daughter was great, but there was something about those few free years that was irreplaceable and something I don't think I'll ever experience again.

I don't know what to do right now, I *need* you to tell me what to do—I can't keep doing this; I don't think any of us can survive you staying in our lives. I just don't want to let you go. To copy your words, it's as simple and as complicated as that. Tonight, I drink to you and all the things you never got to see and I wish that it was you drinking to me. I think about it a lot, what would have happened if I was the one on the street that day; you would have held it together better than me, especially because of Maisy. You would have taken her to your dad's and let him help while you got through it. You could have given her a family, a real family with grandparents and family dinners, you would have known what to do; you wouldn't be crying over stupid things like hair elastics or toothbrushes.

But then again, I'm not sure you could have recovered from it; maybe you would have been just as broken as me. I think a part of me holds onto the brokenness because it means that the pieces are still yours, but the more I feel myself come together, the more I can feel you slipping away. But you would have wanted me to be happy, right? You would have wanted me to live instead of just hiding in the dark for the rest of my life while my family moved on without me. I think today is the last time I am going to sit alone and cry over things I can't change. No more sending everyone away while I try to find you because *you're not here*, and I know that.

So, here's to you my love, happy 32nd birthday. I hope you can hear me.

22

Thursday, February 24th

The day after your birthday was better.

Right after the accident, every day felt longer than the last, like I was constantly walking through quicksand unable to reach solid land, I thought that I was going to drown beneath the weight of it all. But as each day passes, the sand thins, and without even realizing it I go days without the feeling of it tied around my feet. Instead of being in that pit every day, it's more moments; world-shattering moment's where I can't breathe or think of something other than your name, but my therapist said that might happen for years. Years, I still don't like how the word tastes in my mouth.

However, I do have to confess something; a few weeks ago, I kissed a man whose name I never learned.

Well, I did more than that, but that is beside the point.

The point is that for the first time since I was 16, I ran my hands across someone else's skin, I felt someone else's breath on my neck, someone else's lips on my torso; it was someone else, but I swear I still said your name. I woke up the next morning in a stranger's bed and it took me a moment to realize what I had done, and then another moment to not want to throw up. I left his place before the sun was up and I wanted to crawl out of my skin, everything felt as though I was betraying you in some cruel way. I came home to find Jax and Maisy on the couch and the second he looked at me he must have known something was wrong. I watched as he grabbed Maisy and put her in the playpen we had found to keep her from roaming and then I was standing in the entryway with his arms tightly around me, and I cried. Because I didn't know what else to do.

I think a part of me cried because it had felt *so* good to get out of my own head, to be that close to another human being again and it didn't feel wrong like I thought it would, and that was almost worse. The first time was the worst, but after that, it got easier. Spencer said that the only way I was ever going to get through this was to put myself out there again, and a part of me wanted it more than I could say because I've just spent the past seven months alone, but after the first time the guilt in my spine became normal, I stopped caring that it was there at all.

Even as I write this, I'm finishing my second glass of wine. I know that tonight I'll be somewhere else, with someone else, it makes things easier, to drink too much with people I don't know, to have sex without emotions—it makes *everything* easier.

Maybe I can erase your fingerprints if I replace them with someone else's.

. . .

I could spend years writing about the good times during our few years of freedom, and a part of me wants to because it would stall the end from coming, but I can't make this go on forever, and it's almost over.

You were on the brink of turning thirty and I couldn't believe it. We were sitting around on a Saturday morning watching stupid TV, I had a day off and you didn't have to train until the evening, those were my favorite days.

"How does it feel to be old?" I asked as you sat down beside me. You had cut your hair for the first time in years and it was still weird, the way you looked without hair falling against your shoulders was unfamiliar and out of place, but I was trying hard to appreciate it. I ran a hand through the shorter strands as you scoffed.

"Just remember, next year is your turn, and whatever you do to me, I promise I will do ten times worse." You changed the channel absentmindedly. "But it sucks, I think I liked my twenties."

"They were definitely exciting." We were closing in on another decade and it seemed crazy to think about everything that had happened. We were homeless and living on the streets at the beginning of it and most everything that had happened to us, be it good or bad, happened while you were in your twenties and it seemed impossible that it had been that long ago. "But just think about the exciting things that are going to happen in your thirties." I was excited to see where we would end up, whether we would stay in the city forever or move to someplace quieter; if we would ever settle down or keep living life as fast as we could.

"I can't imagine being forty. When I was little, and this is going to sound morbid, but I always thought life ended after twenty-five. I couldn't *imagine* what it would be like to live longer than that and now that I have, I can't imagine what the next ten will bring," you looked at me while moving a piece of hair from your face, "We are going to be old one day, like genuine old people in movies,"

"I don't think forty is considered old," It didn't feel old, considering how fast the last ten years had flown by but I knew that it would seem like a blink of an eye before we were having the conversation again.

"Right now, thirty seems old." And I guess for you it was. If only we had known then that we were living on stolen time, that every single second was getting closer and closer to the end, how were we to know that we wouldn't see forty together, or you at all? How were we to know that you would only celebrate two more birthdays and that I would be celebrating the third one alone? If I had the power to go back to that moment, I don't think I would tell them either. It was beautiful to feel as though the world was still within our grasps, to think that we had forever to make up our minds about what we wanted.

The whole day was spent on the couch with lazy movies and hot drinks, both of us were burnt out and tired, you had a fight on the horizon but I think we both knew the fighting days were coming to an end. You had done everything you had ever wanted; you won world titles and did what you set out to do, and although I think you would have fought forever, you knew that it was almost time to move on. We talked about coaching, you said that you wanted to be there and coach teenagers because you wished someone who actually cared would have coached you. My career was better than ever and I was booked solid for the following two years, things were good.

That night you went to the gym feeling more relaxed than ever and I had resigned myself to TV and green tea, but not long after you left, something happened that changed our world in a second. Someone was knocking on the door, I thought it was Jax or Spencer, or maybe Sam who I hadn't see in a while. But when I opened the door, it wasn't my friends standing on the other side, instead, it was Jaccob looking at me with apologies already spewing from his lips.

"Jaccob—" before I could really understand why he was there, or more importantly, *how* he was there, my 15-year-old sister moved from behind him, and I knew *instantly* that we were screwed. My kid sister was standing there with red, pleading eyes. I didn't say anything, instead, I just looked between the two of them and it took me longer than it should have to realize that something was different about her, I had enough friends with small children to know the reason they were standing on my doorstep with tears in their eyes; Annie was pregnant.

I didn't say anything because I hadn't figured out what to say, she was pregnant, and standing on my doorstep which was the only thing that mattered. Even though we didn't know each other, the first thing I did before anything else I hugged her. The second the door was closed and we were standing in my living room, I hugged her tighter than I think I ever did because I didn't know what else to do. I felt her cry against my chest and ran a hand through her hair, I think Jaccob finally let himself relax.

"I'm sorry." She muffled, I couldn't bare to hear her apology, instead, I pulled away so that she was forced to look at me.

"Hey, don't be sorry, it's okay," I placed a kiss on her forehead and let her fall into me again, I looked at Jaccob over her shoulder. Even though we hadn't been around each other since we were little, when we were all together like that, I was suddenly the older brother; they looked at me as though waiting for me to solve the issue at hand and I looked at them as though no matter the issue, I would do everything I could to fix it. I moved away from her and we all sat down on the couch, I made some tea and when everyone was settled, I looked to Jaccob for an explanation.

"You don't have to tell me anything you don't want to—I don't care what you did or why, but I do need to know why you're here and not at home." I knew why, but I needed to hear. My siblings looked at each other, then at me.

"I only found out a few weeks ago—"

"Me and my boyfriend, well we, you know—it was stupid, I *knew* it was stupid but he talked me into it and then, well this is what happened, I didn't know what else to do." I nodded and put a hand on her knee as though to show her that I was there, no matter what she said next. "I only told Jake a few weeks ago, and then suddenly I couldn't cover it up anymore."

"Does your mom or Noah know your here?" They both shook their heads, and it did cross my mind that Noah would think I had kidnapped her.

"Are you kidding? After what happened to you—Noah would kill me." I nodded, I knew why they were with me; she couldn't be at home, Annie couldn't be at home because—well because there's no way on earth that she wouldn't be subjected to the wrath of the church.

"Do they know you are here?" Jaccob nodded.

"Sorta, I told mom that you were getting married." I hated that, I knew that it would have killed her that they were invited, but whatever they had to do in order to get here safely.

"What about Noah?" He scared me; Noah really did scare me and still does sometimes, if anyone was going to come after them, it would have been him. Neither of them said anything and I knew that she couldn't go home, not until we had figured out some sort of resolution for her predicament.

"I'm glad you guys came here," I looked at Annie "You're okay." I knew that she didn't believe me, I made a mental note to talk to her about it later. I took a sip of tea, my mind was spinning fast with a thousand different ideas of what we were going to do, of what she wanted to do, and how we were going to explain this situation to her mom if we had to. "How are you feeling? Do you know how far along you are? Have you seen a doctor?" There were suddenly so many questions I had for them, I thought of Sam and her new baby, she would know what to do. I also thought of you, and the fact that you needed to know sooner rather than later that I had basically invited my siblings to live with us. She shook her head.

"Maybe two, three months? I'm not sure." I nodded, not wanting her to feel as though she was doing something wrong. Of course she hadn't seen a doctor, where would she have gone that wasn't connected to the people she knew.

"That's alright, the first thing we need to do is get you to a doctor—"

"I can't—I can't afford it."

"But I can, you're crazy If you think I'm going to let you do this alone." I was already making lists in my head of the things that needed to happen, of the people we needed to see, and more importantly, what was she going to do when it was over? There were a lot of big conversations that we needed to have but I needed you to be there for it, it was my family but you were better at this kind of situation. "But we should get Seb, he will be better at this than me." They both nodded, knowing that there was no avoiding him. I knew she was nervous about telling someone she didn't know, especially after the things she went through as a child. I reached out a hand for her to grab, I made sure she could see the cheap ring. "You can trust him. I promise."

Instead of walking all the way there, I called you, and when you didn't answer I called Jax.

"Collin, what's wrong?" I laughed, everyone always assumed something was wrong when I called.

"Nothing, well nothing bad, can you tell Seb to call me?" I walked into the bedroom, giving my siblings some space as well as giving us a chance to speak alone before I threw you into the fray. Jax hung up the phone and less than a minute later you were calling.

"What happened?" I sighed.

"Nothing—nothing to me, I just, I need you to come home. Like right now." It was silent for a moment other than the sound of what I'm sure was you packing your bag.

"what's wrong? Are you okay?"

"I'm fine, Jaccob and Annie just showed up." I heard the background noise stop at that.

"Like your siblings?"

"Yea, but there's more—Annie is pregnant." I knew that you wouldn't react.

"I thought she was in high school—"

"15 actually, but she can't stay with my family—just come home." I knew that you would be back soon. I hung up the phone and moved back to the living room.

"He will be back soon, I promise, everything is going to be okay." She nodded and instead of sitting in silence we talked about what their life had been like. I knew that Jaccob was working towards getting his trade ticket, but Annie was still a mystery to me. Once she started talking, I couldn't get her to stop. I found out that me and her were a lot alike; she talked to me about her favorite books and TV shows, about how school was going and her favorite classes. I saw myself in her, I knew the shame she felt sitting under her skin for going against her God and I wanted to save her from it before it took the things that made her unique. She told me that she loved to write and dreamed of publishing a book one day and I listened as she walked me through idea after idea, it was crazy to listen to what came pouring out of her brain. The more she spoke the more comfortable she got, soon her coat was gone and she had her feet up beside her, I didn't want her to feel afraid, not of us.

In return, I told them about who we were, who I was. I told them about my job and promised that I would take her to a shoot before she left, I told tales of whirlwind adventures and traveling, Spencer's wedding, and all of the crazy things we had done in the last decade. She made me promise that I would introduce them to my friends, I knew that they both wanted more than anything to see the life I had created, maybe Annie was trying to find proof that there could still be life after condemnation. By the time you ran through the door we were laughing and the air was light. You approached us slowly, dropping your bag by the front.

"Seb, you remember Jaccob and Annie, right?" Everyone stood up to make introductions, it was still weird for Jaccob I think because he grew up watching you; you were the athlete who he always wanted to be and now he was sitting in your house as family.

"Course I do, it's great to see you again." You made your face soft and kind, I knew you wanted them to feel welcome. Jaccob shook your hand but Annie moved closer and hugged you, I watched as you held onto her tighter than anyone should hold a stranger. I think the three of us understood each other. When you sat down, you looked between the group as though waiting to see who would tell you the truth.

"Sorry for showing up, I didn't know where else to go—"

"You guys are always welcome here." I knew you wanted to ask more; I was depending on the fact that you would. "If you don't mind me asking, what do you want to do? Are you going to keep it, or adoption is always a good option, what do you want?" We needed to make a plan and I knew that you were already on step five, if she wanted to put it up for adoption then we needed to start the process quickly. "There are private adoptions as well, we will help you do whatever." I started to panic about what we were going to do if she decided to keep it. She couldn't go home, not while Noah was around and she couldn't stay here forever;

we were constantly moving and changing, our house wasn't big enough for both of them and our lifestyle wasn't suitable for an infant, not with our parties or friends, I had no idea what we would do.

"I'm only in grade ten, I can't—I can't keep it, I'm not ready to be a mom." I wanted to say that whether she kept it or not, she was a mom. "But I need it to go to a nice family, not just some random off the street." We both nodded, you more than me because you were already four steps further.

"Okay, then we will start looking into it. In the meantime, we should get you into a doctor to make sure everything's okay." Your words were an echo of mine and I knew who we had to call.

"I wonder if Sam could tell us who she went to," You nodded, and honestly the two of us had no idea what we were doing, neither of us had the slightest amount of knowledge in that department but she was my sister, and I had to try.

"Call her and ask," You turned to her, and I wonder if you thought about the fact that she was the same age as your baby brother. "Can I get you anything?" You were instantly in older brother mode and it was cute, but also heartbreaking. I wonder if they would have been in the same class. It was at that moment that I realized just how young she was.

"No, thank you though, I'm just tired." You nodded and stood up, offering her a hand as you went. We had a spare room with a bed and small couch, between the two of them they could figure out where to sleep. We didn't go to bed right away, instead, we stayed up and talked to Jaccob about what we were going to do next. But that was the thing, there was nothing we could do, not right now anyway. All we could do was make sure Annie and the baby were healthy, and then figure out who was going to get the child in the end. Soon we were all heading our separate ways, we went to bed silently. I didn't know what to do, did I phone her mom? Did she have a right to know that her daughter was going through something traumatic? But I knew that I couldn't. I can't imagine if Masiy was going through something like that and didn't think she could tell us, it would break my heart that she felt as though she had to go through everything alone. You were unusually quiet that night as we laid in bed, we both stared at the ceiling.

"We have to take the kid." Your voice was certain and sure but I couldn't breathe; those single words put a halt to all of my thoughts because—*no*.

"Like the baby? Are you out of your mind?" I sat up and waited for the punch line, there was no way you could be serious. "We definitely *can't* take it; we have to start looking at who can—"

"Collin, we have to take it. It's your family." I shook my head,

"No, Seb our lives they aren't—we aren't ready for that, *I'm* not ready for that—" and I wasn't. I was *not* ready to be responsible for a child, I was still too young. "We are *just* figuring out our own lives plus we are too busy, you are constantly traveling and I am always on the go, we can't just stop everything to raise some kid." The conviction in your voice made my head spin; I wasn't ready—I didn't *want* it. You sat up and grabbed my arm.

"Don't you get it? This is your chance to have what you never did; your family. This child—you share the same blood, it's *yours*. Are you really going to be okay knowing that there is a child out there with your blood, that you *don't* know?" Your eyes were so sure, *horrifyingly* sure and I didn't know what to do, I wasn't ready for a child, I was *still* a child. I never really wanted kids to begin with.

"That's what adoption is, we aren't ready—"

"This isn't about what *we* want," You were getting frustrated as though there was something right in front of my face that I was missing, I didn't understand. "Let's say she gives up the kid, what happens if that kid ends up in a house like we grew up in? What if they end up in a place of violence, or in a constant loop of the system where they think no one wants them? Would you be okay with this child growing up with the same fear you did?" I hadn't thought about it like that.

"We won't let that happen; we can screen families—"

"Because abuse is always obvious right? Take your family, from the outside it looked like a house with loving parents, caring siblings, you looked like the ideal American family. But the cigarette burns on your arms or the scar on your nose would say different," You couldn't live with yourself if the child ended up with someone like our parents because we could stop it. That didn't change the fact that I wasn't ready for it yet. "The only way we can make sure that they are okay is to do it ourselves, to give them a chance we didn't get." I was also starting to realize that your mind had already been made.

"But our lives—neither of us are ever home, my career is still starting out, I can't just put *everything* on hold," I was being selfish but I didn't care. "I just got you back," I said the last words quietly because I felt stupid saying them. "Things *just* became stable; I don't want everything to change yet."

I liked who we were; I liked eating Chinese food on the kitchen table at 2 am or spending an entire day watching movies on the couch or being able to leave and go somewhere new if we wanted to. I wasn't ready to change diapers or buy baby food. You moved closer so that your nose was brushing against mine.

"Nothing important is going to change. It's still you and me. Always." You moved away slightly. "I don't expect you to put your life on hold, I know how long you've worked for it but this is a once in a lifetime chance for us—I'll stop fighting," I just stared at you.

"You can't—"

"We both know that my fighting days are numbered, Rob has offered me full-time work coaching his team and it would mean that I wouldn't have to travel. We *have* to do this C," I looked around the room desperately.

"What if I screw it up? it's not like we had role models, what if—"

"You're not your father. We have to do this, you know it." I felt trapped. I needed to take a minute without your hopeful eyes baring into mine. I'm sure you were horrified; I thought you weren't afraid but I'm sure that you were, you just had the mind to realize that it was bigger than us.

"Okay, I just—I just need a second." You nodded and I got up, quickly making my way to the living room to sit on the couch. I didn't want a baby, but I knew that you did. A part of me knew you would never forgive me if I was the reason why we didn't do it.

I was shocked, if not slightly annoyed, to see Annie sitting on the large couch crying. I really wanted to be alone, but I couldn't turn her away.

"Hey," I said softly, I moved to sit on the other side of the couch in order to give her space. She wiped her eyes.

"Hey." The space around us was filled with years of burdened silence and I wasn't sure how to break it.

"When I was 13, I met a boy named Aaron," Maybe if I told her more about my shame, she could feel better about her own.

"I remember that he had red hair and blue eyes, he always brought a blue water bottle to class." She looked at me. "We became pretty good friends, but then one day I looked at him and realized how much I wanted to kiss him; I thought he was beautiful." I looked at her and wanted her to know that no matter what she had done, it *didn't* change who she was. "You can imagine the panic I felt, I ran home that day and hid under the covers because I thought it would just go away, but then it didn't. I probably prayed four times a day, every day; I remember crying myself to sleep because I thought I was going to hell, I knew it was wrong to feel the way I did, but I couldn't change the way I felt when Aaron smiled." She smiled. "One day, we were sitting in the forest trying to catch bunnies, you know the ones that would run around near the fence behind the school? Those ones, eventually we gave up and ended up sitting side by side on this huge rock playing some stupid game, but then for a reason I don't remember, we kissed, right there on the rock." She moved so that she was facing me instead of facing the wall. "It was my first kiss and I wanted to die. I thought that I had forsaken God and prayed that he would strike me down, I thought my life was over, I wanted it to be." I played with the ring on my finger.

"But then I got older and the world didn't end, there was no magic act to smite me, nothing changed, other than me. And then I met Seb—and I *knew* that there was no way we could possibly be wrong. No matter what happened after that day, I knew that I didn't deserve it and now, well now we have a beautiful life together that I wouldn't give up for anything."

"I'm sorry—"

"I'm not. What I'm trying to say is that no matter what, no matter how much we think we deserve to be condemned, or that we are unforgivable, we *can* create our own salvation. You, Annie, are going to have a *beautiful* life, full of love and adventure and anything else you want it to be. This, none of this means anything because it's just something that happened. You made a stupid mistake but all of us do, I have, but it doesn't define you. Your good, you're so good and you're going to finish high school and do great things in the world." I watched tears run down her face but she smiled, I knew she was trying to be strong in the face of her own fear. I squeezed her hand. "You are *so* much more than the things that you've done." It was a lesson that had taken my entire life to learn, but I wanted her to hear it, to *understand* it because she didn't deserve to carry this burden forever.

"Mom will never forgive me."

"Yea, she might not, but if she doesn't then it's her loss." I knew my words meant nothing; nothing could fix the pain of being abandoned but she wouldn't be alone.

"What if I'm making the wrong choice? What if—what if they end up just another forgotten kid in the system who no one wants? Or worse, what if like on TV they end up a hated child who never knows they are loved, how can I do this—" I pulled her against my chest because I knew her anxiety well. I let her cry against my shirt, I felt her fingers digging into my skin but I just held her tighter. "I can't do this"

I kissed her temple and I knew, despite my own desires, I *knew* what we had to do. You were right, I couldn't live with myself if this child ended up in the wrong hands and more importantly, neither could Annie and the fact that we would forever be left wondering if they were okay—I couldn't put her, or you through that.

"Listen to me, Annie it's going to be okay, we—" I took a deep breath; I was about to change my own life. "We'll take it. Me and

Seb—it's the best option." I felt her cry harder, but then she pulled away with a look of disbelief.

"You would do that for me?" I smiled at her.

If she only knew that I was shitting my pants at the idea of having a kid. My brain was a fog of things I couldn't say.

"This kid deserves a better family than the one we had." She hugged me again and I thought that I might pass out, everything was spinning and my hands were shaking, but I couldn't take the words back.

Sometime after that, I made my way to where you sat waiting for me, this wasn't a decision that should have been made in the middle of the night but it was, for some reason we needed to figure it out before the sun was up. I sat down on the bed and looked at the ground.

"Okay," I whispered despite my brain screaming at me.

"Okay?" You moved closer, running a hand up my arm.

"We have to take the kid—" Your lips were on mine before I could finish and the force knocked us both over, I laid there laughing while you placed soft kisses over the plains of my face. You always wanted a family and I was giving you permission to take It, it was your dream come true.

. . .

That's the story of how we got our daughter, or more so how we decided that we were going to expand our foxhole to three. Although I didn't like the idea at first, now I am grateful *every* day that I get to be her dad. She kept me alive when I didn't find the point in living and I promise to be there for her as long as I'm allowed to be.

But I think I have to cut this short, Jax and Spencer are waiting for me and I still have to get ready, but I'm excited. I think it's going to be fun.

Fun, what a weird word for this alternate version of life.

23

Thursday, March 9th

I think Jax is mad at me.

He hasn't spoken in a few days which is hard considering we live together in a finite space.

I don't know what started it, I can't think of anything I've done to warrant the silent treatment for days on end but here we are. Spencer said maybe he was irritated that I had a social life while he was at home watching a baby that's not his, but he's never cared about it before. This is something else, something I can't put my finger on but I don't like it; I don't like knowing that something I did could have wronged him because he's Jax and I—I don't know, I just need us to be okay. I've been assigned baby duty tonight and it wasn't an option. Apparently, he is going out with some stupid person he met at a coffee shop as though they are the main characters in a YA novel.

I don't care, I hope he and whoever it has a good time, it's just *weird*—he's usually here when I come home and he always leaves a glass of water beside my bed in the morning, it's weird that he's out with someone we have never even heard him talk about. So tonight, I write this with a growing baby on my lap as she laughs at some idiotic TV show playing in the background while I try not to think about whatever the hell he's doing.

. . .

I woke up the morning after we had agreed to take the baby and I almost threw up.

A thousand thoughts were racing through my mind because how was I supposed to be a dad when I never had one to begin with? How did we even go about adopting this kid, would we need a lawyer and legal documents? What about my job? At the time I was booking shoots years in advance, how was I supposed to tackle being a new parent on top of that? But then I thought of your eyes and Annie's cries, and I *knew* there was no other choice. But still, I was more than hesitant about it. You were already awake when I got out of bed, when I walked to the kitchen you were talking to both siblings while making breakfast. I didn't realize you knew how to get up that early.

"Morning, I called Sam and she gave us the name of the doctor, I sent up an appointment this week." I nodded, still half asleep and not wanting to deal with that. Just last night my life was carefree and ever-changing, but now it was changing in a way that I wasn't ready for. Annie smiled at me as I passed her, Jaccob sat with his head on the table.

"What are we going to tell your mom?" I said, the thought popping into my brain as I poured a cup of coffee.

"What do you mean?" Someone asked, I was too tired to care who but I couldn't believe that I hadn't thought of it sooner.

"Your what, three months at most? That means there is still a solid six months of you not being able to go home." Everyone went silent, our little plan was falling apart and you couldn't stop it.

"I could tell mom that I got a job with you, that it's some once in a lifetime opportunity and I have to take it."

"Noah would kill me if he thought I had stolen you away for six months, especially because you're still supposed to be in school."

"It doesn't matter what Noah thinks, he doesn't know where we are, or where you live, mom would let me stay if for no other reason than the fact she can't say no to you." I didn't ask, I couldn't handle the answer to that question, not before coffee.

"What about jake? Don't you have school still?" I finally turned around to look at them and he nodded without hesitation.

"I'm not gonna stay, not right now anyway, if she is here, I know she's safe. I have some stuff to take care of but I could come to visit?" They were still waiting for me to say no, I always had to be the bad guy because you couldn't be.

"Alright. Already gone this far, might as well."

"There's something else, mom will let me stay, but she's going to have to hear it from you." I hung my head. A baby, talking to my mom, the day just got better. I nodded, too tired to fight because I knew it was the only way, I had an idea though.

"Alright ill call her, but I get to pick the name." You smiled because it meant that I still wanted to take it. "If it's going to be our child, then I want to name it." I looked at everyone with an eyebrow raised to tell them I was only slightly joking. Everyone smiled but agreed.

That's how I ended up sitting in my bedroom with shaking hands as I dialed a number I would never forget. I had to do it—Annie needed me to do it.

"Hello?" The sound of her voice hit me the same, despite the fact it had been over ten years since I heard it. She was still my *mom*.

"Hey, Loral? It's Andrew." I took a breath to compose my words, I had to do this right otherwise our scheme would fall apart. I heard her gasp and then she was walking somewhere.

"Andrew—my son Andrew?" I closed my eyes.

"Yea, I need to talk to you."

"Oh my god, Andrew—my son—of course, it's been—it's been so long I just—you must be-" I think she was crying, I started to pace.

"I'm 29, but that's not why I'm calling, it's about Annie—"

"Is everything okay? She said you were getting married—did something happen?"

"Yea I did, but she's fine. At the wedding I let her play around with my camera and turns out she has a natural talent for it," I tried to figure out exactly what I could say to make her agree. "I'm about to start a six-month tour and I think Annie should come with me. It's a once-in-a-lifetime opportunity for her that I think will change her life." There was a beat of silence.

"What about school? She can't just stop going to high school—"

"Ask her yourself, she said that she could do online homeschooling to make up for what she missed, but I really think this is the best thing she could do. But talk to her about it." I walked to the living room in order to give her the phone, I didn't want to be the one to negotiate the details.

"Andrew wait—can we talk—"

"Here's Annie," I handed her the phone before walking to stand next to you.

It turns out that it wasn't all that hard to convince her to let Annie stay, not after I sent her the fake itinerary for what we would be doing and she promised to send updates on her homeschooling—something she would, in fact, be doing because I was *not* going to let her be a drop out like me. That day was the start of six months of baby mania. We said goodbye to Jaccob a few days later and then much to my dismay, you went into full baby mode. You took her to all the doctors' appointments and scans; you took her shopping for new clothes as her stomach grew and helped her with her math homework. Your entire personality changed and I knew that you were going to be the best dad, the kid hadn't been born yet but you already belonged to them. It couldn't have taken more than a month for you to tell Rob you didn't want to fight anymore because you had a baby on the way and wanted to be there for every second of it and thinking back on it now, it seems crazy that you didn't know your last fight was really your last. You had no idea that you would never walk on the canvas again or hear a crowd cheering your name, you just thought it was another Friday night, but you stopped and never looked back. Instead, you started coaching more. There was one young girl you used to come home and talk about all the time, I can't remember her name, but you used to talk about her as though she was going to change the very fabric of the world and we both realized you were going to be a better coach then you ever were a fighter. I for my part, didn't know what to do with the idea of having a kid, I think I thought that if I just continued on with my life then it would make the situation go away, so that's exactly what I did.

I went to shoots and hung out at parties, I hung out with you whenever you weren't in baby mode but I think it started to put a divide between us. You didn't want to do things anymore, you didn't want to go away for the weekend or host huge parties, you grew up in an instant and I was still playing the teenager. A part of me was jealous. I was losing you to something that hadn't been born yet and I didn't know what to do about it.

On March 27th Annie went to the doctor and they asked if she wanted to know the gender, of course you did, but you wanted to wait for me to find out. We all sat around the dinner table with anxiety, me maybe more than anyone else and I just wanted to leave, I think I was uncomfortable because I was so scared that I wasn't going to be enough for this child; that I was just going to screw everything up and it was better if I had nothing to do with it. Sam was there with us, and no one breathed as she opened the envelope.

"Well boys, it looks as though you better start shitting yourselves because your about to have a little girl." You sat there with the biggest smile I think I'd ever seen you make. You looked at me and I couldn't pretend that I didn't feel it. A girl, we were going to have a baby girl. Maybe that's the moment it started to hit me, when it became a person instead of just a thing. Although it never hit me quite as bad as it did you, I think you cried.

I wanted to cry but for completely different reasons. I couldn't raise a girl, oh god—I *still* don't know how to raise a girl. But it seems less scary when she looks at me with her big brown eyes and little nose. You kissed me and I knew it was one of the most exciting moments of your life. That night we sat in bed and you couldn't stop talking about it.

"Imagine her in the gym with little boxing gloves, without a doubt she will be the most badass girl in her class, and we *can't* be those parents who only dress her in pink; screw gender roles if she wants to wear dinosaur shoes then so be it." I was sitting on my phone half listening, it had only been two months but I almost couldn't handle the nonstop baby nonsense. Everything we said or did *had* to revolve around her and she didn't even really exist yet. "Collin, did you hear anything I just said?" I just looked at you, not totally understanding what I had missed.

"I'm just really tired."

"You say that every night." You turned away from me and I knew you were at the end of your rope in the same way I had been when we took our break, I wasn't trying, and I knew it.

"I never thought that I would be a dad," I said and I saw you twitch but still you faced the wall. I played with a loose string. "I just never wanted to be, maybe it's because my dad was such an asshole, I don't know but the idea of having someone rely on me like that—I just never thought I would do it." It wasn't enough, I took a deep breath. "If I screw this up, then she is going to be screwed up forever—look at how screwed up we are, all of our issues started with our parents and how can I be responsible for an entire life, for teaching someone how to survive it when I just finally learned how?" That was it, that was the secret word because you turned to face me and the anger was gone. "I'm going to screw it up, she's going to grow up hating me because of something I didn't even know I was doing wrong and I don't know how to do it."

My dislike of the situation came from a place of complete fear. I thought of my mother crying alone in her house because her kids all ran away, or of your dad trying to desperately fix his past mistakes, they aren't horrible people, they were just in horrible situations and I knew how easy it was for me to get lost in my head.

"You aren't your father C, our parents abandoned us, they stopped being our family and left us to die without a call. You would never do that to *anyone*, let alone a child. We *are* going to mess this up, and I'm sure that she is going to hate us somedays and we will fight as though the worlds ending—but it won't matter, because no matter what she does, or how much trouble she's in, she's still *ours*." You grabbed my hand, and I looked away. This wasn't just some moment of fear that existed in my mind, this was a real human life that I was being given and I didn't know how to handle it. "You and me, we got this. I heard what you said to Annie that night, that was more parenting than I think your parents have ever done." I looked at you and I knew that I was going to have to buck up and become the person everyone seemed to think I was ready to be.

"We are going to have a daughter," I said, trying to make the words real instead of playing pretend.

I think maybe when all is said and done and I'm nothing but dust, I think I want her to read this. I want her to know how much you loved her before she was even born because that's the biggest tragedy of them all. You only got a year, not even. You never got to hear her first word, or take hundreds of videos of her first steps; you won't get to see her graduate or go on her first date, you won't get to walk her down the aisle or meet her children if she has them. All of these milestones that you spent the entire nine months thinking about were stolen away in an instant but it's more than that; she would have *loved* you. I knew right from the day she was born that even though you shared no blood, she was yours.

I wish more than *anything*, that you got to see our little girl grow up.

Honestly, there is not a lot to say about the pregnancy other than what I've already written; you were constantly reading three parenting books at the same time and going to birthing classes with Annie, and I was focused on work and making sure things were ready for when the baby did arrive. I think I may have found it easier after we talked, it helped to know that you were just as afraid as me. Annie was a champ about the entire thing, she didn't complain about her situation, instead, she took it in stride. We all laughed as she video called her friends and introduced us, I helped her with her science homework and couldn't help but think of you the whole time. Eventually, we had to tell our friends about our new lifestyle, we put it off longer than we should have and I'm not sure why, maybe we both thought it wouldn't be real unless we told other people. But I'll never forget the day Spencer and Jax came over. We were all sitting around the living room, Annie must have been six or seven months along by that point and somehow, we had kept the *entire* thing under wraps for the entire time. But I knew we had to say something.

"We should go away for Christmas this year, someplace hot and exciting," Spencer said to no one in particular. Andi was on a work trip which meant he was bored and hanging around us more than usual. Married life suited him. I'm not sure when Jax became a part of our inner circle, he went from a gym friend to a work friend, to a sort of out-of-work friend, to someone I would trust with my life and now—now he lives in my house and lets me *breathe*. I was happy that you two made it work, because the four of us were unstoppable together. "If we go somewhere fun, we can double it as a new year's trip, I am dying to get out of the city for a while." Jax smiled but shook his head.

"Buddy, it's barely July,"

"I know Jaxon, but a man can dream. Besides, things take time to plan, all of us are sadly adults who have to find time off work, lots of prep goes into these things now unlike it did when we were still young." It was true, we used to be able to leave on a whim, and now it was impossible to get away for even a night. You looked at me as though asking permission to share the news, I smiled in response and maybe that was the first time I felt excited about it; my stomach was filled with butterflies because I couldn't believe that this was our life.

"Actually, I think we are going to have to pass this time." You said and everyone stopped to look at us.

"You guys *have* to come with us, I can't just bring Jax, that would be sad even for my standards." Jax hit him and I always secretly thought if not for Andi, Jax and Spencer would have made a good couple. They had that playful banter that never seemed to stop, in another life those two could have been something.

"Sorry, but I think we want the baby to have her first Christmas at home."

"But you'll love it I promise—I'm sorry, what did you just say?" No one spoke, both just looked at us with wide eyes and I watched Jax smile, but his eyes seemed lost somewhere else. "Collin, did he just say the b word?" I nodded and felt my cheeks heat up. they were the first people we had really told.

"He did, yea. Surprise." Spencer sat there as though I had rewired his brain, Jax hugged us both tightly.

"That's freaken amazing you guys, wow—congrats." He sat back down and hit Spencer on the head.

"You're having a baby? For real, like a real pooping, crying, messy baby?" Spencer seemed just as unsure as me. Now, however, it's hard to get him to give her back.

"A real baby, a girl." You said and we laughed as Spencer just stood there, his vacation plans were falling apart indefinitely.

"Holy shit, why?"

"It's a long story, but my sister is pregnant so we are going to take the kid."

"Your sister is here?" Jax commented and I nodded. Spencer just stared at us in his dazed shock.

"Yep, she has been here for about five months actually." I felt bad for a moment that I hadn't told them about it, I told them everything but I left out the biggest news of all. Even Jax seemed shocked at the fact that I kept her hidden but I didn't need a lecture about the ethical consequences of it.

"Your sister has been here for five months and you are just now telling us? Wait -you mean you're having a baby soon, like *really* soon." Jax put the pieces together and I felt his fear.

"Within the next two months." I just kept waiting for Spencer to say something, *anything* but he didn't.

"Again, I'm so happy for you guys, is your sister actually here because I'd love to meet her," Jax said and I nodded, I was happy even though I knew Spencer was feeling betrayed. I was happy because someone else knew, someone outside the two of us knew about her and it made it real. I got Annie; she was more than excited to meet them. Jax hugged her and introduced himself, Spencer sat there and did the same.

"Anyone want a drink? Anyone other than Annie?" You and Jax both nodded, I made my way to the kitchen and knew that Spencer was going to follow me. We both stood in silence for a moment.

"Why—why didn't you tell me? You're going through something life-changing and you didn't tell me." I knew why he was upset; through everything, no matter what, he had been there without question. I felt horrible.

"I didn't really know how," I didn't know how to tell him that my entire life was about to change. "I liked the fact that when I was with you guys, I didn't have to think about it anymore." I got to be the old me with them, the irresponsible kid who just wanted to have a good time instead of a parent.

"You should have told me, this is *huge*—life changingly huge like you're going to be a *dad*—I would have told you." I should have told him and it was disrespectful that I didn't. "Did you think I would be upset or something? Just because I don't want kids doesn't mean I hate them—I could never hate your kid"

"I'm sorry; your right, I should have told you about this—I'm sorry." Instead of saying anything else he hugged me uncharacteristically hard and I let myself be held.

"Just because you're freaking out doesn't mean you get to keep things." I nodded and let myself be afraid before we both returned to the group as though nothing had happened.

If I thought you went overboard with the whole baby fever, Spencer was most definitely worse. He didn't want kids but he was excited for mine, I'm sure he financed her nursery; he bought cribs and strollers, endless amounts of clothes that would be too big for months. He bought art and books and got on board faster than I ever thought he would. You and him together were an unbeatable force and Annie loved every second of it, she loved the attention and love she was getting from the people around us; we were a real family. Not that we weren't before, but having her there, someone from my past, it made it real. Maybe that was training enough for how to raise a baby, I did help raise her and my kid siblings and I did deal with her during her pregnancy, maybe I was more prepared than I thought I was when the day finally came.

And it did, no matter how much I dreaded it, I couldn't help the pit of energy growing in my stomach when I thought about the baby I would hold soon.

On September 27th at 2:34 am our daughter was born. She was 8.5 ounces and as healthy as a baby could be.

I'll never forget what you looked like pacing around the hospital room that night. You were pulling out your hair and I grabbed your hand and made you stop. When you looked at me, I saw for the first time how afraid you were.

"It's never going to be just you and me again. This is it; she's coming right now—we aren't ready—" You were frantic as you grabbed onto my shirt and for the first time I was at peace with the situation. I pulled you against my chest and took in the last seconds of us; the two broke runaways who loved each other more than logic allowed. I said goodbye to who we used to be as we stood there and got myself ready for the people we were about to become.

"We are as ready as possible, we got this." For the first time I comforted you about our impending doom because there was nothing, we could do about it now, this was happening and we couldn't change it; all we could do was embrace the life we had chosen. You nodded your head and we stood like that for a long time, I think we were both trying to remember what it felt like to belong to each other instead of a screaming infant. But your fears were gone the second Jaccob walked into the room with what looked like a bundle of blankets in his arms. You didn't cry a lot, but you cried that day.

"I'd like to introduce your daughter."

"Andrew," you whispered my name while grabbing my hand, and I couldn't look away from her. The moment was surreal, nothing about it seeming like it could possibly be happening but then Jaccob was right in front of us and we were looking down at her. I think I watched your face first; I watched your eyes go wide and the tears form, I watched as you subconsciously gave everything you were or ever would be to her because she owned you from that very first second. I was so afraid when I finally let myself look down at her tiny form, but when I did, she was *so* beautiful. I didn't feel like the movies said I would; my fear didn't disappear and I didn't instantly think that things were going to be okay, but when I looked at her wrapped in that hospital blanket, I knew that I would do anything for her; that no matter what, she was *mine* and I would protect her in a way my parents never could.

"Did you ever think of a name?" Jaccob said and his face was split with a grin, I saw tears in his eyes as he handed you his niece. This was the moment everyone had been waiting for, the name that I said I wanted to choose and I had thought about it for months. I had thousands of ideas; Andromache, Aris, Shane, Greyson, the list went on and on for pages, but I kept coming back to one. There was no meaning behind her name, other than the fact I heard it while watching interviews and knew that it was meant for her. No one had heard it, not even you. I don't think you really cared because you were building a new life right there in that room, your mind was spanning the next twenty years and all the things we were going to do, everything seemed new now that we got to do it with her and I wish that you would have gotten to see the future you were so passionate about living.

"I did—Maisy. Her name is Maisy." You looked at me and there was *so* much love in your eyes, so much adoration for the fact that you were really living in that moment. You held her so gently yet it was fierce, I watched your hands shake as you ran a finger over her tiny face. "Maisy-Ann Spencer Morgan." I wanted her mother to be a part of her name, it was her mother's strength that brought her into the world but I also wanted Spencer to be there too. He saved me—time and time again without needing anything in return, he was there. I wouldn't have made it to that day if not for him and I would never be able to thank him for it, but it felt right to honor him in the way we did.

"It's beautiful." Your voice was so soft, so *impossibly* soft as you looked down at her. "Welcome to the world little one." You whispered, I watched as you kissed her forehead gently, then you passed her to me and I didn't know what to do. She was so light, so small and fragile that I was afraid to break her. I couldn't look away, how was it possible that humans were ever that small.

"I *promise*," I whispered, it was meant for no one but her, I'm not even sure that you heard me but I didn't want you to and I couldn't think of anything else to say, other than promising her a thousand things I couldn't articulate. It's safe to say that I loved her from the first day, although I got lost for a while after you left. Jax sees her more than me sometimes I think, he likes the company or maybe it's because I'm not home enough, I don't know, but she was the love of your life and it was the purest thing I'd ever seen.

Just like that we were parents and in charge of a real human, the fear hadn't sunk back in and for a moment we were just in awe of how precious she was. She still is.

The end is close, I don't know how long I should keep writing this, do I wait until the past is gone and the only thing, I'm left with is my present? Or do I leave you unfinished so that we never have to say goodbye? That's a question for another night, tonight I have Maisy, and my mind won't stop thinking about when Jax is coming back.

24

Saturday, June 27th

Its summer now; the weather is sticky and hot; the kids are running around the streets looking for water to cool off in.

I didn't think I would ever see summer again—but here I am, and I feel better than I have all year. Our story might be running out of lines, but maybe *mine* doesn't have to be. Before we can continue in the past, I think I owe it to you to catch you up on my future.

. . .

After the last entry, which must have been a month or two ago, Jax and I were still fighting, although we never said any words.

Instead, he stayed silent every time I went out and left him at home, he never complained or outright said anything against it but I knew he was harboring some feelings, he didn't look at me anymore, he didn't try and talk to me or wait around to hear the crazy stuff me and Spencer had done, he started retreating in on himself and I absolutely *hated* it. His rejection made me go out more, and every time I kissed someone new, I thought less about you but one night with horrifying shock, I realized that I was thinking about *him*. I was thinking about his eyes and the way his lip turns up slightly when he is trying not to laugh, I thought of the way his hair fell against his face no matter how hard he tried to keep it up, I was thinking about all his details while I kissed someone I had never met and I didn't know what to do, so like the adult that I am, I completely ignored what it might mean and chose to do anything I could to push it away.

But then one night as I was leaving, I saw him sitting on the couch and something about the sight made my heart break. I sighed and walked over to him, to which he of course tried to act as though I wasn't standing there at all.

"It's been weeks since you spoke to me, are we ever going to talk about it?" I sat down a few feet away and he seemed to be fighting some conflict, the evidence was written on his face.

"Fine," he turned to me, his red hair seemed like fire under the bright overhead light. "I understand that you're going through something and you are doing what you have to do but Collin, you still have a child who needs you—you can't just go out every single night and pretend as though she doesn't exist because she does." It was honestly not the fight I thought he was going to make. I watched Masiy play with her toys, I knew he was right

"Im not trying to ignore her." I couldn't look at him, instead, I looked at the floor.

"And what are you thinking sleeping around like this, as though some twenty-year-old with no responsibilities, I have a life too. I can't just keep sitting here with everything on hold because you are figuring yourself out, it's been a year." He didn't raise his voice but I could hear the emotion in it, I knew that for whatever reason he was hurting and it was my fault. I couldn't read him the same way I could read you; I didn't know what the right thing to say was or how to make it better.

"I'm sorry, but no one is making you stay, you are choosing to be here—" I knew I was making the wrong choice before I could finish my sentence. I took a breath. "I know that this has been a lot for you, but you don't have to keep doing this. Your right, it's not your kid, which means that you have the choice every day to walk away, why don't you take it if you're so unhappy?" I'd asked myself that question a lot; no matter what, he *always* came back even though he had absolutely no reason to. He looked at me and I didn't understand, there were new emotions that I hadn't seen before stuck in his eyes.

"I'm not unhappy, I just—" he took a second to find his composure. "Don't you get it? I stay because of *you*."

The words were quiet but there, and I wanted to hear them again and again and again because my heart was racing with new anticipation. He looked away. "It's *always* been because of you." I knew what he was saying without him needing to explain and I had to make a choice whether to stay in the past with you or take a chance at having a future with someone else and *finally*, I knew what I wanted.

"I'm sorry—I know that you are still trying to move on and I'll never expect *anything* fr—" before he could finish whatever he was saying, I kissed him. Right there on the living room couch, I kissed Jax. And best of all, he kissed me back.

His hand moved to the back of my neck softly and to be honest, it felt *wonderful*. Everything made sense, the horrible feeling in my stomach whenever he went out on a date, the way he always looked at me when he thought I wasn't looking. Somehow, he had made himself an indispensable part of my life, and somewhere along the way, I decided that I wanted him to kiss me. I moved away slightly but he chased my lips as though afraid that once the moment stopped there would never be another one.

"I've—I've wanted you to do that since we met." I kissed him again instead of responding because I liked the way it felt. He had turned into my best friend without my consent and suddenly I became aware of how badly I wanted him to stay. He wasn't you, and what I have with him will *never* be anything like what we had, but I'm happy, and I think that's enough.

Anyways, back to the story.

The bliss of having a newborn wore off quickly.

Before long we were exhausted beyond belief and at each other's throats. I think I may have hated you by the end of the fourth week, genuine and utter hate as I was getting up to feed her at 3 am. Even you were tired and worn, although you didn't complain nearly as much as me. The hardest thing about those first few weeks was saying goodbye to Annie. After she had recovered for a bit, we knew it was time for her to leave. I kept waiting for her to have a moment of motherly affection for Masiy but she never did, I don't think she ever really felt as though the kid belonged to her because she wasn't ready for it, she didn't want it and knew it was going to people who did. But through the sleep depravity, I remember the day Jaccob came to pick her up and take her home because I hugged her tighter than I had ever hugged anyone before.

"Call me as soon as you get home," I said into her ear, she let herself cry and I wiped away the tears. We had bonded for life over the past six months, never again would we be estranged siblings, she was forever going to be a part of our lives and I held onto that when I thought of her leaving.

"This Is your second chance, finish school and do the things I wish I could have," I told her and she nodded swiftly. I don't remember much else other than the empty hole I felt when she was gone. I should call her; she calls a lot, her and Jaccob both do and I don't respond as much as I should.

If I'm being honest a lot of the first month or two are a blur, Jax and Spencer fell in love the second they saw her and Andi wouldn't stop posting about how adorable she was on social media, but we—mainly I, suffered while trying to get used to it. The number of times we thought she was dying is pathetic and our doctor was basically on speed dial because every time something small changed we both immediately thought we had screwed it up. I remember you frantically running around the house while trying to describe what kind of poop she was having. But of course, with the stress and pain, there were amazing moments too. Like the day I walked in and saw you asleep on the couch with her perched on your chest, or the moment's she would laugh and we would both suddenly feel less tired. I took more photos than I had ever taken before because I wanted to document it all, every single moment we had with her was one worth saving and I did. I don't know what I'm going to do with all those photos now, I think most of them are going to stay in a box along with everything else until I decide it's time to unpack it.

I don't think—please forgive me for this, but I don't think I'm going to tell her about you. On one hand, I feel as though I am erasing you from our lives, but that's the thing, no matter what I want, you aren't in them anymore. Whether she should have or not, she is *never* going to know you and I think me and Jax have to bare that knowledge alone. How can I tell her about who you were and show her a life that was stolen from her fingers, when she will never be able to fix that pain—the feeling of missing someone she never even met and I just *can't* let her carry that too. She deserves to start life unburdened by your ghost.

But I'm going to teach her to live as you did; I'm going to tell her about the rain and why it falls, Jax is going to teach her how to fight and even though she won't know you, everything about her will come from pieces of you. That, I can promise.

I took so many photos of the two of you; at the gym, at home, on the couch, and on the floor, hundreds of moments forever captured in film and we really did become stereotypical parents who talked about their kid at events or showed poor unsuspecting strangers' photos of the cute things she did, and eventually, we did create a new normal together. By December we even snuck away a few times in order to remember each other.

We would watch TV in some random hotel room and do everything we could not to think of her, it got easier after the first few times and then those few nights without the white noise of a crying baby became my lifeline. We would drink expensive wine on the floor and play cards, or sit on the balcony and remember what it felt like to be young enough to believe the whole wide world was ours. We would sleep through the night without being concerned over if she was okay and it was wonderful bliss.

Christmas was unlike anything I had ever seen. As a kid, my family never had a lot of money, we grew up okay but could have had more. Christmas was always about the church so it wasn't until I was older that we started doing Christmas our way; we always stayed small, just personal things to each other while we sat around our dry tree. The first year with Maisy however, was very different. We had everyone over, including your dad who had only recently joined our lives after the baby but had been around enough that our friends knew his name and weren't unsure when he sat beside them on Christmas day. Spencer and you should never have been allowed to have money because of the ridiculous things you bought for her—it was *insane*. Truly and utterly insane. So many things that she was far too young to use, I think the thing she liked most out of the thousands of dollars spent was the wrapping paper used to wrap It all. It was a perfect day though, we sat around drinking eggnog while she played with various things and cheesy Christmas movies playing in the background.

It seems impossible that it was only a year ago because I don't recognize the person I was in those photos, but without knowing it, we were celebrating the last Christmas you would see. The last time you got to play Santa or sing off-key carols, the last time you got to decorate the tree, that was it; that was the last time you would see the holy day and we didn't know it. Instead, we all celebrated into the new year as though there would be more, you kissed me on New Year's Eve as the confetti fell around us and it was like a dream. The whole ten months that we got to have you like that was a dream.

When your birthday finally came around again, I could hardly believe how much we had changed in only 12 months.

"Thirty-one, how does it feel?" I asked in the morning. Masiy was with Spencer and it was only the two of us in the quiet house.

"Like I should be forty-one instead." I felt that.

Instead of partying like you normally liked to do, or drinking until we were dizzy and making out on the balcony, we stayed on the couch and watched movies because we had a day off for the first time in months. We ate cheap take-out food and frozen chocolate cake; we drank wine from the bottle and when you slowly kissed me, I could still taste it on your lips. Nothing was rushed that day, instead, we enjoyed each other and the feeling of being alone. At some point, I remembered about the box sitting on the floor of our closet and smiled against your chest before getting up. It wasn't anything crazy but I knew you would like it and it had been almost impossible for me to find it. I walked back over to you with a secretive smile.

"This has a story, but you need to see it first." I gave it to you and sat back down. It had taken a lot of collaboration to acquire the gift, but I knew it was worth it. You unwrapped the box and my heart jumped because I *really* wanted you to like it. When you lifted it up, I saw the way your face changed. In your hand was a piece of stained wood, in the middle of it were our worn-out initials still visible after over ten years of use.

"Is this—"

"Yea. That old playground finally got taken down after a kid almost fell through a piece of rotten wood, but before they could dump the rest of it, I had Jaccob steal this from the pile." The playground where we fell in love was finally gone, but thankfully my brother was willing to sort through rotting wood to find the one we claimed when we were 16. "Do you remember when we wrote that?" I asked, watching as you ran a hand over the indented letters.

"Yea—I think you were mad, your dad did something and you were mad so you took out a pen and wrote our names where no one would see them." I nodded, it was our history; our story forever on the wall and it's the only thing I didn't put away in a box. Even in this new house, with my new life, that piece of wood still hangs on the wall because it wasn't just you, it was *me*. It was the start of *my* story and I couldn't just erase it. You were kissing me before I could say anything else, your hand went to my waist as I smiled. "Thank you." You mumbled before moving away and it was amazing.

Everything had changed; we grew up and aged, our faces were a little different and there were new lines on our skin but it was still us; we were still the same kids who just wanted the world to remember that we existed.

Your last birthday was perfect, and after it, nothing else really happened.

Nothing else happened.

Nothing else happened because—because I've finally run out of time.

There is no more history to share, no more words to write about the people we were because I've already said it all, I've said everything other than the one part I've been too afraid to write, but I owe it to you to finish your story; you deserve an ending even if I don't deserve to write one. It's taken me close to a year to write down the people we used to be, maybe now I am ready to talk about the person I am becoming; maybe I'm finally ready to write about the last day you woke up next to me.

But not tonight. Tonight, I think I want to explore my present where Jax has an arm draped over my side while he kisses me as though he's waited a lifetime to do it.

25

August 3rd.

It's been exactly one year since it happened.

365 days later and I think I'm ready to talk about it.

Instead of sitting alone in a dark room with an endless supply of alcohol, I'm with my family. Jax and I are sitting on the couch; he has an arm around me tightly as a silly movie plays on the TV. It was easy to adapt to our new roles, easier than I ever thought it would be but it is. He knows that I am still learning to let go of the past and he doesn't push, instead he lets us move at my pace and I'm grateful for it. I think it's easier to talk about the past now that I feel safe in the present, so even if I don't know how to write this part, I am going to try.

. . .

August 3rd started out like any other day.

It was hot in the city and kids were running up and down the streets, Maisy was crawling around the apartment faster than you could chase after her and it was a seemingly normal, mundane day.

We were having Spencer and Andi over for dinner and spent the whole day preparing food. Around three I went to grab the milk and realized that we didn't have any left. It was my own fault, I had used it the day before and forgot to get more, but instead of owning up to my mistake and walking the five minutes to the store, I looked at you with pleading eyes. Every day I wonder what would have happened if I just got it myself.

But I didn't.

I looked at you and you laughed.

"What did you forget?" You were playing with Maisy; you picked her up and walked over to find out what disaster had unfolded in front of me.

"I may have forgotten that I used the rest of the milk yesterday." I wrapped an arm around your middle and kissed you, hoping the small act of affection would get me out of grocery duty.

"And I suppose you want me to get some more?" I nodded, completely unsuspecting of what that one action would mean.

"I don't have my phone remember? And I have no idea when they are showing up so someone has to stay here and keep getting things ready." You moved away with a knowing look.

"Luckily for you, I have to drop off some stuff at the gym, so I'll pick up milk on the way back." You had found a bunch of old workout clothes that Rob wanted for the younger kids who didn't have a lot of money, you were more than happy to help out any way you could. That was it, that was how it started that day. A few minutes later you handed me the baby and put on your shoes.

"Jax is coming to get her later," I said offhandedly, he had offered to babysit while we had a fun night with the adults.

"He really is the best." You said and he is, he is one of the best people I've ever met. You came over one more time and kissed her forehead, then mine. "I'll be back soon." You said and I nodded, not thinking twice about the action, and then you were walking out the door.

That was the last time I was *ever* going to see you alive, and I just let you walk out the door without argument.

I just let you walk away.

268 ~ BRENNA JARDINE

Hours passed and you still hadn't returned. I couldn't call you since my phone had ended up in the toilet due to our child but I assumed that you had gotten caught teaching a class or something at the gym, or maybe you started talking to someone and never stopped, I didn't really think about it very much, that is until it was getting dark and I still hadn't heard anything, it wasn't until that point that my chest started to feel heavy with familiar anxiety. Those were the last few seconds of normality. It couldn't have been more than a few minutes later someone was knocking on the door.

"Hey, Sebs is still gone but—" I stopped in my tracks when I looked up to see Jax and Spencer standing in the doorway with tears in their eyes. Jax wouldn't look at me, all he did was move past me and grabbed Maisy. I watched wordlessly as he hung onto her tightly. I swear I heard him crying.

"What's going on?" I asked, the anxiety now growing to my throat because something—something was *wrong*, I could see it in their eyes. Spencer put a hand on my arm.

"Lets—let's go for a walk." He said but his voice broke on the first word, I didn't want to, I didn't want to move because I *knew* something was wrong.

"What happened?" I said again but this time my voice was weaker, my brain was in a fog as though I was trying to steel myself for what was about to happen. Spencer looked at Jax, then back to me. He didn't try to wipe the tears out of his eyes; I wanted to throw up with the pure despair written on every inch of his face.

"Something happened—" he was crying, and I hadn't seen him cry before, not like that. He took a deep breath but it didn't help the way I watch him swallow a cry.

"Is Andi alright? Did something happen?" I was worried for him, did something happen to Andi, was he okay? Jax walked past me carrying Masiy and I didn't know yet that I should have been worried about you.

"Andi is fine, Jax is gonna take her for a minute because we—Collin—something happened." I barely noticed Jax leaving but he did, I couldn't move from the doorway.

"Tell me." The words weren't mine, they sounded hollow and frail and so far away. I honestly don't remember a lot of this, my words are coming from the people who were there the day it happened and had to watch me fall apart.

"There was an accident—Collin, I'm *so* sorry." He tried to hug me but I pushed him away, my brain wasn't processing what he was saying.

"What accident—"

"Seb—" I didn't hear anything he said after that, I didn't hear the explanation; I didn't hear him talk about the car that hit you or that they had pronounced you dead at the scene, I didn't hear *any* of it because everything around me was spinning and disfigured, I couldn't hear anything other than my heart racing in my ears because no—*no*, there *had* to be a mistake because it *couldn't* be you—but I could *feel* it. Some part of me could feel it and I couldn't—I *couldn't* breathe.

My knees smashed against the floor as I *screamed* against the carpet, my nails bled as I dug them into the floor but it didn't matter, all I remember is the absolute *agony* that ripped me apart from the inside, leaving everything numb in its wake.

I wanted to die; I didn't care about anything else or anyone else because I—I couldn't move, or speak because *everything* hurt—I couldn't bare it.

Eventually, Spencer must have gotten me inside the door and I remember him pinning me to the concrete because he was too afraid of what I would do if I got up. I think I pleaded with him and kept saying that it was okay, it was okay and you were okay because—because he was wrong, but he *wasn't*. You were *gone*.

Jax heard me screaming as he walked down the stairs; he said that he sat with my daughter and cried against the staircase.

At some point that night we made our way to the hospital, although I only remember moments of it; I remember watching the lights outside my window, I remember your dad sobbing in the lobby and that's when it really hit me, the real truth of what I had lost and I was paralyzed. He came over and together we stood in the waiting room like others had done before and cried. I gripped onto his jacket hard enough that it broke the skin of his back, but I didn't care.

"He—he was just getting milk." I sobbed into his shoulder, he held me tighter as my knees hit the floor.

I remember a staff member handing me a bag of things that you had when it happened, I saw the blood on your wallet and the ring—I threw up in a trash can after Spencer dragged me from the room. Most of all, I just remember feeling nothing but yet *everything* all at once. Spencer and Jax stayed with me all the time, I don't think I was ever alone for those first few days but I didn't care. I'm glad someone was there to watch Maisy though; she had just lost her dad and had no idea it happen, but I did. I couldn't look at her, not without thinking of you and I couldn't—I *couldn't* think of you. My siblings both showed up but I'm not sure they recognized me anymore.

I was happy to die with you, but my stupid friends kept me alive.

I'll never be able to repay them for that.

At some point, we had a funeral and a hundred people asked me if I was okay, what a stupid thing to ask someone. Of course I *wasn't* okay; the person I loved for 16 years of my life was just—he was just *gone* without ever saying goodbye, how was I *ever* supposed to be okay again?

I couldn't stand it, the people and their questions, I just wanted everyone to go away and leave me to die in my own home. I think I spoke at the funeral, or maybe I didn't, the entire thing is a blur that I don't really want to think about because that was it, you were gone and I was alone.

Later that day we stood in the field where you were being buried and I couldn't leave, I must have sat there for the entire day because you—it was *you* laying in that box; not someone else but *you*. The headstone should have had my name on it instead of yours because I couldn't stomach the idea of living now that you weren't. Your dad stayed with me for a while but I couldn't look at him, I think he knew it too because before long he was saying goodbye, then Jax showed up and you've already heard the rest.

Those first few weeks, were by far the worst weeks of my entire life,

It took me most of them to realize that you were actually gone—that's the thing about death, just because it happened and you know it happened, doesn't mean that your mind can believe it. For weeks, even months, I still expected you to walk through the doors every morning. I would have dreams where you would come home with your duffle bag and talk about the flight or traffic, I would wake up sobbing because you were just gone, and our 16 years of history were gone with it.

I thought it would kill me—I *wanted* so badly for it to kill me but then it didn't. Then hours turned into days, days turned into weeks and suddenly months had gone by and I was somehow still standing. Now it's been a year and there are days where I don't think about you anymore, because whether I liked it or not, life went on without you, and so did I.

Maybe that's the point of this whole thing, to keep moving forwards.

I meant what I said before, I'm never going to love someone the way I loved you; there is never going to be another person who makes me feel the way you did or gets me the way you did without having to try and I *promise* that I'm going to hold a piece of you in my heart until the day I die. I'm always going to see your face in every fighter I meet, I'm going to hear your laugh whenever someone makes a joke you would have liked and I'm *always* going to think of your voice every time it rains. But Jax makes me smile. every single day and I owe it to everyone, including you, to give it the best chance that I can.

So that's it, that's our story from the beginning to the end and now that it's out there on paper in front of me, I can't believe that I actually got to live it.

These pages really are a beautiful collection of pieces; each one of them like a puzzle that can't exist without the rest and I think that's okay; maybe my life is always going to be in pieces, but instead of seeing a thousand of them scattered across the floor I think I am starting to see the first stages of a picture. Maybe the trick to this whole life thing is learning how to be happy without always knowing what the full picture is going to be.

To be honest, I'm not sure if I'm ever going to write again, not to you. Maybe one day if I feel as though I need to, or if I have a new story to tell, but for now I think it's time to let you go.

You get to rest now because I'm okay—I'm *going* to be okay and thank you for patiently holding my hand as I learned how to walk again. But the rain is softly falling against the window and I know; it's time to start again.

But if this really is the last time that I sit and write to you, Sebastian Morgan, let me promise you one last thing;

I, Andrew Collins, am *going* to make it.

Acknowledgments

This book started out as a project for my grade 12 creative writing class. Me and my teacher would sit and talk about the idea for hours after school while painting the set for my school's musical, and I was certain that the idea would take off. But then COVID-19 spread across the world and things got a bit screwed up and I started to get lost. It took me almost two years to come back to this world and these characters, and I did right when I needed it most. This book was born from my own heartbreak and confusion, I got to put myself into Collins's shoes as he dealt with the world around him and it helped me figure out my own; Writing about their story helped me figure out what I wanted mine to look like and I can't believe its all actually over.

This was only made possible by the support systems around me, although not many people knew that I was writing this at all; Suprise!

When I was upset or having a bad day, my mom would start asking me about this book, about the characters, and what would happen next; she would sit with me for hours as I talked my way through it, she read each chapter as I was writing it so that she knew what to say all because she knew I needed it, and I am forever grateful for it.

A shout-out should go to my brother for endlessly listening to me talk about this without complaining, and to my friends for standing by me through the last few months despite how rough things seemed to get for all of us.

And lastly, I owe a huge thank you to all the people following my journey online, none of this would have been possible without your constant support, and im eternally grateful for the chance you've given me.

I hoped someone else out there saw themselves in the pages of this book, because i know that i am scattered through every line.

CPSIA information can be obtained
at www.ICGtesting.com
Printed in the USA
LVHW111803181021
700771LV00012B/797/J